# STATEMENTS 2

# Statements 2:

## NEW FICTION

edited by
Jonathan Baumbach and Peter Spielberg

with an introduction by Robert Coover

Fiction Collective △ New York

The publication of this book is made possible
by a grant from the Brooklyn College Press.

First Edition

Library of Congress Catalog No. 76-56053
ISBN:—0-914590-36-7—(cloth)
ISBN:—0-914590-37-5—(paper)

Published by FICTION COLLECTIVE
Distributed by George Braziller, Inc.
One Park Avenue
New York, N.Y. 10016

# CONTENTS

| | | |
|---|---|---|
| ROBERT COOVER | Statement | |
| WALTER ABISH | Parting Shot | 11 |
| GLENDA ADAMS | The Music Masters | 30 |
| MIMI ALBERT | Rock Bottom | 35 |
| RUSSELL BANKS | By Way of an Introduction to the Novel, This or Any | 46 |
| JONATHAN BAUMBACH | Tooth | 59 |
| BURT BRITTON | Self-Portrait | 69 |
| JERRY BUMPUS | from *Lutz* | 70 |
| JEROME CHARYN | from *King Jude* | 78 |
| ROBERT COOVER | The Clemency Appeals | 87 |
| RAYMOND FEDERMAN | The Voice in the Closet | 95 |
| B. H. FRIEDMAN | P____: A Case History | 106 |
| THOMAS GLYNN | Bo and Be | 122 |
| RICHARD GRAYSON | Au Milieu Intérieur | 133 |
| MARIANNE HAUSER | Ashes | 141 |
| STEVE KATZ | Two Seaside Yarns | 145 |
| BRUCE KLEINMAN | The Misplaced Trout | 149 |
| ELAINE KRAF | Men | 155 |
| LAURA KRAMER | Shoes | 161 |
| CLARENCE MAJOR | from *Inlet* | 168 |
| URSULE MOLINARO | The Ghosts of Leaves on Winter Trees | 175 |
| LEON ROOKE | The Broad Back of the Angel | 182 |
| STEVEN SCHRADER | Whole | 195 |
| R. D. SKILLINGS | from *The Meatrack* | 198 |
| PETER SPIELBERG | The Hermetic Whore | 201 |
| RONALD SUKENICK | The Endless Short Story: Dong Wang | 212 |
| | Notes on Contributors | 219 |

# STATEMENT

America is, at best, a strange place for an artist to work in. On the one hand there is the illusion of artistic freedom, constitutionally protected; on the other, there's the operative dogma of the marketplace: will it sell? In America, art—like everything else (knowledge, condoms, religion, etc.)—is a product. The discovery of this is the capstone to the artist's alienation process in America. He knows there is no relation between what is good and what sells, nor between what he's made and how it's used by the market managers. He is often made rich by his worst work, if he gets anything for his work at all. Critics may eventually discover his best work, but then it is they who get rich off it, not he. Most often he sees others—hacks, imitators, faddists—get rich while he is entirely ignored. Or patronized: "This is a very original and interesting manuscript (play, painting, composition, etc.), but I'm afraid that in the present economic conditions . . .". No need for censorship: trust the general banality of the marketplace.

Three times already I have used the word "rich." It is true, America is a large and prosperous country, there is money to be made. American artists are the envy of the world. People have been made millionaires off a single book, a film, a few paintings. Which draws a lot of people into the arts world who know nothing about art, nor remotely give a shit. And since quality, innovation, profundity, seriousness of purpose tend on the whole to reduce the product's marketability, it's the "tough-minded" (generally a euphemism for "stupid but lucky") entrepreneur who has the best chance of making it into the main power positions. Ditto for the people further down in the hierarchy, editors for example. Most of whom, as far as I can tell, don't even have the time to read books, even if they do remember once liking them.

The immediate consequence of this dictatorship of the market-place is that it's all rags or riches. You make a million or you don't even get printed. Rockefeller collects you or you don't get hung. The meathead distributor gives you the nod (and chops up your product) or the film stays in the can. You play the mindless Broadway game or your play gets crapped on, disappears. Good work slips through, of course. Since the entrepreneurs are generally unable to tell the difference between good work and bad, it's natural that they'd choose some good work from time to time, just as snake-eyes turn up once in every 36 dice throws.

In the old days (so they say) book publishers took it as part of their responsibility to publish works they knew would not be easy to sell, being too difficult or too innovative, for example, using some of their profits from their popular works to support less popular (or developing) writing. Not altogether selflessly: it was hoped that such books might add "prestige" to the house. Most publishers now, however, are owned by multinational corporations who are interested only in the profit margins, and what middle ground there might have been has been pretty well shot away by the company accountants. Or anyway that's what's implied in the rejection notes.

Out of a desire to recover (or perhaps to create for the first time) that middle ground, the Fiction Collective was invented. It has been criticized for being self-serving, and in a sense it is: certainly the founders, having a tough time of it in the Knowledge & Entertainment Industry, banded together in order to get their own work into print. (Those who have followed have had to pass through an editorial screening process: democratic, sympathetic, but serious.) But the implication of the criticism—which comes mostly from the "professionals" in the Industry—is that the Collective therefore publishes inferior work. Well, no one is claiming that it's all great writing, and least of all the Collective; they even encourage their own authors to go to the highest bidder if they write a book the Industry seems to want, and so are openly willing to publish an author's earlier work, help him get established, then let him go just when he's accomplishing his more mature and perhaps his best work. But the Collective *has* published a lot of good writing, and even the less convincing material has generally been interesting even in failure.

I will go further than that: comparing the Fiction Collective list to the recent fiction list of all the other major publishers, I would say that it has been this past couple of years one of the half dozen most consistent and most exciting in America. It lacks the old established masterpiece some of the older houses can brag of perhaps, but it also lacks the list-thickening mass of commercial shit. Which is to say, it's about time people—in particular, critics of contemporary culture, who should know better—stopped looking down their noses at it and started taking it seriously.

*Statements* is, in effect, though only a casual publication, its house organ. It is, like the Collective, a cooperative venture. All the material in it in fact is donated: a gift, as it were, to the American reading public from its working writers. There aren't many publications in America in which you can find this much contemporary fiction in one place. It deserves a moment of serious attention, a fair read, its writers' only reward.

*Robert Coover*

# PARTING SHOT

*Walter Abish*

1.

I returned from Morocco in September in time for my exhibition
of photographs at the Light Gallery on Madison Avenue. Most of
the exhibition was devoted to photographs I had taken of the
Mosque of Kairouan, and of the city of Kairouan which is
surrounded on all sides by desert. At the very last moment, before
the exhibition was to open, I decided to include a photograph I had
taken of Irma on the West Side pier a week or two before my
departure for North Africa. I was fully aware that the photograph
was out of context with the exhibition, and might even be
disconcerting to a viewer looking at the Great Mosque, and the
innumerable shots I had taken of the shrouded women in the city. I
included the photograph of Irma for no particular reason that I can
understand. I had invited her to accompany me to Morocco and
Tunis, but she couldn't make up her mind, and I finally left without
her. I worked in my darkroom on the print of Irma in her one-piece
bathing suit only after my return from North Africa. At the opening
the gallery was packed with people, and in general the show was
well received. I sold about a dozen prints the first night. In all I sold
eight prints of the photograph of Irma sunning herself on a bench at
one hundred and twenty-five dollars each, but of the eight buyers
only Gregory Brinn called me to invite me to his place on Central
Park West for a drink. I remember looking everywhere for Irma at
the opening, but apparently she never made it.

A friend of mine informed me that Gregory Brinn was an authority on Guy de Maupassant, who incidentally had visited and admired the Great Mosque of Kairouan in 1889. Brinn was also a literary critic, and his wife was the daughter of Emmanuel F. Hugo, a well-known and extremely popular writer. Somehow, I had not expected to be the only guest invited that afternoon; however, both Gregory Brinn and his wife, Maude, were extremely cordial. Somewhat furtively I looked around for the photograph he had bought, and finally located it on a bookshelf in his study. The photograph was inside a Kulick frame.

From his desk Gregory Brinn had a superb view of Central Park eighteen floors below, and, whenever he chose to turn his head slightly to the left, a view of Irma in her one-piece bathing suit. I must admit I was somewhat disappointed that he had not picked one of the photographs of the Great Mosque. As an authority on Maupassant who had written with great eloquence of the latter's visit to the Mosque, Brinn's failure to choose one of the Kairouan photographs struck me as odd. She has a striking face, he said, referring to Irma. He then asked me if I was attracted to the kind of cold sensuality Irma exuded. I couldn't think of an appropriate answer.

What makes you decide to photograph someone, Gregory asked me just before I left. I walked out of their apartment with a vague sense of having been used. I felt that I had been asked over in order to supply Gregory Brinn with information regarding the woman on the photograph he had bought. Perhaps he felt that for the price he had paid I should provide the information. When I had said that I knew Irma quite well, he had promptly asked me if I ever had an affair with someone simply as a result of having taken their photograph. Well, Irma is always photographically available, I replied, expecting him to laugh. With no change of expression on his face, he stared at me, apparently trying to evaluate what I had said.

The following day his wife went to the gallery and bought one of the photographs of the Great Mosque, one that had two men in white cloaks standing in the background. She paid with her own personal check. I think she bought the print purely as a way of apologizing for her husband's behavior. I had been invited over on a false pretense, and she knew it. My first impulse was to ring her up and thank her for buying the print, but then realized how awkward and stilted the conversation would be, since her purchase had only been a gesture, and what I was thanking her for as a professional photographer was her supposed good taste, and her admiration for my work.

Months later I ran into her on Madison Avenue. She was looking at a blue blazer on display in one of the shopwindows at Triplers. Do you like it, she asked anxiously, momentarily leaving me with the impression that she intended to buy it for me. It's very handsome, I said. I'm so glad you like it. I intend to get it for Gregory. He looks so good in a blazer. I could tell that she was very much in love with him.

By the way, what's the name of the woman in the photograph you took?

Irma, I said reluctantly, Irma Dashgold.

She's awfully attractive. I believe Gregory's fallen in love with her. Do you see her often?

Now and then.

You must come and see us again, she said politely. Gregory and I enjoyed your visit immensely. I wanted to thank her for buying the print of the Great Mosque, but didn't.

I fell in love with Irma the first time I saw her. I was much younger, and it was easy to fall in love with her, or perhaps I should correct that and say, that she made it easy for one by treating love the way she treated everything else, with a kind of elegant casualness.

What does she do? Maude asked.

Who?

Irma.

I really don't know.

She said goodbye, and then entered Triplers, I assume to buy the blazer. I hoped I would not run into her again, since the encounter had made me remember her gesture, it also reminded me of her husband, and their very beautiful apartment on the eighteenth floor. I remembered the view from the apartment, as well as the gleaming parquet floor, and the way each object in the apartment appeared to have been carefully placed where it was in order not to detract from the beauty of another object. Visiting their place was a little bit like going to a museum. Although Gregory Brinn was successful, it was mostly if not entirely her money, or more precisely, her father's money that had paid for everything in the apartment. I could not efface the photograph of Irma sitting on his bookshelf within close proximity of his desk. It may have been the reason why I never displayed Irma's photograph in my place, although I was greatly tempted to.

2.

The large plate glass windows of the stores on Madison Avenue are there to protect the intrinsic value of the plaid suit, of the hounds-tooth hunting jacket, of the blue blazer, the purple polo shirt, the polka dot scarf and what are essentially tastefully arranged objects in the shopwindow, without for a second depriving the passerby of the perfection of the merchandise.

Does the accumulation of what is perfect indicate wealth. The large plate glass windows are always clean. They not only permit a viewer to see what is inside the shopwindow, they also reflect what stands and moves outside the store. It is not entirely uncommon to see a man wearing a blue blazer stop to look at what appears to be the exact replica of his jacket in a shopwindow. It is, in fact, wealth that permits the easy replication of what is perfect, despite Whitehead's admonition: *Even perfection will not bear the tedium of indefinite repetition.*

Did Whitehead know that wealth enables people to acquire the perfect apartment, the perfect country house, the perfect haircut, the perfect English suits, the perfect leather and chrome armchair, the perfect shower curtain, the perfect tiles for the kitchen floor, and a perfect quiche available only from a small French bakery near Madison Avenue, and the perfect Italian boots that look like English boots but are more elegant, and the perfect mate, and the perfect stereo, and the perfect books that have received or undoubtedly are just about to receive a glowing review in the *Saturday Review*. Wealth makes it so much easier to have the perfect encounter with a stranger, enjoy the perfect afternoon, make perfect love, a sexual encounter that is enhanced by the objects that are in the room, objects that may at one time have attracted a good deal of attention while on display in a Madison Avenue shopwindow.

I do not feel well, said Maude. I distrust Gregory with all my heart. I also distrust my own acquisitiveness, and my occasional generosity. Why on earth did I buy Gregory that 200 dollar jacket? What I really would like is to spend my life somewhere in the country, away from the stores. I would like to stroll down a country lane, surrounded by horses and whitewashed barns, and wave to friendly yet aloof farmers with weatherbeaten faces. I do not feel that the perfection of anything in this apartment has enriched my life in the slightest. All it has done is to protect me from what I consider garish and crude. I walk around in the nude to combat the incipient coldness of Gregory. How easy it is to give in to his remoteness and to surrender and embrace his sexual indifference . . . We no longer make love. We occasionally fuck . . . two collectors of the perfect experience, assessing the degree to which we have arrived at the state of perfection.

3.

Gregory does not know where in the city I had taken the photograph of Irma. It will take him some time to find the pier with the double row of benches on either side. People who visit the pier walk up one side and then return by the other. When I took the photograph early in the morning most of the benches were not occupied. I let Irma pick one. What do you want me to do. Anything you like, I said. She was wearing her one-piece bathing suit. Her feet resting on the bench in front of her, she leaned back, and shut her eyes. She was posing, she was also trying to decide whether of not to accompany me to North Africa.

Everyone who enters Gregory's study, comments on the photograph.
Isn't that a Kulick frame?
Yea.
Who is she?
I saw the photograph at a gallery on Madison. She possesses a certain almost undefinable sensual coldness that I find attractive.
They stare at Irma. Their eyes dissect her. I see what you mean.

I wonder what she does, Maude remarked to Gregory.
Why don't you ask the photographer.
She smiled. I will, the next time I see him.

Why don't you give him a ring? He's in the book.

4.

Don't you think you ought to put on a robe instead of parading naked around the house, said Gregory. There are people out there. Gregory pointed at the houses on the other side of the park. You may not know it. It may not occur to you, but anyone looking into our apartment must get a curious impression of the way we live.

We're on the eighteenth floor, she reminded him.

I still wish you wouldn't walk around in the nude.

I wonder if you have the vaguest idea of how irritating you are, said Maude.

I merely suggested that you put on a robe. People talk. The doorman has been giving me the strangest looks for the past month.

People talk. Is that what you would say to that glorious beauty in your study. You'd be off like a shot if you had the teeniest chance of fucking her.

Oh well, said Gregory, I better take a walk. I don't want to stand in the way of one of your little melodramas.

From their apartment on the eighteenth floor Maude can see the buildings on Fifth Avenue across the park. Using Gregory's binoculars, she can make out Gregory's tall figure in his blue blazer as he heads for the other side of the park, turning occasionally to look at someone who has attracted his attention. Once he turned around, as if sensing that he was being observed, and shading his eyes against the sun with one hand, stared at their building, at their floor, at her standing naked at the window. But at that distance she could not make out the expression on his face. There really was no need to see his expression. It never changed. He was going over to Madison to look at the latest exhibition of photographs at the Light Gallery.

5.

Maude called her closest and dearest friend Muriel. Tell me, she asked impulsively. Have you and Gregory ever fucked? I won't be mad if you say yes.

So you take me for some kind of shit, said Muriel. I don't screw around with married men if I happen to know their wives.

Then what about Bob?

But that's different. I can't stand Cynthia. Look, why don't you come over and talk about it?

What's there to talk.

Whatever's on your mind. Whatever made you pick up your phone.

I can't make it today, said Maude firmly. Maybe tomorrow.

Not before eleven, said Muriel.

Do you ever sunbathe on a park bench?

Never, said Muriel emphatically. I can't bear the sun.

Maude studied Irma's photograph, and realized that Irma resembled her slightly. Yes, there was a distinct resemblance. One of these days, she decided, I'll go to a park or to one of those piers on the West Side wearing only my skimpiest bathing suit, and then, among all the freaks and weirdos with their Great Danes, I'll stretch out on a bench, my eyes shut, soaking in the sun, oblivious to everything and everyone around me . . .

When Gregory had stepped out of their apartment to walk across to the Light Gallery he was wearing a blue gingham shirt she had bought him for his thirty-eighth birthday, and the blue blazer she had bought him at Triplers. She had spotted it in the shopwindow. She had not even intended to buy him anything that day. Yes, he said, when he tried it on. It's a nifty jacket. She had also bought him three silk shirts, two ties, and a belt. Seeing him for the first time, a woman, any woman might think that Gregory was a really sexy sort of guy. He loved to leave women with that impression.

6.

Maude is quite prepared to acknowledge that the instability of every object around her, the instability of her vision, the instability of her fragile demands upon herself and others may have paved the way to what had happened, at the same time that it steeled her for the eventuality of Gregory's abrupt departure. Perhaps *unannounced* was the word for which she was searching, not *abrupt*. His departure being unannounced appeared as abrupt. He left saying that he was going to take in a show at the Light Gallery. The mere mention of the gallery brought to mind the acquisition of the photograph, and then the presence of the photographer in their apartment, a somewhat hostile presence, she felt.

She watches Gregory leave, and with the aid of his binoculars follows his progress across the park. Most likely he will proceed straight to the Light Gallery, but the possibility that he will fail to return cannot be ruled out . . . He'll do anything to demolish her, destroy her, intensify the agony she suffers daily at the instability, the fragility, the ambiguity, the indirectness of everything that is said and done.

But despite the aforementioned instability of her vision, she can easily run up a flight of stairs,
she can also sew on a button,
prepare a mushroom omelette,
calmly undress in front of an open window,
grip a head between her thighs,
turn her head ever so slightly to the left and then to the right at the dinner table and gravely listen to what the men on either side of her are saying.
What else can she do?
Afflicted with the grave insecurity that measures the exact, the precise breaking point of every object, she can also muffle her screams.
She can wait in a panic for Gregory's return.
She can kill some time by writing a letter to her father who is spending the summer as usual in his rundown country place.

7.

This is an introduction to the father. His left eye twitches at what appear to be regular intervals. But his handwriting is quite controlled, quite steady, almost appearing confident and over-bearing. Wherever he happens to be, he is waiting for the mailman, waiting for the envelope bearing her nervous scrawl.

Why am I writing this letter to my father, Maude asks herself. I am writing this letter to cause him pain.

It is one of those beautiful days in early June or late August. In one week Maude has received half-a-dozen picture postcards from friends vacationing abroad. Most of the postcards show a good deal of blue sky, an excessive amount when you come to think of it. It is the color so dearly loved by the suntanned men and women stretched out on the white beach, their blank-looking faces turned skywards. The postcards she receives are all cheerfully cryptic. If you only knew who is screwing Lou. P and S have separated again. He is trying to persuade me to leave F. Who is Lou. Who is P and S. And who is F? The postcards allude to exotic Persian rituals in the caves. The cards are all addressed to her and Gregory, it being taken for granted that they, for the time being at least, are still sharing the same perfect apartment overlooking Central Park. That they are still sharing the same magnificent blue tiled bathroom with the sunken tub, and that occasionally, when the situation demands it, they compare each other favorably to someone else, someone who may have suddenly cropped up in their life, someone who smiled at one of them invitingly, a smile that could not have been mistaken for anything else . . . For all Maude knows, everyone who has been writing and calling her on the phone may know more about the woman in the photograph than she does. For all she knows, Gregory may at this moment be seeing the woman. It might have been he who requested the photographer to take the photograph of her in the black bathing suit. Nothing could possibly surprise her now.

All the same, despite her almost detached awareness of Gregory's ongoing unfaithfulness (what an old-fashioned word) she is mistaken in her belief that anything she might write her father could possibly cause him pain. He is inured to her attempts to cause him pain, because he recognizes her intent to do so. No, her letter will not cause him pain. When someone stole his new bike, that caused him pain, and whenever he misses a train back to the city, it causes him a terrible and agonizing pain.

What is her father doing at this precise moment. He is working on his eighteenth novel. His principal character, Agnes, a divorcee, is walking along Madison Avenue, musing to herself as she glances at the more attractive shopwindows. It would never, for instance, occur to Maude's father to question the fragility of glass, or ponder the intrinsic function of the large plate glass windows in a post-industrial society. Not unlike his daughter, his character Agnes can run up a flight of stairs,
    sew on a button,
    prepare a spinach pie for seven,
    toss a vase across the room,

set the dial correctly on the small washing machine in the kitchen,
and determinately search for a specific word in the dictionary, a
word that would spell a certain release, that would indicate a
lightening of the burden some people suddenly, when they least
expect it, feel in their hearts, or roughly in the area where they
suspect their heart to be, somewhere below the left shoulder, and a
bit to the right.

Like his daughter, his character, Agnes, can lightheartedly chat
for hours on the phone with her best friend. It is part of the novel's
format. The conversation may appear banal, but it is pertinent to
the novel's development. Still, Maude's father is terribly selective in
his choice of details he wishes to magnify and details he wishes to
omit. If the doorman is about to collapse, and if Agnes, his
character, mistakenly presses the wrong elevator button, he neglects
to mention it. He glosses over the universal dread people have that
someone may change the locks on their doors while they are out.
All his male characters are somewhat heavy-handed but brave.
They seem to show a marked preference for fur collars on their
wintercoats, and stare expectantly at the naked woman in their
bedroom. The woman, in this case, is Agnes. She is standing
proudly (?) erect, her legs slightly parted. All the men agree that she
has superb legs. Fleshy calves. In chapter three of his eighteenth
novel Agnes is about to be screwed. This she knows. She anticipates
it. One might say she was aware of it the moment she woke up that
morning. It will happen today, she said to herself. Not that she
could possibly anticipate it all in its minute details, but only in a
broad sense that did not, however, diminish the clarity of her vision
of the event that was to take place. It could happen at any moment.
She may, for the duration of the climactic encounter, lie on her
back, or sit on a tabletop, or crouch on the floor. The positions, for
that is what they are called, are as recognizable as the objects that
are so carefully and meticulously displayed in any one of the
shopwindows on Madison Avenue. A woman can easily spend an
hour selecting a blouse, asking herself: shall I buy this one or that.
A woman can always recognize a beautiful blouse. A woman can
also recognize a prick, even in its flaccid state. Each recognition
presents a different problem to the mind. What is my correct
response, asks the character in her father's novel. Clearly it is to
arouse the man. In doing so, the man, as it were, recedes into the
background, becoming one with the wallpaper, as Agnes concentrates her entire attention on the man's prick.

If only all my father's female characters did not resemble me, sighed Maude.

As stated previously, the unreliability of Maude's vision, the unreliability of each telephone conversation she has, the unreliability of every encounter with a friend, acquaintance, or past lover, has prepared Maude for Gregory's disappearance. It was really astonishing, when she thought of it, that his disappearance had not occurred at an earlier date. That he had waited five-and-a-half years to disappear. A few characters in her father's novels had on one occasion or another dropped out of sight, but they were all minor characters, and never missed by the reader. Evidently her father had no use for disappearances. He did not care to create ambiguous situations that required a great deal of explanations. Instinctively, he understood the readers' distaste for the gratuitous act. He knew his women readers, and his readers were predominantly women. He interviewed them in the supermarket. A woman was not bewildered when she saw a naked man in front of her. She can readily grasp in a man's excitement the great need that manifests itself daily in all human beings. A woman can to a great extent determine her own response to that need.

She can run up a flight of stairs,
undress,
examine herself in the mirror with narrowed eyes,
and ask herself: Will they like me?
before entering the adjacent room where the two men she had met an hour earlier are waiting.

It is taken for granted that a woman has certain preferences.
She prefers one bedspread to another,
one man to another,
one position to another,
one picture frame to another,
although at times all things tend to blur, to become indistinct, so that each choice becomes increasingly difficult.

What would Maude say if asked, what is it that you now want most?

8.

Are you aware, Gregory had told Maude shortly after they were married, that all the women in your father's novels are exact replicas of you? They're all highly sexed women with splendid legs who tend to be nearsighted. They all seem to spend a good deal of time writing lengthy confessional letters to their fathers. She hadn't noticed until Gregory brought it to her attention. If not for Gregory she would still be reading her father's novels without a clue as to the true identity of his principal female characters. In her father's latest novel, Agnes, the ash blonde divorcee was gazing raptly at a shopwindow on Madison Avenue when a young athletic-looking man with a slightly protruding cleft chin stopped at her side, to contemplate the objects that were on view behind the thick plate glass window. She felt her pulse quicken. The two of them stared at the imported leather suitcases, the leather briefcases, the leather handbags, the gloves, hats, slippers, all of leather, and all imported. She could see his face reflected on the shopwindow. The protruding cleft chin was a minor flaw, easily overlooked. He wore a winter coat with a fur collar. The coat was unbuttoned, and she could see the vested plaid suit he wore. Cooly he studied her reflection on the plate glass window, debating whether or not to speak to her.

At night, alone in bed, Maude tosses about in her sleep. Whose head is she gripping between her thighs. Is it Gregory's, or is it the head of the man in the winter coat with the fur collar?

Although the world is filled with doubtful and dubious information, a woman can tell at once when a man is trying to pick her up. A woman, by the time she reaches thirty, has seen her share of men, dressed and undressed, singlemindedly striding towards her. It is consistent with this singleminded sexual pursuit that a woman will daily, sometimes hourly, examine herself in the bedroom or bathroom mirror with narrowed eyes, asking herself: Will he like me?

Everytime we fuck, Gregory once confided to Maude, with a slight almost imperceptable grimace of distaste, I feel as if I am one of the characters in your father's latest novel.

Why the detestation, Maude asks herself. Does he dislike me, or does he merely dislike the women in Dad's novels, in which event I could try to persuade Dad to alter them somewhat, to make them less demanding.

9.

Please do not be distressed by this letter, she wrote her father. I really expect Gregory to return within the hour. He went to look at the latest photographic exhibition at the Light Gallery on Madison. An hour after he left I fixed myself a light lunch. Tomato soup with an egg in it, and a tuna sandwich on rye bread. At four in the morning I called Muriel. I had to speak to someone. I would have preferred to speak to you, but I know how you hate to have anyone call you when you are at work . . . and I can never tell when you're not either at work on your novel or asleep.

Gregory left Maude on a Tuesday. He walked out of the apartment just as she was getting ready to plan her day. He looked his usual unconcerned self as he stepped out of their eight-room apartment on the eighteenth floor, an apartment containing two color tv sets, approximately eight thousand books and two thousand records. Most of the books had been signed by their authors. To Gregory with the deepest gratitude, and such shit.

When Maude runs into an acquaintance in the park who inquires what she has been doing with herself, Maude replies: I am presently working on a long letter.

10.

Writers receive long letters with grave misgivings, particularly when the letter appears to have been written by a close member of the family. Lengthy letters have a way of becoming books. They are a pretext to enable the letter's author to enter the combative world of literature. How many people have squeezed their unwelcome presence into literary history just by writing a long revealing letter to their father.

I fully comprehend, wrote Maude to her father, that when Gregory went off to see the exhibition at the Light Gallery, it may not yet have dawned on him that he might not return. I clearly recall saying: Give me half-an-hour, and I'll get dressed and come with you. No, no, he said. He was only going to take a quick look at some photographs. On his way back he would pick up the *Times*. I never saw the *Times* that day. I was so certain he would get it. The next day I couldn't get a copy of Tuesday's *Times*, for love or money. When I called Muriel, she at once asked me what's wrong. I asked her if she had Tuesday's *Times*. She said no.

I think you are well rid of Gregory, Muriel had said. What you need is a stable, strong, and emotional man.

No, said Maude. What I now need is a smaller apartment.

What I now need is a smaller apartment, she writes her father. I also need a place to store the books and records. Could you possibly take a few days off and drive over in the station wagon? You always wanted that entire set of Maupassant. Remember?

How odd, thinks Maude, that under the circumstances I am not discontent. How odd that I did not become a prisoner of my marriage to Gregory. How bizarre that he should have walked out of my life on a Tuesday before breakfast. How fortunate I am not to have any children to worry about. The oddest thing of all was the fact that she could no longer remember his face. It worried her. Poor Gregory's face had been effaced from her memory. Try as she did she could not put Gregory's handsome face together in her mind. She managed the lips and the eyebrows and even the hair, but she could not assemble the total face. The total face escaped her. She succeeded, however, at the first try with the face of the young photographer, thinking to herself, what a sweet face. I bet he's an awfully sweet guy.

11.

This is an introduction to the nervous handwriting of Maude. She is sitting at her little writing desk, writing a long letter to her father. She can see her father in his large rather neglected country house impatiently waiting for the mailman, impatiently waiting for her letter. Her father is wearing his old Harris Tweed. He and the mailman go through their familiar routine, speaking about the weather, the crops, the livestock, before the mailman reluctantly hands over the mail.

She could have typed her letter, but she preferred to write it by hand, infecting the desperate message her letter conveyed with the angular nervousness of her handwriting. Her handwriting accentuated the intensity of her feelings. It clamored for attention. It also demanded an immediate sympathetic response.

Everything that you see and hear is plausible, her father had once said. At the same time, it can also remain highly questionable. All the things in this house, the house included, more or less reflect a certain taste. Is it my taste? Take this couch, for instance. Why is it still here when it should have been sitting in the garbage dump years ago? If I were to sit down and write about the couch I would probably write that I was attached to it, in order to make plausible its presence in my study.

In her letter Maude casually mentions that George had briefly stepped out to see an exhibition at the Light Gallery two weeks ago. She had intended to accompany him, but he had reminded her that she owed her father a letter. If not for the letter she might have accompanied Gregory to the gallery. In the late afternoon, when Gregory failed to return, she called the gallery, identifying herself as the lady who some time ago had purchased a print of the Great Mosque of Kairouan. She wondered if there were any other prints left of the Mosque, and incidentally, had her husband, Gregory Brinn, been in that day to purchase another photograph of the lady in the one-piece bathing suit sunning herself on a park bench?

## 12.

Every evening Maude walks naked to the window and takes a deep breath. She is relaxing. She is also asking herself: What will I do tonight? She can always take in a movie, or go to a concert, or see a play, or read a good book, or watch an old movie on TV, or do some Yoga excercises, or bake a cake. She can also, on the spur of the moment, invite someone to dinner.

Are you free tonight, she asked me on the phone. I thought you might like to come over for dinner. I know this is terribly impromptu. You can bring your friend. The woman in the photograph. Oh, by the way, Gregory is away on business. It'll just be the two or three of us.

She can also go to one of the neighborhood bars and strike up a conversation with a stranger, someone who will undoubtedly have read one if not more of her father's eighteen books. Whenever she mentions her maiden name, the response is immediate: Good God, you're the daughter of Emmanuel F. Hugo. I firmly believe he's the greatest writer since Maupassant. She used to have her father read Maupassant to her when she was a child. The mere mention of Maupassant makes her weep.

She can also, just to show that she doesn't give the slightest damn, throw a gigantic party, inviting all her friends and their friends, and just people her friends may know or run into. I've been looking for you, she said severely. I was afraid that you mightn't show up. I don't know half of these people. Did you bring her along? I introduced Irma to Maude.

Why did I bring Irma along?

Did I want her to see her photograph in Gregory's study?

Did I want her to see the view from the eighteenth floor?

Did I want her to savor the perfection of the apartment? The perfection of every object in the apartment? The perfection, consequently, attained by her photograph in being in such close proximity to the other carefully selected objects in the study.

Goodnight. Maude kissed me on the lips. I left without Irma. I couldn't locate her in the dense crowd. Thank you for bringing her, said Maude.

13.

On the spur of the moment I decided to throw a large party, Maude writes her father. It may cause him pain. It is intended to cause him pain. She describes the people who came to her party, she also describes Irma, describes her in a way to cause her father anguish.

Maude likes to write letters. She's quite an accomplished letter writer. The letters are breezy, informative and even witty. She likes to make fun of herself. She writes of the time she and Gregory spent a week in Jamaica. They had been making love when the door of their hotel room was opened by the chamber maid. Just put it on the table, said Gregory without even turning around. The maid placed his polished shoes on the table and quickly stepped out of their room. They burst out laughing hysterically as soon as the maid had left, but when her father made use of the incident in one of his novels, Gregory actually threatened to take him to court. He's really totally humorless, said her father. My poor child, married to a humorless man.

She married a man who was an authority on Maupassant, and who was also a book reviewer for one of the major journals in the country, because it was so refreshing to have someone who could analyze so thoughtfully all the women characters in her father's books. Of course, that one is you too, Gregory would say. Can't you see how your father is trying to disguise her to lead us astray? That first year she spent with Gregory was the most exciting time in her life. Suddenly she was able to cope with her fear of the elevator going out of control, and plunging eighteen floors to the ground floor.

I wonder what I should do with all the books the publishers keep sending to Gregory, she asked me. I didn't feel like inquiring if she had seen Irma since the party. It wasn't any of my business. I realized that for the second time I was the recipient of an invitation from one of the Brinns that was given in bad faith. Maude had wanted me to bring Irma to her, and I had complied.
Why? Why? Why?

14.

Without the slightest trepidation Maude enters the room in which the two men are sitting on the couch with Irma. No one prevents her from walking to the window and looking at the West Side Drive, as she pretends not to notice that the two are quite openly caressing Irma's small white breasts, breasts that resemble her breasts. In order not to see the men and Irma, Maude is compelled to partly close her eyes, or focus them elsewhere, on the wallpaper for instance. It is a pity about the wallpaper. The wallpaper destroys the room. It makes the room smaller and less attractive. Obviously Irma had little sense for color or design. Maude would have suggested a bolder pattern. But Irma had an incredible body. Most men noticed her body. Irma, at their first encounter had quite casually mentioned that her legs were her best feature. What an amazing thing to say, Maude had thought at the time. For some reason the two men were not touching Irma's legs.

Perhaps, it occurred to Maude, they were saving Irma's legs for later. Perhaps they were satisfied to look at the legs while concentrating on other parts of Irma's anatomy. Who can say? Who can tell what is on the mind of a man who is caressing a woman? One of the two men was rather attractive. He had bony hands and blue eyes. For no discernable reason he looked at Maude, and said: I expect to make a lot of money next year. At least twenty thousand. Maude was not impressed. Her father made eight times as much after taxes each year. She watched the two men who might easily have stepped out of one of her father's novels strip Irma naked. She had expected Irma to offer a certain amount of resistance. A certain struggle was called for, Maude felt. Instead, all she saw was total compliance. It is depressing, she thought, to see an attractive woman give in so easily. In her father's books the women always put up a certain struggle. Even in Maupassant it was not merely, one, two, three. Is Irma, she wondered, without backbone. She tries to stiffle a yawn. Her yawn is an unabashed admission that she is becoming bored by the spectacle and by her role as captive audience. She is thirty-five and easily bored, but she makes no move to leave the apartment. Having read the *Story of O,* she knows what would happen if she did. She knows how the men would respond.

I can take a taxi home, thinks Maude. She is disconcerted to find Irma staring at her. It's not more than ten, at the most fourteen steps to the door, another twelve to the elevator.

She would describe what had taken place in a letter to her father. She would go into great detail to cause him anguish. I was afraid, she would write, I was so afraid, and yet, I was so excited, so excited.

Her father wrote big fat American books. At this moment he is sitting at his typewriter turning out beautiful books for America. He is a man of letters. He is a man America respects. He is a man who understands the quintessential American need for friendship. It is this fundamental understanding that has enabled him to sell his books in the hundred thousands. People crave friendship, not sex. Her father's face is recognized by millions. Each time he takes the BMT he is besieged by the readers of his books. She adores her father. She adores the poignant titles of his books. Books, in which all the principal female characters resemble her. It is only to be expected, she thinks. She can also recognize the figure of her father in his books: Her father at the age of four, seven, eighteen, twenty-two, forty-nine, sixty-seven, eighty-one, one hundred and two.

15.

Maude is compelled to concede that one of the two men, the more agreeable-looking one, is screwing Irma in her presence. She stares at Irma's face in amazement. It is a face she can no longer recognize. It could be me, thinks Maude, how easily it could be me.

Where the hell have you been, shouted Gregory furiously when she got back to the apartment at four a.m. I've been going stark raving mad. He kept pounding the table as he spoke. She had never seen him looking so agitated. I want an explanation.

You . . . you . . . you dare ask me where I have been. Her voice was quivering with indignation. You've been gone for over two weeks.

Oh no, cried Gregory. Not again. It's going to be one of those long drawn out melodramas. I can't take it. I simply can't take it. Not at four in the morning.

16.

I really don't know why you wish me to take your photograph in a black bathing suit in a park, but if you insist, I will.

It's a going away present, Maude explained.

A parting shot, I said.

I like the view from the eighteenth floor. I like everything about this apartment. From my desk I can see Central Park, and when I turn my head slightly to the left sitting on the second shelf is a photograph I took some time ago. My father-in-law wants to use it on the cover of his next book. Sure, I said, if Maude doesn't object.

Maude, naked as usual, enters my room.

# THE MUSIC MASTERS

*Glenda Adams*

Everybody knows that men are the true artists. Where are your great women composers, conductors? Some women think they can sing, but it's more often a screech or a scream. They can also dance a little. But where are your famous women painters, comedians? Women have no sense of humor. But they are educable.

The father sits at the kitchen table with his daughter, listening to the Spike Jones Half Hour on the radio. She isn't allowed to talk or clatter plates, because he doesn't want her to miss a word. Chewing Gum on the rail, Cabbage ahead, and Here Comes Beezelbom—are among the funniest lines ever written.

This father travels the length and breadth of the city for a Marx Brothers rerun. He takes the daughter to the Prince Edward to see *Night at the Opera* and *Duck Soup,* to supplement her regular education.

When Gummo's sweetheart sings a love song from the deck of the passenger liner taking her to New York, the father groans and holds his ears.

"God love a duck," he says. "Screeching women."

During the intermission, the spotlight falls on the orchestra pit. A trapdoor opens and Noreen and her Hammond organ, a special feature, soar upwards. Noreen wears a strapless blue lamé evening dress. Her sparkling silver hair is set in corrugated waves. Her back is as fresh and round and pink as a new velvet pincushion. She sways and bends over the organ, pressing out "Melody of Love."

Take me in your arms dear
Ten-der-ly.

"Why did they have to bring her on and spoil it all," the father says.

It's a jolly day, today's the wedding
Of the little painted doll.

"God stiffen the crows," the father hoots. He hates Noreen and her organ. The daughter thinks she is rather beautiful.

When it is time for *Duck Soup*. Noreen turns to the audience and, still sitting on her stool and playing with one hand, she bows. The lights go off and Noreen and the organ descend into the pit.

"There ought to be a law," the father says.

His favorite scene in *Duck Soup* is at the end, when they all throw edible items at the female singer. He laughs so hard he has to push his dentures back into place.

On the way home, the father tells the daughter that the best movie ever made is *Treasure Island,* because there is only one woman in it, right at the beginning. Once you bring women into it, art is ruined. The Marx Brothers do very well, considering.

The father plays the piano. He specializes in honky tonk and thinks Knuckles O'Toole is the greatest.

The father can play any tune in the world. The daughter can ask for anything at all and he can play it. He always plays in G major, with the left hand very low and the right hand very high, so that it is impossible to sing with him.

When he plays he beats his foot on the floor. He has worn a hole in the carpet. The daughter stands beside him, waiting for a space between the songs to ask him something. He is playing a medley and there is no space. He calls to her to speak up, because he can play and keep time with his foot and listen to her, too.

The mother likes to sing as she hangs out the clothes. Usually she sings

I'll be loving you, always.
With a love that's true, always.

She also likes to sing

Now at last the door of my dreams is
       swinging wide
There upon the threshold stands the
       blushing bride.

Often the father requests that she put clothes pins in her mouth.

The son plays the drums. He has a rubber practice pad that he takes with him everywhere. Whenever he has a spare moment, he takes his sticks out of his back pocket and beats out a two-four, or a four-four, or a six-eight. When anyone speaks to him, he frowns and keeps on playing, his head held critically to one side. People give up trying to talk to him.

The daughter thinks that perhaps she will be a dancer. She has seen every ballet movie.
    She has seen *Tales of Hoffman*. Olympia, the wooden doll, is so lifelike that a young student falls in love with her. But she is only a piece of wood, a puppet.
    She has seen *The Red Shoes*. When the girl accepts the red shoes and puts them on, she dances forever. The shoes don't let her rest and they dance her to death.
    She has seen *Giselle,* who is loved for a day by the prince. When he forsakes her for a princess, Giselle goes crazy.
    She has seen *The Story of Three Loves*. The beautiful young ballerina dances for the artist she loves, even though she knows she has a weak heart and it will kill her. But she does it for him, to help him through an artistic block.
    She asks for the *Nutcracker Suite* for Christmas. The father obliges. Six 78 rpms.
    She puts on her ballet slippers, puts on side one, and prepares to dance. But instead of flutes and piccolos, there come a banging of tin, a kind of hiccupping, and a bunch of high-pitched voices singing

Dja ever see a tin flute dancing?
Nothing is so funny as a hunka tin.

She bursts into tears. It is Spike Jones's version, and there is hardly any music at all. The father tells her not to be silly. The record is a marriage of two great arts—music and humor.

Bill Haley and his Comets come to town. Also Freddy Bell and the Bellboys. The son gets tickets and buys the record. He wants to know all the words of "Rock Around the Clock" and perfect his jitterbugging so that he can get up and dance in the aisles at the concert.

He puts the record on repeat and sits beside the record player all morning, writing down the words. He says he doesn't mind practicing certain steps with his sister, since she is at least a better partner than his dressing gown cord hooked around the bed post.

The daughter falls in love with a young man who can pom-pom the Barber of Seville from start to finish. He can sing the Freudeschone-Gotter-funken from Beethoven's ninth, and he knows all the *Carmina Burana* in Medieval Latin.

He takes her home with him to listen to his record collection.

She chooses *Petrouschka,* planning to tell him about the doll with the heart. Then he sits up and sings "Nessun Dorma," pounding on the arm of the couch with his fist.

Next he plays *The Song of the Earth* and sings along with Fischer-Dieskau about the glowing knife in his breast.

The daughter gets home at two o'clock.

The father asks where the hell she's been and what the hell she's been doing. She tells him she has been listening to records.

The daughter falls in love with another man who can read the newspaper, eat a sandwich, talk on the telephone, watch television and memorize songs on the radio, almost simultaneously, or at least in quick succession.

She waits for the TV commercials to tell him something. But he also likes commercials and can sing most of them.

After the 11:30 movie, he turns up the radio and reads a back issue of *The New Yorker.* She curls up beside him. He is reading the history of the orange. She takes the magazine from him and tells him he's the only one. He closes his eyes, smiles and nods his head. He reaches out his arm and turns up the volume on the radio and sings

If you can't be with the one you love

Love the one you're with.

He snaps his fingers to the beat. Next he sings

Bye, bye, Miss American Pie

and falls asleep.

# ROCK BOTTOM

## *Mimi Albert*

"You look like you could use a friend," she said. She sat at the next desk to mine in the Madison Avenue office in which we worked. Under yellow lights her brown hair bobbed, her green eyes squinted at the page. Our typewriters clacked in unison. We weren't allowed to smoke. When I got up to go to the bathroom she followed me. Did she want to hear me fart or urinate?

"I just need a couple drags, that's all," she said. Could she read my mind? I didn't trust her, even later on. But I liked her looks. She was both tough and soft. She was only twenty years old and had a thick, tense, overstuffed body. She crammed her ass into leather skirts and corduroy dresses, buttoned tailored blouses across her full chest. Her eyes bulged from their sockets, her lips pouted. She had sophistication. Two years younger, I did my best to imitate. I always fell flat on my face when I put on the high spiked heels she wore so casually. My stockings were always ripped.

Starved for friendship I ended by accepting hers. We guzzled sandwiches together during the half hours we were given for our lunch.

"So tell me Anna. Are you still a virgin?" she asked me during our second break together.

"No."

"How did you lose it?"

"I can't remember," I lied between bites.

This seemed to satisfy her. She wanted to talk about herself anyway.

"I've been laid by forty fellows," she informed me. "Now I've got a crush on somebody new. Promise not to tell?"

"Who would I tell?"

"It's my acting teacher."

She whipped out his photograph which she carried around in her wallet. He was a short fat man with a bird's beak for a nose and no chin to speak of.

"Isn't he gorgeous?" She already had the answer. "So distinguished. He's absolutely marvelous as a lover." She lied to her husband every night so she could couple with this hero in the back seat of his family station wagon. They drove off after acting classes and screwed in the darkness of a Long Island City garbage dump, his children's rubber ducks and xylophones squeaking on the car seats around them.

"Do your parents make things hot for you? I'm lucky. I got married. Do you live at home?"

I didn't. I had run away. My parents knew nothing of me. Not even my address. I had eluded them and eventually they had given me up. They had stopped even the lost, hurt searching. But I was afraid to tell her anything. Fugitive, moving frequently, I had learned to be suspicious of everyone. I had even changed my name to get the job.

"I've got an apartment," I evaded.

"Lucky stiff."

"What are you talking about? You're married."

"Yeah. You've gotta meet my husband, he's the most exciting man I ever knew." She stared into space.

"This is the first real job I ever had," she told me later. She typed her letters with energy. Her "territory" was northern Florida. "Before I had to hustle if I wanted even a little pocket money. You can believe I never told my husband. He thinks I was cocktail waitressing in a place uptown."

Nancy was an actress and had been to the better schools, she said. "I'm on the lam from Finch's." She brimmed with giggles. I thought she didn't look like she had gone to Finch's.

"I'm a college dropout too." A lie for a lie.

"What a waste of time, would you believe it? I wanna get into the Actor's Studio. That's more like it. Do you know about the Method?"

I knew about the Method. In my last year at the School of

Theatrical Arts I had found a single acting job, the part of a child in a good off-Broadway play. I was no child but the play ran for months. Soon the smell of cosmetics nauseated me. The hot lights made me want to faint. The other actors bustled and pushed me onto my marks when I wasn't paying attention.

"Look where you're going for God's sake," they whispered to me under their lines. I was demoted to understudy within two weeks.

"I studied but I'm not a very good actress," I said now.

"Oh bullshit," Nancy said. "I can see you haven't got confidence in yourself. Listen, come home and meet my husband. He's the smartest guy I ever met, he'll set you straight."

When she brought me into her dingy sitting room on Christopher Street I was filled with apprehension. They had a black cat which they tied with strings to the bathroom sink. The husband, Phillip, sat hunched over a typewriter, his black eyes too bright, his hair lank. Still I consented to place myself upon his knee at his request.

"So this is Anna." Phillip breathed cigarette smoke into my ear. "I've heard so much about you, Anna. Tell me, what would you rather do more than anything in the world?"

"I don't know."

"In this house you can do anything you want. We run a free house here. What do you really want to do?"

"I don't know."

"I'm a writer," said Phillip. "I'm a merchant of words. I know about people. I know what you want."

He kissed me. He was right. Tied up under the bathroom sink in yards of cheap Woolworth string, the poor black cat started yowling, pulling with its paws at the cords and knots.

The next day I returned home alone. I wore one of Nancy's sweaters. It was too large for me. I came into my apartment and lay down on the single piece of furniture, an old studio cot. I hadn't slept all night.

But my apartment was so cold by then that I couldn't sleep. November, and the cold was an iron maiden. I had moved into a rock-bottom low rent walkup in a building on East 72nd Street. There in the territory of airline stewardesses, models and insurance men was my building, left from another era, the neighborhood eyesore. Once it had been either a prison or a fortress; some said during the Civil War. Six stories high, it snaked around the block and flanked  an inner courtyard where children shouted and sometimes an old man came to play the violin. There was no bathtub, no refrigerator, no stove, and the toilet was a box with a commode across a freezing cement hallway. Later it was torn down and replaced by a thirty-story marble temple in which only millionaires could afford to live.

I had fled Brooklyn and run to the Lower East Side of Manhattan, and I had fled the Lower East Side to end up here. From Hell to Hell I realized, balanced between the elements of past damnation and future possibility. Like the embryo which passes through all the stages of human evolution and beyond, I was living through each stage of a lifetime, in rapid succession and without thought. I even felt like an embryo in my freezing room on 72nd Street. I climbed into bed wearing all my sweaters and all my underwear and my winter coat and three pairs of socks, and listened to the winds of autumn rising in the streets outside. And I wondered what I would become and how and if I was going to survive. And why I was wandering from Hell to Hell like a sinner in search of her punishment. I awoke with the blankets tangled in a mass above my head, the sourness of my empty cot beneath me.

"Look at you," said Nancy the next day at work. She took control of me. It was only right. She was older than I and married. "Your neck is filthy. Don't you wash?"

There was a thick line of black around my short thin neck. My hair was dingy.

"It's from the coal," I said.

"Coal?"

"I light coal fires in the fireplace because my apartment hasn't any heat."

Nancy began to laugh. The next day she brought me an electric heater and a hotplate. She took them to my apartment and installed them a few feet from the bed, and from then on I slept facing the electric flames.

Every night I returned to my apartment and endured my Hell. When the cheerful copywriters in my office greeted me in the mornings I answered them with a cold stare and a nod. I read the story of the Snow Queen who captured her prey by dropping a bit of ice into his heart. I too had been captured. I was numb and calm. As the sidewalks froze, the people in my building shuddered in their rooms. I could hear them. I could listen to the passing of their lives in the wind that penetrated my walls. One night I heard a man screaming in the hall. I thought of looking out to see what was the matter. But I was cold, and I was afraid it might mean trouble. What if he was a madman, waiting for me to step into the hall so he could pull a knife under my throat and slit me open from ear to ear?

"A man died in my building last night," I told Nancy the following day. "He died of a burst appendix. I saw the ambulance standing in the street in the morning when I went to work."

"That's horrible," said Nancy.

"I could have helped him but I didn't. I heard him screaming in the middle of the night but I didn't help."

"That's horrible," said Nancy.

We went back to work.

Nancy's hotplate fell off the table where I had placed it and set my bed on fire. Like a maniac or a Buddhist I awoke to see myself burning slowly. Then I rolled down onto the floor and put out the flames.

It was too late. I was grilled. But I pulled the cord of the hotplate and the fire went out.

I decided to think of what to do. Should I call for help? But no one had come to help the dying man, and who did I have to call anyway? I thought of calling Nancy. She would come and put her soft arms around me and call me stupid.

"Stupid, why do you have so many accidents?"

"I don't know. I just have them all the time. I must be uncoordinated or something."

I did have accidents all the time. I slipped on ice. If I carried an umbrella it wrapped itself around my legs and tipped me over. Certain flights of stairs were impossible for me to navigate.

"How are you going to be an actress if you can't stand up for fifteen minutes without bumping into something?" Phillip asked me.

"Well, I thought that maybe I wouldn't be an actress any more. I don't really seem to have the knack for acting anyway."

"What are you going to do then?" Phillip occasionally became impatient. In a state of exasperation he seemed more like a real person, even like one of my relatives. Otherwise he was always gentle, always soft-spoken. Which is why I returned to him again and again, I suppose.

"I thought I'd do something that lets me sit a lot. Like writing," I suggested.

Phillip turned away.

But now I couldn't call them. I had no telephone, for one thing. For another, it was two a.m. Still, I thought of calling someone. I thought of calling the police.

That seemed like a good idea.

I put a coat on and went down to the phone booth on the corner. I dialed 0 and asked for the police.

"Well, what do you want?" said the policeman at the other end.

"I don't know what I want. I've burned myself."

"You want an ambulance, lady?"

I thought. Should an ambulance come I would be brought to a hospital. I had already been in a hospital.

"No hospital," I said now.

"No ambulance? What do you want then, lady?"

"Couldn't I just have a doctor? Just an ordinary doctor, to give me something for the pain?"

I stood alone in an open phone booth, moored like a houseboat in the frozen night. Shaking, I was as shattered as the bits of glass that flew against the wind, making a faintly musical sound in the gutters. Under my open coat I wore a flowered nightgown; one of my mother's old nightgowns that she thought had been thrown away. I could imagine her wearing it with a pink bedjacket, woolly socks protecting her feet. She would be sinking just now into her own bed with a new book by some French novelist, something about love affairs and good food and the lights of the seasonless Riviera.

"So!" said the doctor. "To my apartment! Come!"

Like a lover he crouched above my body. What wasn't burned was white and girl-soft. Flabby. I was eighteen years old with round, dark eyes.

Scratched, scarred legs. Babyfat. Dimples.

"To where?"

It was three a.m. I loved the night but I was weary. Maybe a hospital would have been better after all. He led the way down the stairs.

He was a dreary and fastidious doctor. He had been sent at long last by an emergency service of the A.M.A. He had come from a party. I could see that. His good suit was rumpled, his breath smelled of scotch. What opportunities had he missed on my behalf, the worthy doctor? But he was babyfat himself, and wrinkled. His forehead was as pink as the patch of baldness above his hair. He was past his moment. Still. His doctor's bag had the odor of leather so indulgently fine that it sang slightly in the ill-lit discomfort of my room.

"You live alone here?"

By then I had turned into Cleopatra, embarked upon adventure, cloaked in my usual black dress and bright green stockings. I combed my black hair into my eyes and even applied pencil to my lids and brows, maybe just to prove to myself that I wasn't dead yet.

"Yes."

"You like living alone?"

A clue, that question. I followed him down the staircase, feeling myself buckle and tremble with pain.

"Why are we going?"

"To get medication for your burns."

"Why don't you have it with you?"

No answer. His sports car glimmered at the curb. The only possession I have ever really coveted is a sports car. Sleek and fast. In which to obscure my own shy fatness and make an exit through the curtain of reality like a serpent. Maybe he had the same idea. At this time of morning there was no traffic to evade. We glided to 57th Street on slithery Pirellis.

"My building."

There were four doormen in the lobby which was hung with mottled mirrors and blue rococo cornices in very bad taste. I saw myself six times over as I stepped into the elevator. I wasn't beautiful, as I had imagined while getting dressed. (I always imagine that I am beautiful while getting dressed.) Beside the six-foot-tall gilded women still (or already) waiting in the lobby I was very small and shabby, barely able to walk. There were six elevators, we took only one. We traveled swiftly upwards to something like the 34th floor. I had never known anyone who lived on a 34th floor before.

"Have some vodka. Orange juice is good for you."

He poured the drink even before removing his topcoat with the velvet collar. I sank into baby blue carpeting and looked at his apartment. Carefully anonymous sofas. Padded armchairs. Discretely illuminating lamps. It was like a thickly upholstered cell. In one corner was a brief rise on which like a utilitarian throne his bed resided.

"Sleeping alcove."

"Oh."

I felt sorry for him suddenly. Here he lived, alone and swiftly fading, cradled by his soft and colorless replica of wealth. What hadn't he achieved, this aging baby? Shining car, expensive address. Once in a while even a divorcee or a schoolgirl fell to him as his proper share. What difference did it make to him that her side was slightly baked?

Earlier that evening I had been hungry. I realized that if I had met him then I might have hustled him for a steak, then done my usual swift ballet-turn at my apartment door and slammed it in his face. I was very good at that and I was even sorry for him now, although he'd missed it. What did he have after all? Education, wealth, some power. I had only youth. And pity.

"I'm getting out," I said.

"No, no, it's too cold outside." He was settling down, beginning to squirm onto the sofa beside me. "It won't be good for you."

"Getting out anyway."

I wanted to splash the orange juice into his face. He was doing nothing for me. It was useless to stay. I stood up.

"I'll treat that wound now," he said.

It was about time.

He took off my dress. His attention wasn't purely medical. He pored over my burns as he had in my apartment.

"You know, they're not very serious. They won't become infected. I wouldn't worry."

Out of his pocket he took some salve, a roll of gauze. I began to cry, silently and without much hope. He had had these all along.

"But I wouldn't leave here if I were you, not for a while at least." He was hopeful. I could imagine him in the morning. Having squashed himself against me, what would he offer? Twenty dollars?

"I think I need more medicine," I said. Tears fell along my cheeks and neck. It didn't matter. I knew how totally it didn't matter, not to myself and not to anyone else. The entire city, the entire world was sleeping. Only he and I were awake in this overstuffed room, bargaining for my flesh. I knew that I wouldn't be surprised when by morning the bandages would stick to my stomach and arm, and I would be left with ugly scars which would puff away from my body. But if I hit him with one of his thick lamps it would matter. I was sure of that.

"I think this is the worst." I watched him swab the arm too carelessly.

"Sure. It can only get better. It isn't serious, you know." He scanned my face.

That wasn't what I meant. I took my coat and went out into the light blue corridor.

"I don't advise . . . ."

"I think this is the worst," I said again, ringing for the elevator. "I mean it can't get any lower, can it?"

"You ought to take better care of yourself," said Phillip, who watched me limp through the door. Nancy didn't say anything, but blew cigarette rings towards me as I slipped out of my sweater. Which after all she had seen me do so many times before.

I sensed that they were becoming bored with me.

But when she saw the burns she became animated again. She jumped to her feet and ran around the room.

"What the hell do you think you're doing, Nan?" drawled Phillip. He was already reaching for the phone.

"Getting some ointment. I've got to take care of her."

The room seemed to swell under a glowing orange lamp. I felt that I could no longer stand up. Here at least there was the illusion that someone cared about me.

"The doctor neglected me," I said, and began to cry.

They sent for one of their own friends who also happened to be a doctor. John. He was delicate, soft-spoken, his hair thinning. Later he lost his license and performed abortions in order to pay the bills. Now he came in with his small shabby bag and looked down at my stomach. Then he sent Nancy out for special bandages, dressings and salve.

"This isn't going to hurt," he reassured me. It didn't. "Isn't she pretty?" he demanded earnestly of the three of us, looking from Nancy to Phillip to me. I saw at once the way it would go. It always did.

"I'm only seventeen," I lied.

"Don't say that. Sh. That would be against the law, dear. Do you use birth control?"

Nancy and Phillip retired discreetly and left us alone to figure out positions that wouldn't irritate my wounds. Eventually we came up with nothing. My affection for John doubled.

To return to my job was impossible. I could do little more than lie in bed and sip cool drinks. Nancy, having gotten over her excitement at taking care of me, chafed with boredom.

"What's the matter with you?" she began to scold. "Why are you always in trouble when you've got good friends? You ought to be grateful for such friends." She rested one of her fat hands against the edge of my pillow. Obviously she thought a man had done this to me, proof of my infidelity to Phillip.

Soon she wanted to throw me out but I couldn't move. She sent in her own father, a fat sleepy man, to help look after me.

"Look at this," he said, entering the bedroom. "These are photographs taken by a friend of mine of a Venusian standing in his backyard in Brockport, New Jersey."

"The Venusian's backyard?"

"No. My friend's."

"I don't see anything."

"It's special photography. Called Kirlian photography. You see the fuzzy circle in the center of the photo? That's the Venusian. That, right there."

I thought I saw. "Yes, I see," I said.

"It's irrefutable proof, isn't it?" He waved the photograph. "You'd think the newspapers would be interested, wouldn't you?"

I couldn't turn or look away because my side was throbbing. Shafts of pain ran up and down my ribs and into the flesh above my groin. But John's bandages were expert and he carefully changed them every evening. He came and bent above my body with the tenderness of an angel. I began to feel that my whole existence had turned into something floating in air, hanging above the surface of the earth on winds created by the whims of other people. I too had become a Venusian; my form had changed to shadow, to a fuzzy substance in the center of a photograph. As he bent over me one night to change the dressings, I whispered, "Take me with you, John. I'd be happier at your place."

He burst out laughing. "I can't dear. Of course I'm married. What would the wife say?"

I hadn't thought of that.

Unluckily Nancy had heard me, and looked up from the television set where she sat watching Miss Kim Stanley in an off-beat dramatic presentation, and scratching her husband's shoulders with his riding crop.

When the wounds had healed enough for me to walk, she threw me out.

By then I could just about hobble. One of my arms was in a sling, my hips were bandaged. There must have been some unknown charm in my ailment, because I became the center of attention wherever I went. Men wanted to walk behind me, ogling my limp and making various suggestions as I passed. Young boys swished up and asked my name. I sensed at once that there was something enticing and provocative about a female cripple.

I returned to my cold apartment, to my frozen rooms.

Nancy and Phillip deserted me.

"You're no fun any more," said Phillip.

"But it hurts too much."

Still, I sensed that Nancy was relieved. In some peculiar way she'd been jealous of me. Phillip had always been excited by the soft guilt on my face. "What's the matter, honey?" he always asked me. "Don't you know we're family? You can do anything you want with us, just anything. We'll never mind. And this is the essential human contact, the spiritual awakening."

# BY WAY OF AN INTRODUCTION TO THE NOVEL, THIS OR ANY

## *Russell Banks*

It didn't occur to me to write a novel with A. as the prototype for its hero, Hamilton Stark, until fairly recently, a year ago this spring, as a matter of fact, when I drove the forty miles from my home in Northwood across New Hampshire to his home outside the town of B. Upon written invitation (*via* post card, as was his habit), I was going to visit him for the afternoon and possibly the evening. The post card read:

> *4/12/73. If you don't show up here Sat. with a fifth of CC and a case of Molson I'll stop up your plumbing with my toe. Number 5 has gone back to Mother and I've gone back to my old habits. Bring me a box of 30.06 rifle shells too. We'll do some shooting. A.*

Typically he had typed his message, and the four color photograph printed on the reverse side was of a building he had helped construct, in this case a Tampax factory in the southwestern part of the state. A. was a pipefitter with a wide range of practical engineering skills, and on that job he had been the foreman for all the plumbing, heating and air-conditioning systems. He's quite a character, I thought as I read his card, and then decided that someday I would write a novel about him.

It was with considerable excitement, then, that I approached the turn-off to the road, from the paved to a dirt road, practically a trail, that led through a quarter mile of approximately flat and unkempt fields to A's home. The fields on both sides of the deeply rutted road, lined with slowly collapsing stone walls, had retreated to furzy bushes and scrambling tangles of wild blackberries, sumac, and poison ivy. Scattered over the fields in no discernible pattern were ten or twelve rustling shells of windowless cars and trucks, some of them further decomposed and more nearly destroyed than others, also several farm vehicles—harrows, plows, cultivators—, a one-handled wheelbarrow, an outhouse lying awkwardly on its side, rusty bedsprings and swollen mattresses spitting yellowish stuffing onto the ground, a pile of fifty-gallon oil drums, an engine block and a transmission housing, both lying atop a child's crushed red wagon which lay atop an American Flyer sled in splinters, next to a refrigerator (with the door invitingly open, I noticed), and a red, overstuffed couch which had been partially destroyed by fire. None of this wreckage was new to me. I had observed, enumerated, and reflected on all of it many times.

The fields and the road on which I was driving were all part of A.'s property, but a stranger, noting the broad, carefully mown lawns, gardens, house and outbuildings that spread out from the closed gate at the end of the cluttered fields, would surely infer two separate and probably quarreling owners, one for the fields and badly maintained roadway, and another for the house and grounds. But that was not the case. A. was fastidious and energetic, even compulsive, about the maintenance of the house and the yards, gardens and outbuildings that surrounded it. The region that lay beyond the white, iron-rail fence, however, he cared for not at all, even though some seven hundred acres of that region was his private property, had been deeded to him with the house and outbuildings by his parents.

Actually, it was fortunate that so much of the world beyond the fence was A.'s private property, because for years he had been tossing his garbage over that fence, throwing his rubbish, all his used-up tools, vehicles, furniture, even his old newspapers, over the fence and into the field. Every now and then, perhaps once a year, depending on domestic changes, he rented a bulldozer, took down a section of the fence, and pushed the rotting garbage and trash roughly towards the main road and away from the house, to make more room near the fence. It was a casual operation. The vehicles stayed pretty much where he had left them, and he usually left them where they had got stopped, either because of running aground on a huge boulder, of which the field had an abundance, stalling or coughing out of gas, getting stuck in the mucky, tangled ground or ramming into another car or truck from the previous year's trash.

He used his vehicles until they were too weary and broken to drive any further than to this odd burial ground, and he always tried to make that last drive as exciting as possible. Then he would hitchhike twenty miles to Concord, where there were half a dozen automobile dealers, and buy a new vehicle, usually a different type from the one he had just interred, a pickup truck if last year's had been a sedan, a station wagon if a convertible. Because of the intense way he drove them, his new vehicles rarely lasted longer than a year.

Similarly, whenever he disposed of furniture, tools, garden implements, waste or rubbish of any kind, he took from the act whatever last pleasure he could wring from it—making bets, and usually winning them, that he could lift and throw a sofa over the fence, or hurl a transmission housing from his pickup bed onto a pile of children's old toys, and then an engine block onto the transmission housing, or that he could carry a refrigerator in a broken wheelbarrow for a quarter of a mile over a rough surface under a hot August sun. Afterwards, to complete the act, he liked to sit up on his porch, usually in the admiring company of a friend or one of the local adolescent boys he permitted to hang around him, and while guzzling Canadian whiskey and ale, fire his rifle at the new trash. He shot his rifle at many things, animate and inanimate, but he always seemed to enjoy it most when he was shooting at the things he had used up and thrown out.

On this particular day, a blotchy, glutinous gray afternoon with a cold rain lightly falling, as I neared the gate where the road ended and A.'s wide, paved driveway began, I noticed a high, wobbling stack of what appeared to be new furniture—a Danish modern diningroom set, a formica-topped kitchen table and four chairs, a double bed with bookcase-headboard and matching dresser, several table lamps, and two or three cardboard cartons filled with pastel-colored articles of clothing and possibly curtains and bedding. This carefully constructed stack, with all the articles balanced and counterbalanced, was located a few feet from the fence and about twenty feet from the roadway, and I had never seen it before. I assumed, therefore, that these were his fifth wife's leavings, her effects, an assumption which later proved correct.

I got out of my car, walked up to the gate, unlatched it and swung it open. I could see A. in the distance, sitting on the porch of the house at the far side, swinging slowly in the wood glider. Neither of us waved or signalled to the other. That was customary. I returned to my car, drove it through the gate, got out again and closed the gate behind me, as I knew I was supposed to do, and then drove up the long, curving driveway past the smooth, freshly green lawns to the house, parking next to the house on the side opposite the porch, where the driveway ended, facing the entrance to the small barn, which under A.'s care had been converted after his father's death into a modern garage and workshop. Behind the house loomed the hump-backed profile of the mountain, Blue Job, adding its shadow to the day's gray light and casting the darker light like a negating sun across the house and onto the fields in front.

You know, it occurs to me that I really needn't bother with all this. Certainly not at this point. Perhaps later in the narrative such descriptions will be of significance, but here, now, I'm merely attempting to explain how I, Russell Banks, came to write a novel with a hero whose "real life" prototype is my friend, my own "hero", as a matter of fact. And though that notion had *occurred* to me barely moments before, by the time I had parked my car and started walking around the front of the house to greet A. at the porch, I had already completely forgotten the idea. I was worrying over whether or not I had properly secured the gate at the end of the driveway.

We spent the remainder of the day and most of the evening cheerfully drinking, first out on the porch, where until dark we sat and took turns shooting at the furniture A., and his fifth wife had bought as newlyweds the previous September. After dark, we lurched into the house and sprawled on the floor of the kitchen (the chairs and table were all in the field, ripped apart by high-powered rifle slugs), finishing the bottle of whiskey and the case of ale. I remember that A. had recently installed a central vacuum-cleaning system in the house, so that one could simply plug the hose into outlets located in the baseboards of every room without having to drag the heavy cannister or tank along behind from room to room, and he was quite proud of the system. He said to me, "I've got a dishwasher, a clothes washer and dryer, and a radar range that bakes a potato in forty-six seconds. And now I've got this vac' system. Now, you tell me, Russ, what the hell do I need a woman for?"

I said nothing. I was too drunk to speak clearly, and also his question had seemed rhetorical.

Then he said, "I can get laid when I want to get laid. And if the day ever comes when I can't get it, Russ, it'll only be because I don't want it enough."

This last statement seemed wise to me then, and it does now, too.

I was quite drunk, naturally, but I somehow got myself safely home, and that was the end of the day last spring when it first occurred to me to write a novel about A., or rather, someone very much like A., so much like him that I would have to give him the name of Hamilton Stark, or A. would know that the novel was about him, a thing he would hate me for. I did not want A. to hate me. Luckily, he is no longer alive, or naturally, I would not be writing this introduction.

(I should say that I *believe* he is no longer alive, and although technically he does not exist, that is, his body has never been located, it would certainly be strange and ironic if the publication of this novel brought him out of a hiding place. I can imagine the letter I would receive, postmarked in some tiny, far-northern, Canadian village where he is thought of as a hermit:

> *The only reason I'm not suing you is that a lawyer would cost me more than you could make from such a piece of crap as your so-called novel. Just know that if I ever run into you I'll run right over you. You are an asshole. And a lousy writer too. You're going to get everything you deserve, you faggot.*

And then, for the rest of my life, silence. Cold, stony silence. It would be a hard thing to bear. But that's the chance I must take, the chance all artists must take.)

It wasn't until almost a full year later, a Sunday late in February of this year, when A. disappeared for a while (not the first time), that I again thought of writing about him. This is how it happened.

I was in the neighborhood, as they say in New Hampshire when you are within ten miles of a place, photographing birds in winter scenery at a state park not far from A.'s home, and as it was still early in the afternoon when I finished, I decided to stop by for a brief visit. I rarely visited him unannounced or uninvited, but for vague reasons (too vague and smokily intuitive to go into here), decided that this time it would be permitted and perhaps even welcomed.

When I arrived, I immediately noticed that he had parked his car in the driveway outside the garage, which was not his habit. At this time he was driving a pale green, Chrysler, airport limousine, an unusually long vehicle that he took considerable pride in being able to park wholly inside his garage, and therefore he rarely missed an opportunity to do so. Swinging open the garage door, raising it like the curtain at a stage play, and revealing the blunt green tail of an automobile that, like an overweight dragon, seemed to go on forever, disappearing into the far, cavernous darkness of the converted barn, was an exquisite pleasure for him. As a matter of fact, on several occasions I myself, as a member of the audience, had found the experience oddly satisfying and had broken spontaneously into applause.

But on this day the car was parked outside the garage, and the garage door was locked. I walked quickly around to the side door at the porch, knocked, and then called. That door, too, when I tried it, was locked. It was a cold, diamond-clear day, with about eight inches of dry, week-old snow on the ground, and there were hundreds of footprints in the snow, most of them probably A.'s. But fresh prints could not be distinguished from week-old ones. A narrow path had been tramped from the porch down to the fence in front of the house, and on the other side of the fence was a waist-high pyramid of the last week's garbage and trash, most of it frozen solid. Across the snow-covered, bumpy fields in front and into the woods behind the house and on either side were numerous chains of footprints—but it was impossible to tell when in the previous week any of the chains had been laid down. Beyond the woods hunched the mountain, mute, seeming almost smug.

It wasn't that I couldn't understand A.'s absence as that I could not understand both his absence and the car's presence. Except under severe duress or drunkenness, he never rode in anyone else's vehicle. I knew he must still be on the premises. On the other hand, if he were just out for a walk in the woods, a normal activity on such a crisp, clear afternoon, why did he leave his car parked outside the garage? That was not normal. (Rather, it was not *usual.*)

I decided to examine the car more closely. Perhaps there was a note, or a clue. After circling the enormous, green Chrysler twice, I finally noticed the three holes in the front window on the driver's side, holes surrounded by interconnected cracks, like spider webs, holes that could have been made only by high-powered rifle bullets.

This was certainly a curious, if not ominous, development, I thought.

I called out his name, several times, doubtless with fear in my voice and surely with urgency. No answer. Silence—except for the whisper of the cold wind riffling through the pines and the distant, harsh cries of a pair of crows from somewhere in the woods behind the house.

What could I do? I couldn't ask any of A.'s neighbors, those folks in the trailers and shacks back along the road, if they had seen him recently. The mere mention of his name and myself as a concerned friend would have invited any one of those folks to slam his door in my face, or worse. Years of living in A.'s proximity had created in his neighbors a certain amount of anger. I couldn't call the police. To a stranger, especially to a law enforcement official, the circumstances simply weren't that ominous. The police chief, A.'s brother-in-law, as a matter of fact, but no help for that, doubtless would have advised me to drop by again in a day or two, and if A. still hadn't moved his car, then perhaps an inquiry could begin. And of course at this time, A.'s divorce from "Number Five", as he called her, had not yet been legally consummated, and he was still living alone, so there was no spouse, no proper "next-of-kin" to alert and interrogate.

Feeling puzzled, helpless, and increasingly alarmed, I got back into my car and started the long drive home to Northwood. I had not gone many miles when I imagined, successively, three separate events, or eventualities, which, successively, I believed true—that is, I believed in turn that each event sufficiently explained the peculiar circumstances surrounding A.'s absence.

*Event #1:* Upon arriving at my home in Northwood, I built a fire in the fireplace in the library and was about to fix myself a cognac and soda, when the phone rang. It was A. His voice was sharp, harsh, annoyed with me, as if he had been trying to reach me for several hours.

I tried to explain that I had spent most of the day photographing jays and chickadees in the snow and had stopped by his house on the way home, but he interrupted me, barking that he didn't give a damn where I'd been, he'd been arrested by his own brother-in-law, Chub Blount (let us call him), and had been charged with the murder of Miranda, who was A.'s fifth wife. He told me that he'd been permitted one call, and he'd called me, and then, when I hadn't answered the phone, he'd decided I was probably in on the arrest somehow, so now he was calling to let me know what he thought of that kind of betrayal.

I was shocked. I assured him that I was shocked. "I didn't even know Miranda was *dead,* for God's sake! And you know what I think of your brother-in-law," I reminded him. "If I had known that Miranda was dead, murdered, I mean, and if for whatever reason I had thought you were responsible, you *know* I'd never have called

Chub in. I probably would have called the state police, not *that* idiot," I reassured him. "Assuming, of course, that I would've called anyone. I mean, what the hell, A., you know what I thought of Miranda," I said.

Apparently my words soothed him, as good sense inevitably did. Above all else, even in distress, A. was a reasonable man. In a calm voice now, he told me that he wanted me to hire a lawyer for him.

"Did you do it, I mean, you know, kill her?" I asked. Perhaps he'd shot her with his 30.06 while she was sitting in his car—though I could not imagine circumstances under which Miranda might have ended up sitting in the driver's seat of A.'s Chrysler while he stood outside with his rifle. But I did want those bullet holes explained.

For several uncomfortable seconds, A. snarled at me, literally snarled, like a bobcat or cougar interrupted at a meal. Then he shouted that he hadn't called me so he could confess to me, and he hadn't called to protest innocently that he was being framed by his brother-in-law. He'd called me, first, to tell me what he thought of me if I had been a party to his arrest, and then to instruct me to hire a lawyer for him. Not a shyster, a *lawyer* he bellowed. He figured it was a job that fitted my natural and acquired skills rather well. (A.'s sarcasm rarely failed to make a point, though often an obscure one.) As to whether or not he had in fact murdered his ex-wife, A. told me that if the lawyer I hired was able to convince a jury that he didn't do it, that would be the truth. If he failed, that would be the truth too, A. explained. That was why he wanted the best lawyer in the state of New Hampshire, he shouted. Did I understand?

"Yes, I understand. How do you think it happened, though? I mean, how do you think Miranda was killed? How does Chub, the police, explain those bullet holes in the Chrysler?"

A. uttered a low, sneaky-sounding giggle, almost a cackle, except that he was genuinely amused. He was intrigued, he said, by my knowledge of those holes. Until now, until I had asked about them, he himself had been wondering who killed Miranda. But now . . ., and his voice drifted back into that low, sneaky giggle.

"Now, look A., you don't think that *I* . . ."

He assured me that he thought nothing of the kind. Besides, he pointed out, it didn't matter *what* he thought, *who* he thought had killed her. All that mattered to him was getting his case presented to a jury by the best damned lawyer in New Hampshire, and if I could find him the best damned lawyer in New Hampshire, he'd forget all about my knowledge of the three bullet holes in the Chrysler.

I agreed to the terms. I had no choice. But who could such a marvelous attorney be? I wondered. In a backward state like New Hampshire, how could there be a barrister sufficiently gifted to create the kind of awful truth A. had defined? The task of locating and hiring such a person frightened me. I am an ordinary man. I felt alone, young, inadequate.

*Event #2:* I departed from A.'s house, driving carefully along the rutted, rock-snared roadway to the main road, where I turned left, and in a moment I was beyond A.'s property and was passing the battered house trailers, tarpaper covered shanties, and those all but deserted farmhouses. Then there was a stretch of road where for about a half-mile there were no dwellings and the dark spruce and scotch pine woods came scruffily up to the edge of the road, darkening the road, creating the effect of a shaggy tunnel or a narrow pass through a range of craggy mountains. As I entered this stretch of road, I saw a young woman standing by the side of the road and was about to pass her when I realized who she was and what she was carrying in her arms.

It was Rochelle, A.'s twenty-two year old daughter, his only child and, at that, the child of his own late childhood. A lovely red-haired girl with long thin arms and legs, dressed in a forest-green wool parka, hatless with the hood laid back beneath her dark, tumbling, red river of hair—she was a startling figure to behold, and especially when she was the last person in the world one expected to see out here, and even more especially when one realized that she was carrying a rifle, which, because of the telescopic sight attached to it, I instantly recognized as A.'s own Winchester 30.06. She had the rifle cradled under her right arm and across the front of her flat belly, with her left hand gripping the bolt, as if she had just fired off a round, or was about to. She seemed distraught, shaking, green eyes darting wildly, roughly and in the direction of the woods on the left side of the road. She did not seem to notice my car as I slowed, crossed over, and stopped beside her.

Leaning out the open window, so that she could recognize me, I cried, *"Rochelle!* What's the matter? What are you doing out here?"

"I'll *kill* him!" she screamed into the woods, as if I were located in that darkness rather than behind her in my car. "I'll *kill* the bastard! I'll *kill* him!"

"Where is he?"

"In there someplace," she said in a hoarse voice, as if she had been screaming for hours and had exhausted all her vocal resources but the roar. All she had left was her maximum effort; anything less collapsed of its own weight. "I know he's in there," she croaked, motioning towards the woods with the tip of the barrel. "I think I hit him once, maybe twice, at the house when he drove up. When I chased him down here, I could see he was bleeding, his face was bleeding, all over his lousy face, the bastard!" Her own face was gathered up like a fist, her green eyes agate hard. Her fine, even teeth were clenched, and the muscles of her long jaw worked ferociously in and out. Her delicately freckled hands had turned chalk white from the force of her grip on the rifle.

Though she had acknowledged my question by shouting her answer into the woods, she had not acknowledged my presence yet and continued to stare searchingly into the tangled darkness of the woods. With extreme care, moving slowly yet smoothly and, I hoped, gently, I got out of my car. She seemed not to notice, so I took a single step towards her, when she wheeled about on her heels and swung the gun up, slapped the butt against her right shoulder and pointed the tip at my heart. She sighted down the barrel with care, focussing the telescope with her left hand as if she were tuning in a distant radio station.

*"Don't"* she ordered.

I froze, one foot held delicately off the ground, both hands palm-down and off to my sides, as if quieting an orchestra. "Rochelle," I said in a calm voice, "give me the gun. C'mon, honey, let ol' Russ have the gun now, you don't want to kill your dad. I know you're mad at him, I know he's upset you, but you don't want to *kill* him for it, now do you, honey? C'mon, honey, let ol' buddy Russ have the gun, then we can sit down and talk about it . . ." I slowly let my foot descend to the ground, and I had taken a second step.

I was terrified—the sight of one of the most stable creatures I had ever known, one of the most admirably predictable and rational women I had ever met, standing wild-eyed before me with a high-powered rifle zeroed in on my thundering heart, so upset my notion of the real and expected world, that anything could happen, anything, and it would have seemed appropriate. Rochelle could have broken into a Cole Porter song and started tap-dancing her way down the road, using the rifle as a cane, waving over her shoulder at me as she pranced out of sight, the end of a musical comedy based on the exciting life of a girl revolutionary. Or she could have suddenly opened her mouth wide, as if to eat a pear, and shoving the tip of the barrel in, jammed her thumb against the trigger and blown the top of her lovely head away. Or she could have simply squeezed one finger, nothing more than that, just wrinkled her trigger finger one-sixteenth of an inch, and I would have heard the explosion, possibly would have smelled the fire and smoke, seen a shred of the narrow belt of blue sky fall into my face as I was blown back against the side of my car, my chest an erupting volcano for no more than a split second, and then nothing.

With a shudder, I decided it didn't matter what happened, so long as anything could happen, and hopelessly, I took another step, then yet another, and gradually as I neared her she lowered the barrel of the gun, until, by the time I could reach out and touch her shoulder, the gun was pointing at the ground. With my left hand I took the gun from her, and with my right I reached around her shoulders and drew her to me.

Suddenly she was sobbing, her boney, fragile shoulders hunched and twitching with the sobs. And then it all came out, what he had said in his answer to her letter, what her letter had said about her mother, A.'s first wife, until finally she was blubbering wetly against my chest, "Oh, Russ, I don't understand, I just don't *understand,* why does he have to *be* that way, why is he so *awful? Why?"*

I sighed. It was not going to be easy for me to explain. After all, she was his daughter, his only child. And she loved him.

*Event #3:*

(From *The New York Times,* Wednesday, May 1, 19—.)

ABERDEEN LAKE, Dist. of Keewatin (AP)—On and off for the last twenty-four years a man with a long grey beard has lived in an empty tomb in a little-used cemetery in this tiny (pop. 49) village one hundred miles below the Arctic Circle. He says, "It's nice and peaceful."

"Well, it's waterproof and nobody is going to trouble a fella living in a tomb," says the 65-year-old man, who goes only by the name of Ham.

"They call it a receiving tomb. They put the bodies in there until the ground thaws and they can bury them. But they haven't used it in a long time," says the old-timer, an American who refuses to talk about his past.

He considers himself a retiree and draws a $62.50

monthly Social Security check. Does it bother him
living in a cemetery?

"No, I kind of like it," he says. "You know, we all got
to die sometime and this just helps a fella get used to the
idea. Besides, it's kind of nice here."

Where did he come from? What kind of life did he
lead that brought him to this end. "I'm luckier than
most," he says. "I got what I wanted, not what I
deserved."

I read the article with slight, barely conscious interest, prodded by
my daily habit of reading every article in the newspaper from
beginning to end diligently, regardless of the content, but perhaps
also prodded by the vaguely familiar tone of the somewhat cryptic
remarks attributed to the old man, an assertiveness tempered by a
strangely familiar form of personal humility, a kind of matter-of-
fact pride and wisdom that I had not heard in many years. There
was a small wirephoto of the graybeard above the article, and when
I studied the blurred face, I recognized, in spite of the long beard,
the hair, the stooped posture and the obvious aging that had taken
place, my friend of long, long ago. It was A. And thus, once again,
after a lapse of what seemed an entire lifetime, I began thinking
obsessively about the man. "Where did he come from? What kind of
life did he lead that brought him to this end?" I chuckled to myself
at the poor, befuddled reporter's questions and imagined A.,
frustrating the fellow with half-truths and outright lies, flattery and
aggression. The person the reporter should have been talking to was
not A., I snorte, but me! He'd never learn the truth from A., not in a
million years.

Believing as I did that each of the above three events, taken
separately, explained A.'s, to me, peculiar absence that Sunday
afternoon in February 1974, I had reached a point in my relation to
him where almost anything could happen and where whatever did
happen would be believable to me. It would seem "natural" to me,
"right", consistent with all I had known of him before. In other
words, the man had become sufficiently real to me that I could, and
therefore should, write a novel about him—even if that "reality"
were nothing more than a projection extruded by my unconscious
life, even if it were no more than imaginary.

It was almost four o'clock by the time I arrived at my home in
Northwood. The sun was setting coldly behind the low hills,
dragging a darkening grey blanket across the snowy fields and

woods while the temperature tumbled fast towards zero and below. Then, as the sun dropped wholly behind the furthest hill, leaving only a sky fading from red to peach to sooty gray to deep, starry blue, a low cold wind cruised across the snow, from the colder, eastern horizon to the slightly-less cold western, as if following the waning light. Then the wind was gone, like a pack of silent dogs, and the night settled motionlessly down to its business of making the icy lakes creak and boom, of making trees snap, the streams whimper, the hibernating animals underground turn worriedly in their sleep, of making the rocks beneath the snow concentrate their mass.

Inside my house, as soon as I had built the fire to blazing in the fireplace in the library, I sat down at my desk, plucked my pen from the holder, and opening a blank notebook before me, wrote in large letters on the first page, *Hamilton Stark a Novel by Russell Banks*. I turned the page, and continued to write.

# TOOTH

*Jonathan Baumbach*

One day a man swimming off the point returned to shore with much, if not most, of his left leg missing. He was as surprised as the rest of us to discover what had happened.

The incident put a damper on our vacation. It was as if an alien force, boding no good, had entered our world.

We continued our summer routine, continued to do the things we had been doing, as if to admit the reality of this intrusion was to give up everything.

Some of the summer people kept their children out of the water for a week or so after the incident though most of us felt that what had happened to the man (the loss of half of his left leg) was a singular occurrence and of little consequence to the rest of us.

(Little did we know.)

Not five days after the man (a stranger to most of us) had lost his left leg in the water, Alfie Knopf (12), who was a strong swimmer for his size, emerged from a dive into the waves with his head torn off.

This was different. Alfie Knopf was known, more or less, to all of us. He played the outfield in our weekly softball games. Whatever had killed poor Alfie in such a pitiless manner could not be countenanced indefinitely.

This was the beginning—the early volleys so to speak—of what has been called *The Great Cape Cod Bicentennial Shock Scare*. No shock at that time had been sighted but we all assumed that that's what it was.

All of us assumed the obvious except my wife Genevieve, who put it down to providence. "There's something there that doesn't want us in the water," she would say, only partly (one half to one fourth) kidding.

The rest of us tended to make light of her portentousness and she took a lot of teasing that summer from our friends. Time would vindicate her. She had a history of being vindicated by time.

A side effect of the crisis was a run on books in the local libraries dealing with ocean predators. We were hungry to know what the adversary did in his spare time, what his habits were and habitat, his modus vivendi. There were not enough books on shocks to go around so some of us became experts on stingrays, piranhas and poisonous underwater plants.

It was mostly unspoken, though clearly it was on everyone's mind: When would the killer of the sea strike again?

We didn't, as it turned out, have long to wait.

An old man named Perez, casting for his dinner in a rickety fishing boat, became the dinner of someone or something else. He was a brave old man, who had once seen Joe DiMaggio play centerfield for the Yankees, though had been fishing out of his depths. We learned from this incident that being in a boat was no guarantor of safe passage.

A few days after that—it was on August 1, as I remember—the first shock hunting party set out. On August 5, an empty boat returned.

The hunt was our main topic of conversation when we got together over cocktails each evening. Rumors and fantasies passed among us, enlivened by irony and the postures of sophistication.

My friend Ugo had fantasies of taking on the shock single-handedly, mano a mano, and talked for days of little else.

The cocktail parties were particularly hard on the women who tended to be bored by all the shock talk. "I've had it," Genevieve announced one night after leaving the Lipman's. "No one talks about books or movies or whose marriage is breaking up anymore. If you want to go to those parties, you'll have to go without me."

I told her that I didn't enjoy the parties any more than she did, and added that the shock talk was merely fad and would pass in time.

"If it wasn't the shock, it would be some other unnatural disaster," she said. "The shock fulfills a real need for this community. I'm surprised you don't see that. It gives it a center of focus without which it cannot do."

I tended to think that everything was both true and false that summer so I didn't argue the point with her. Meanwhile the mutilations and deaths were piling up in unobtrusive profusion. The shock, if that's what it was (no one had seen it or too many had seen it in too many different places), could be ignored only at our peril.

The second hunting party spent six days and five nights without making contact with the predator. No one knew quite what to make of it. The shock, it seemed, had a predilection for the defenseless.

It touched us and it didn't. Although we followed the exploits of shock and shock-hunter with a certain fascination, the actual events seemed remote from our lives like a film we had seen on television and forgotten the next day.

Genevieve in bed one night: "Your shock is pressing up against my thigh."

So it was that the predator insinuated itself into our daily vocabulary.

Our neighbor, Anna, joking about her children, would say, "I wonder where my little predators are."

Little jokes covered over unspoken, perhaps unspeakable terrors.

We could only guess at what was going on in the mind of the shock, though there was no paucity of theories. He hated the human race, a visiting psychologist posited, for its presumptive superiority to his own.

Anna's husband, Ugo, had a dream in which he captured and killed the shock, stabbing the sea monster repeatedly in the tail with a fish-cleaning knife.

The dream, as it might, fired Ugo's imagination. He read it as an omen, a strategy from the unconscious. "The trick is," he said over drinks at our house that night, "is to take him from behind. If you stay away from his teeth, he can't do any great damage to you."

Genevieve had her hands over her ears.

"In this dream, I held the sonofabitch around the tail, my knife between my teeth, and he thrashed about in the water, trying to shake me loose. He couldn't do it. No matter what he did, I held fast, my hands coated with a stickum substance that professional footballers use. He couldn't understand why he couldn't free himself of me and eventually, you could tell, it broke his spirit.

Then—the timing had to be perfect or I was dead—I went for the kill."

Throughout the recounting of this dream, Anna had this big sly smile on her face. We all knew, though never talked about it directly, that their marriage was in trouble.

"The shock has put Ugo in a very macho mood," said Anna.

The next day at The Grand Union, while we were checking out the groceries, Ugo suggested with a wink that we go out together in his cabin cruiser tomorrow and do some deep-water fishing.

I didn't mind, I said, but it would have to be after lunch as I used the mornings to write.

If what I said registered, there was no indication of it on Ugo's face. "We'll need a crew of four," he was saying. "What do you think? I'd like to get Norman and Ron or Hennessey and Eastlake. Do you see what I'm aiming at? The right combination of chemistries, a self-generating tension."

There was something solid about Ugo beneath the quirkiness. If I was going to risk my life in some quixotic pursuit, there was no one among our acquaintances I would rather have on my side.

We didn't set out the next day or the next one either, although we had an understanding, Ugo and I. We talked about it as our impending deep-sea fishing expedition.

On a Friday, twelve perhaps thirteen days after the first shock incident, we received a verifiable sighting of the predator. He had been seen ten miles off the coast of North Truro, cavorting in the waves with what appeared to be a human hand in his mouth. The hand to this day remains unidentified, one of the continuing mysteries of the whole affair.

On Saturday at 10 A.M., we started out on our expedition. There were four of us, Ugo, myself, Hank Kissinger, and a fat southern Irishman named Forster Hennessey. "With a crew like that," said Genevieve, who had been against my going, "you don't have to look outside the boat for an enemy."

She might have said the same thing about any four or five of us that summer, but as it turned out she was more than usually right. While Hank, who is an inveterate complainer and intellectual, seems to enjoy physical labor—some compensatory principle operating there—Forster Hennessey, a mountainous man given to sloth and fat, generally does as little work as the traffic will bear, preferring talk and drink and the violence of metaphor.

We were a mile or two off shore, Hennessey on his fourth ale and in the middle of what seemed like an endless monologue, when Ugo called us all together to assert his authority.

"There can be only one captain on a ship," he started out. "I'd like to get that out of the way so that there'll be no misunderstanding later on. I served in the Navy in the last war so I know what I'm talking about when I say that our survival may depend on how decisively the captain gives orders and how quickly the crew responds to them."

Hennessey belched again. "Come off it Ugo," he said. "If you want to be captain, you can be captain. It's your boat, man. Just don't be so heavy about it, huh?"

Ugo transformed himself before our eyes into some self-created image of captaincy, puffing out his cheeks like Charles Laughton as he informed us of our duties. I was to be second in command, or first mate as he called it, to become captain if the original were in some manner incapacitated. (I would have declined if given the choice—but no choice was forthcoming.) Kissinger and Hennessey were to share, no status distinction between them, the remaining chores of crew. Ugo would treat us as men, he said, so long as we behaved as men. He wore a pistol and walked up and down the deck, as he delivered himself of the terms of his command. If I hadn't known him as well as I had, I would have thought that he had taken leave of his senses, had moved beyond the pale of eccentricity into outright madness.

Before he dismissed us, Ugo produced a pint bottle of blood—for a moment I thought he was going to ask us to drink from it—which was to be the bait to lure the shock from its depths. "It is my blood," he said, "and it will do what is expected of it."

The next morning Hennessey was ordered to paint a thick stripe of blood on the right side of the boat, an order he accepted to our surprise without even an obligatory display of resistance.

"What if the shock finds Ugo's blood unappetizing?" Hennessey asked me later just loud enough for the captain to hear.

"Cool it," said Hank.

"In that case," said the captain, "we'll have to use Mr. Hennessey's blood."

Hennessey had painted the stripe and dribbled some blood on the outside of the boat as an added fillip and we waited at our posts for the predator to declare himself.

It was a clear mild day but the ocean was inexplicably choppy, perhaps from some storm recently passed or some foreboding of one to come. The boat, especially at the trolling speed Ugo had set for it, tended to rock back and forth at the pleasure of the waves. We were all at this point a little queasy.

Hennessey was in the worst shape of all, his face drained of color. He was leaning over the deck rail awaiting the call when Ugo stepped out of his cabin.

At first he didn't appear to notice Hennessey although he seemed to be staring directly at him. After some minutes of this odd, distracted behavior, Ugo brought a bottle of anti-motion pills from his cabin and instructed us to take two each without water.

Hennessey could barely get his pills down, then retched them over the side the next moment. Ugo said nothing, merely turned on his heels and marched off. It was not something, you knew, he would easily forgive.

"Didn't do me much good," said Hennessey as soon as he could talk again.

Hank took me aside. "What do you make of his behavior?" he asked.

I pretended to miss his meaning, said *whose* behavior, Hennessey's?

"I think you know who I'm talking about. There is no point in mentioning his name or that we may be dealing with an acute paranoic suffering from delusions of grandeur." All of this was said in a sibilant whisper, a sound not unlike the lapping of the waves against our hull.

The boat began to lurch more violently than before, knocking us across the deck and into the railing.

"Battle stations," Ugo called over the loudspeaker.

Hennessey, who had fallen down, was sitting in a puddle of water, laughing hysterically. Hank was kneeling over him, whispering I could imagine what in his ear.

"Battle stations," Ugo called again. When we didn't move he pushed us decisively, each in turn, in the direction he wanted us to go, shouting some unintelligible command that sounded like "Birrip, birrip."

"Do you see it?" he cried. He was staring into the ocean, his gun drawn. "My God, don't you see it?" Two shots sounded. His thick black hair seemed to be standing on end.

We (I speak for myself at least) saw nothing, only an opaque and implacable sea, boundless and mysterious, a mirror without reflection.

"I order you to see it," Ugo shouted. And then we did, though not before the boat seemed to lift in the air. It was as if Ugo's gun shots had roused the monster from its deep, had challenged it into self-declaration. I was not alone in holding him responsible for its presence.

"You're mad," Hennessey yelled at Ugo or the thing in the water, one and the other. He had a harpoon in his hand, though seemed unable to let it go, paralyzed by drink and terror.

I had never been so frightened in my life and it is unlikely that I shall ever be as frightened again.

Ugo was leaning over the rail firing his pistol at the spectre of the giant fish.

I had long since disemburdened myself of the harpoon I had been assigned and it hung like a decoration from the side of the huge predator.

"Damn you," Hennessey yelled and turning let fly his harpoon at Ugo's head. The shifts and turns of the small boat saved the captain's life for something more in keeping with his obsession to end it. The harpoon caromed blindly off the railing inches from Ugo's shoulder and lodged itself in his shoe.

"Will somebody pull this son of a bitch out," he said, never once taking his eye off the predator. When the pistol was empty he reloaded it and continued his single-minded assault on the moving shock, one or two of his bullets apparently striking home, though to insignificant effect.

He turned to me when his gun was empty a second time and said, "Joshua, the operating manual is in the second drawer on the left in my cabin. I want you to take an oath that you'll get the Discontent II back to port and that you'll tell them, those that didn't make this voyage, what it was like. Can I have your promise here in front of the others?"

I was about to say that my chances of returning were no greater than his—we had already succeeded in unstapling his foot from the deck—when the giant shock leapt from the water to take possession of Ugo's gun hand, removing the weapon at the elbow. The captain's cry was barely heard over the roar of the boat.

He held up his bloody stump like a torch. "Where is it gone?" he seemed to ask.

Hank, who had fainted, rolled across the deck like a log, one lens of his glasses cracked.

I took out my handkerchief, thinking to bandage Ugo's arm,

though it was clearly too late for that. Holding onto the rail to keep my balance, I gave Ugo my word that I would honor his request. The shock was gone, had disappeared beneath the surface, and I remember calling to him in rage and anguish as if he had stolen something from me.

Using his remaining hand, which I clearly remember as the left, Ugo tore the harpoon from his foot. "Stand back," he grunted, a fountain of blood rising miraculously from his boot. His seersucker jacket, what was left of it, had turned a darkening pink. I looked around for Hennessey and didn't see him, called his name three times.

Ugo leaned over the railing, studying the ocean, harpoon drawn back in anticipation, bloody stump inside his jacket. He muttered in Italian, reverting in crisis to the language of his childhood. I had never seen him quite so beside himself.

The waters were mysteriously calm. As unobtrusively as it had come into our lives, the sea monster had returned to the deep, leaving us, as before, as always perhaps, unsatisfied.

There was something in the water, flailing about, which I took at first to be the shock returned. Ugo made the same mistake. It is a common illusion to perceive the thing you anticipate despite an opposing reality. The mind is its own place, after all. Still, I make no excuses for Ugo here. He was a man bent on revenging himself, a man, who in all the years I'd known him, had never let the real world intrude on his chimeras.

Ugo flung the harpoon, though the weapon never left his hand. I would never know whether it was Ugo's intention to follow his fling or whether he was unable to let the weapon go. He was a man from the outset, his wife would report, obsessed with holding on to what he had.

There was nothing anyone could do for Ugo after that. His flight was conclusive. He pursued his weapon to its misperceived target.

Ugo and Forster Hennessey rose and fell in the waves, tied together by rope and blood. I threw a life preserver over—it was the least I could do—though neither made any effort to secure it. It was hard to tell whether they were fighting to survive or to destroy the other.

Moments later, the great gray shock, as we had dreamed him, joined them in their final dance.

I did then what I had to do, what Ugo had he remained in command would have done himself. I made my way into the cabin and took command of the Discontent II, turning the boat forty-five degrees around so that the nose of the cruiser was in the direct line of the three forms in the water. I handled the controls without difficulty and had no doubt, an illusion perhaps though a useful one, that the boat would move exactly as I directed it. The shock was struggling to unseat Ugo who had attached himself to its tail, who in fact seemed to be sodomizing the sea creature, a look of delirious pleasure on his face. When the moment seemed right I drove the boat at full speed at the distracted predator. The creature, though diminished by its wounds, was still a frightening adversary, its eye peering at me with vengeful recognition.

"Don't," screamed Hank from somewhere on the deck. Or perhaps what I heard was the keening of the wind. Once started there was no holding back.

The collision, the shock of impact, knocked me backwards and into an ever receding dark space where monstrous teeth and eye floated over me and under, until I too was in that dance of death with the sea monster and Ugo and Hennessey, the last light of day breaking up in my head like shards of fire.

I had no way of knowing how many hours or days had passed when I came to consciousness again. I was lying in a bunk in the captain's cabin, the surroundings unfamiliar as if erased from memory, a compress on my forehead. Hank was there, sitting next to me, his eyeglasses reduced to one cracked lens, an uncanny effect.

"It's over," he said when he saw that I was awake.

"Is it?"

"It's over and done."

That's all that was said, though I have to think that we understood each other as well as we ever had.

What had happened—the details tend to rearrange themselves each time I look them over—revealed things about and to ourselves we had not been prepared to face.

What remained were the explanations to the authorities and some word or two of condolence to the wives of the deceased. Hank and I worked out a story between us, which had little relation to the real experience, but was less susceptible to disbelief.

We invented a reality just incredible enough to give it the ring of arbitrary rightness. In a certain sense, the story I would come to tell made itself up. I take no more credit for it than I do for the accidents of day-to-day experience.

So I told the story. And told the story. I told the story not only to those to whom it had to be recounted but to anyone who would pretend to listen. It got better with each retelling, achieved surprises of form, though lost something of its original freshness.

Hank, so the coda to the story goes, became morose and unable to hold a job, became an habitué of certain fashionable drugs, and drifted, downward step by downward step, into oblivion.

Ugo's wife, Anna, remarried twice within a year, losing husbands and discarding them, and kept a pet snake in a terrarium for her oldest boy, Garo, who talks of becoming a shock-hunter like his old man.

My own life goes on much as before.

I keep telling the story of the shock hunt, revising it as the imagination wills, inventing new possibilities, always veering cautiously from the truth.

And here I told it again, trying with each false variation to make it true.

## SELF-PORTRAIT

*Burt Britton*

# from LUTZ

*Jerry Bumpus*

*Special Yearning* was going unnoticed—this, the novel dedicated to the memory of my wife who, half-way through the ms. in one last hurried reading, told me in a note (cancer had taken her voice) that except for a blunder here and there it was my best effort yet. *Honestly!*—double-underlined. That night as I slept on the floor in the next room, she died, the pages of the last chapter scattered among the bedcovers and indecipherable notes she had been scribbling at the end.

Finding a company to publish the book took some doing, but at last it saw print. Months slipped by, and no reviews of it appeared—not one. In desperation I used the name B. Arthur Lutz and, disguised by a style that did a lot of huffing and puffing, wrote a piece on Hobart Stull's *Special Yearning*. But I was too late.

The day after I mailed Lutz's essay, I received the first annual statement from my publisher, a poet-novelist, small press entrepreneur, and overseer on a chicken ranch outside Salt Lake City. He said he had moved seventy-one copies of a printing of two thousand. Sixty-eight were complimentary copies he sent to reviewers, editors, writers, old school chums, aunts, uncles . . . He had sold three.

"Your novel is good, Hobart," my publisher wrote. We had known each other for years but, as was the case with most of my friends, only through our correspondence; we had never laid eyes on each other. Still, I picture my friend—not young or old, not large and not small, ink-stained and harried and shaggy with feathers—sitting on a stool in the doorway of a coop on a rainy day, his charges crowding around and watching as he writes, cocking their heads this way and that, and clucking softly as though to say, *Three. Hm. Could be better, could be worse.* "We know it's good," his letter went on, "but no one wants it. It has sunk like a rock. Now what? Do we try again? Do we wait? Wait for what?"

I never heard from him again, and my unopened letters returned rubber-stamped *No Such Person.* I pictured him driving across Utah, Idaho, Wyoming, in an old pick-up. He gives rides to hitch-hiking Indians and fills them in on the literary business. At the crossroads where he leaves them off he hands out copies of *Special Yearning* which they accept with solemn thanks. Or I see him back at the ranch, lighting a pyre of the books. Standing among the stunned and blinking chickens, he watches my novel whisper into the black bowl of night above the Great Salt Lake. The fire dwindles. He tramples the embers to darkness and jumps into his truck. He waves to the chickens—a few are scratching in the ashes—and drives off.

But B. Arthur Lutz penned his essay before I knew my novel was out of print.

And in the weeks following the essay's appearance, Lutz received a dozen letters from editors requesting similar pieces, but, as one put it, "on less obscure works and on writers not so backwatered as Hubert Strulle."

I instantly realized that if Lutz were successful, his essays might someday be collected into a book, and this collection might conceivably contain the piece on *Special Yearning* which might in this way not altogether perish but tag along, far back, like some distant and unillustrious relative walking through the thickets at the edge of genealogy's great wilderness.

Being Lutz would take work. He must be complete and consistent. Much completer than myself, of course—and marvel-ously, grotesquely consistent. But nimble, too, capable of neat cruelty, and hyperpedagogic, and full of syllables, walking with utmost obliviousness up and down the work of his betters while blatting his own wondrous version of the language. In the notes I was continuously jotting, a habit I had recently formed, I reminded Lutz that he had from the beginning seen through modern fiction as the wobbly work of jerrybuilders and dabblers. And late of a winter afternoon he could expect to realize that the situation was even worse—and better! He would hear himself whisper to the gray world that the work of the masters, even, is tenuous, with gaping, open areas, vacuums dogging the work, reminding us that these words are not reality, reminding us that even beyond what *is* real there is an infinite blank which absorbs meaning at roughly the same rate it absorbs light. Gaps! Vacuums! Even the best work is a shared deception, author and reader agreeing to lie with each other for a while—Oh, Lutz would like that! *What a mockery,* he whispered, his heart pounding loud. One night I heard him harrumph and pronounce, *Seen in this light, James is an old girl stuffed with words . . .* He went on, chortling, discovering what fun it is to shame the work with the artist. He danced in the dark, knocking books from their shelves, braying and sobbing, crunching mouthfuls of pencils and spewing splinters, until at last he flung open the window and hung his head out in the night air . . . *Where was I born?* a note demanded. The handwriting wasn't mine. Another asserted

> *N.B.* I am prepared at the flick of a page to scramble up a wall and gouge my hieroglyphics on any man's monument, not utterly defacing it but making my cats and geese sufficiently distinct to last a lifetime.

> Yrs trly, BAL

He was all about, waking me as he paced up and down muttering, shaping phrases, reading the compact O.E.D. without a magnifying glass, translating Proust into Lutz, Dostoyevski into Lutz, Faulkner too, everyone—all in all quite becoming himself and leaving samples of his prose in the typewriter for me to find: at its best his style had a certain abstruse bulk of the density and lucidity of lard. (Or so Hobart Stull saw it; farewell to the good old blowziness *he* had scrapped around with for years.)

One night I saw my wife dining with strange fellows. There she was, discussing *Special Yearning,* laughing in an uncharacteristic saucy manner and gesturing with both hands, while the men carved notes in the table with paring knives. As I peered through the window I recognized them—a band of critics! My wife, who had for so long shared with me the peculiar loneliness of my work, my dear wife had become their muse! One of them rose—I couldn't see him clearly—and going to her leaned down to whisper in her ear. *I am Lutz and you are dead*—and his lips touched my own ear. I woke trembling in the bed where my wife and I had slept, in the small room where I had worked all these years.

With monolithic ease Lutz burbled forth essay after essay, his dinosauric prose surfacing in every literary pond. He worked night and day, the clank of the typewriter waking me from dreams in which I was a boy named Homer Stone. After long periods of writing, Lutz researched maniacally, tearing books apart, literally, consuming the whole body of a writer's work in one sitting. Lutz discovered he had a photographic memory! And even as he slept, pen in hand and a pad on his chest where he jotted notes without needing to wake, paragraph after paragraph flowed before him, which he sometimes read aloud, waking me to stare out the window at the stars.

Then a tragic and hopeful development: after a year of this revelry, this wordy rampage, after a year of appalling success, Lutz published a piece on Canada's most ignored poet, Hershel Abbott. The essay was profound, sweetly written, and full of loving-kindness. Like a stone marker on a forgotten road, it was a tribute to hard thought and the long journey of the soul.

Lutz flooded the journals with essays on Abbott—and discovered he had made a world of enemies. There sprang up three dozen attacks on Lutz and Abbott. The *coup de grace* was a "revaluation of Lutz's recent criticism" by an eminent fellow whose forte was flamboyant irascibility: he concluded that after a mediocre beginning, marked by a paucity of scholarship and consistently dim vision, Lutz had fizzled, sinking to the lowest of lit crit tricks: pretending to find value in flops too cowardly to admit their life work had come to nothing.

Prior to his Abbott essays, Lutz had been invited to a conference of critics at Dunmunler College. The invitation was reluctantly honored when he had the nerve to show up—in tweed and spectacles, with the meerschaum stuck in his mouth. During the week of lectures, panels, hobnobbing and general palaver, all the others ignored him and, when cornered, pretended never to have heard of him or, for that matter, Hershel Abbott. Lutz's name had been struck from the speakers' program, but at his insistence it was added: at 5:55 p.m. on Friday, the last day of the conference, Lutz could address his colleagues. He spent the afternoon rehearsing his talk on Abbott, but when he arrived at the lecture hall it was empty. He looked in the adjoining rooms and all around outside the hall, but found no one, and because Dunmunler is a very small college in a very small town, he was able to look in a matter of minutes from one end of town to the other, but without success. Returning to the lecture hall, he heard a sound like thunder or rumbling, distant laughter. He found the narrow staircase to the attic, silently climbed it, swung open the trap door, and rose up just as a photographer snapped a shot of all the other critics.

In that picture, which would grace the front page of a literary newsletter, all the rest are smiling dourly or scowling with sublime, angelic disdain. Only Lutz, at the end of the front row, knee-high, has that mild look of bemusement customary to our species.

Two months after the picture's appearance, Lutz received a letter from Hershel Abbott.

As the ancient train rolled north, I stared into the letter, listening for murmurs and trying to see the man beyond the words and the "H.A." scrawled above the typed signature. He praised the essays on his work—and asked if I would serve as his secretary! I would receive room and board, and be free to gather material for a biographical-critical study. What an opportunity! For Lutz's research had disclosed that Hershel Abbott was a recluse about whom absolutely nothing was known of a personal nature. Lutz would be the first representative of the literary world to meet Canada's finest poet face to face! Abbott's letter went on to say the essays and my face in the Dunmunler photo showed Lutz had "some sense" and the "modicum of spiritual quietude" prerequisite to the position! Lutz treasured the paper on which this judgment was so clumsily typed, with many X-outs and scribbled corrections—and he fired off a reply accepting the job. Abbott's address was his publisher's in Montreal; however, the train ticket which came several weeks later was for a destination in Saskatchewan—and not a place-name but a railway code number of a dozen digits.

The train made a few stops the first day, refueling and letting off passengers—none boarded—and fewer stops the second. By the third day the train had shrunk to one car and a handful of passengers, mainly Indians, none sitting together, none talking. The train labored for hours up long hills, and I found myself leaning forward, my teeth clenched—then I would slump back, muttering Abbott's verse as the train coasted downhill, slowly at first, then faster and faster. We passed the latitude beyond which days in that season are continually late afternoon, the lights in the car burning round the clock; at night I watched the empty gray seats, facing resolutely forward row on row, ascend the reflection of my window like runt seraphims on a special mission through a hole in space. Morning would find me roaming through the train, standing on the

caboose platform, watching the world come up again from
darkness. Once as I was returning I found someone dozing in my
seat, a crumpled raccoonish fellow with a narrow, pointed face and
dark-ringed eyes, clutching one of Abbott's books, a finger stuck
inside to mark his place . . . It was Lutz!

But of course my seat was farther on—and the book wasn't one
of Abbott's, and the man wasn't at all literary, he was a cowboy
who when he woke firmly ignored me as I stood staring.

I seldom slept, and when I did I only wandered off a ways into the
shallows and woke hurrying back, finding myself already on my feet
or talking out loud to someone standing, to my surprise, in the aisle
by my seat—the conductor, or, once, a fellow passenger asking to
borrow a pencil. Then I woke and a man was helping me down the
aisle, leaning me against him in the same way I had helped my wife
to the bathroom before she became too ill to leave her bed. The
conductor stood at the end of the car holding open the door. They
got off with me and I saw my trunks stacked before a shed with
numbers painted on it corresponding to those on my ticket. The
conductor and the other fellow got back on and shut the door. The
train started rolling backward down the hill, the engineer, his face
vague beyond the narrow window of the locomotive, looking down
at me. The train rolled away, swiftly shrinking far down the hill to a
gray dot which vanished when I blinked.

The shed wasn't locked. The door had no latch or hinges and was
wedged in its frame. Inside was a dirt floor and a yellowed timetable
nailed opposite a window so dirty I could barely see through it.

I dragged in one of my trunks as night fell, and after unpacking
some of the things, slept in it, shivering, waking again and again
from the same long dream in which I was skating on a lake. I woke
believing someone had called my name. Lifting the lid, I looked out
and of course there was no one. I had been talking in my sleep.
Through the window the moon was brown.

In the morning I lay listening to the wind which in that northern
world has a throaty rumble like the laughter of large animals.
Suddenly I realized the sound was the idling of an automobile!

I climbed out of the trunk and pushed the door out. A large dark
green car, an ancient Daimler, was parked by my trunks.

The man at the wheel wore a wide-brimmed black hat and he sat
staring down the hill. The door swung open and he got out—tall,
gaunt, wearing a loose black coat that flapped as he leaned into the

wind. He turned toward me. But I couldn't see his face. It was too dim, gray, narrow . . .

I refused to see it, suddenly immensely weary: having come all this distance I must now try believing there was a poet within those abject yellow eyes and that narrow triangular face, a wizened Valentine heart carved from bone, and I knew again, with all the loneliness I had spent so many words and a lifetime trying to populate, just how wonderful and bitter a sham is art, that first it hides the artist from himself and then, after sublimely making separate beings of him and his work, succeeds in totally disguising him from others, and, if the work is great, ennobling him through his work, a beautiful but utterly false semblance of "himself," that will carry his name up the steps and down the marble halls to the long shelves of perpetuity.

He slammed the car door and I saw what at first looked like long black pistol barrels at the end of his arm, as if he had guns up his sleeve. But then I saw they were the steel fingers of a huge prosthesis.

"So you're a day early." He was looking beyond me.

"A day early? No, I . . ." I turned, suddenly believing some—Lutz?—had stepped from the shed. I looked back to him.

He had taken advantage of my glancing away to open one of my trunks. "Coming a day early is a trick," he said into the trunk. He scooped up a handful of manuscripts. "Why do you trick people, eh?"

"I don't trick people. The train was faster than anyone expected."

He looked through the manuscripts, his mouth pinching tight with distaste, his eyes squinting then as splinters. "You typed all this?"

"Yes." Which was a lie; before her illness my wife had done much of the typing.

"Huh. I guess he'll like it good enough."

"He?"

Reaching down with two steel fingers, he picked up another manuscript. "Why, Mr. Abbott," he said as if he had uncovered the poet's face.

I felt nothing at learning that this individual was not himself Hershel Abbott, for seeing him staring into the trunk triggered a memory that sank me into numbness . . .

As I had been carrying our old crank-up Wuxell record player into an alcove of the funeral parlor, a plump young man rushed up and begged me to let him perform my wife's service. Though I had planned a small funeral, just the two of us, I heard him out. He was an unemployed minister, he explained, his eyes filling with tears as he stared down at my feet. His career was finished before it had even begun, and his marriage was nearly done for . . . He had lost his first job after only two Sundays. "I'm not good yet at eye contact," he whispered and looked at me for two seconds, then away. I of course agreed to his offer, and he waved to a plump young woman, his wife, who so resembled him they could easily have passed for twins. The three of us stepped into the alcove where the casket waited.

The young man started off well enough, addressing general remarks to the floor and ceiling. Then he began the eulogy I had written—and very distractingly he paused, not once or twice but repeatedly, and each time he did he stared over the side of the casket. And though I tried to resist, I, too, looked each time, in spite of myself hoping, and inevitably expecting, to see some sign from my wife, some vague movement, a hand lifting to pass up a note . . . At last the plump young man finished the eulogy. He stepped down, took a seat, and wiped his forehead with a Kleenex his wife handed him. We sat there until the young man coughed and his wife nudged me. I cranked up the Wuxell and put on a piece by Brahms that played a little too slowly and was rather scratchy. It had been her favorite . . .

The man in the black coat and hat was staring at me. He had spoken.

"Lutz," I answered loudly.

He stared at me with what seemed like disdain. For he of course already knew my name; Hershel Abbott had told him.

He wagged his steel hand, the fingers rattling. "Ekersly," he said. "Give a hand"—and we loaded the trunks into the car.

# from KING JUDE

*Jerome Charyn*

He'd been a worthy student spy. Packed off to Germany by his father and Admiral Max, who expected him to destroy the republican stinkholes in France and the British Isles, Jude was declared unfit by the regular army on account of his age (fourteen) and pitiful upbringing (tutor Matthew, in his passion to teach Jude the names of Balleneran objects and institutions, hadn't bothered to stuff the infante's head with the practical matters of long division, and the irrational laws of grammar). The secret service took him with all his deficiencies; the aristocratic colonels in the Abwehr offices of Hamburg and Berlin thought it handsome to have a prince on their rosters.

Jude got along well with his gentlemen spymasters. They introduced him to schnapps and Saxon wine, and talked about that ape in the Chancellery, Uncle Adolf, who chewed carpets for breakfast and sucked his fingers. They would outwit the fat sea horses of British intelligence for their love of Germany, not for the Nazi rabbits whom they despised. Jude was one of their own, a prince from "Country 89" (the *Abwehr* name for Whalebone). He was given the code name "Miriam," because the colonels admired the womanly grace of clean hands, quiet speech, and a smooth chin (Jude acquired his beard and slovenly habits at Wormwood Scrubs). Then the colonels changed their minds. If the smug little democrats of Paris, or the loathsome Londoners, who worshiped their King George, but hated foreign royalty, ever unmasked Jude, traced him back to the *Abwehr,* the boy would be butchered. So the colonels struck "Miriam" off the rosters and listed him as

"Ungenannt" (unnamed). Thus, they told their superiors, they had a spy of such value to the *Abwehr,* they couldn't risk tagging him with name or registry number.

The colonels pampered Jude at their spy school in Hamburg. They recited whole snatches out of Hofmannsthal and Kleist, while teaching him the formulas of their best secret inks. Soon the boy could tap out messages on the Afu (the special spy radio and transmitter developed by the German secret service) with an expert "fist". The colonels had precious little spying for the prince to do; they didn't want to soil Jude with the muck of explosive jelly or the swinish art of disembowelment, which they reserved for other candidates at spy school. Instead, the prince became an all-around angel of mercy, clearing debris after the British strafed the docks of Hamburg with their low-flying fighter planes, helping to evacuate children (some of whom were older than Jude) into the Hamburg suburbs of Blankenese and Wohldorf, shoveling out inmates—dead and alive—of the epileptic hospital near the Lombardsbrucke, after a bombing raid.

It became increasingly difficult for the colonels to carry Jude on their books as an unnamed spy from "Country 89." *Abwehr* headquarters in Berlin expected sensational results from this "Ungenannt". The colonels managed to delay their Berlin chiefs. They turned Jude into a *Schweigeagent,* or S-man, who could only be activated for assignments of an extraordinary nature. Jude remained frozen for another thirteen months, but there was no possibility of a permanent sleep. The Berlin chiefs removed him from his handlers. In a tumult over the expected Allied *Grosslandung* (invasion), they were desperate for an S-man who could speak English, even the oddities of Balleneran English.

After a round of schnapps and goodbyes with the colonels (they hugged him and sniffled into his overcoat), Jude was sent to Norway, where a German seaplane ferried him to a point off the coast of York between Scarborough Castle and Robin Hood's Bay. He landed with a spy kit of binoculars, secret inks, and Afu radio in a suitcase, passport and identity card under the name of Mr. Andrew Foldstone of Derbyshire, and £15 in a watertight jar (Berlin expected its unfrozen S-man to rough it in England). Jude was meant to nose out preparations for the *Grosslandung,* and signal back to the colonels in Hamburg, who were familiar with his "fist", his distinctive touch on the Afu. Ignorant of English geography, Jude wandered about in the Yorkshire Moors until two men in brown jackets seized him by the ankles, flipped him over, and shook him free of his spy kit, his travel documents, and his watertight jar. A prince who had never once been squeezed by his own father, he was unused to this rough treatment. The two brown jackets pushed him half a mile, then drove him up to London in an old furniture lorry.

He was sneaked into an insane asylum close to Battersea Park and left in a pit that doubled as a prisoner-of-war cage. He had to scrounge on his knees amid his own wormy stools (his captors gave him nothing solid to eat). Finally they interrogated him, after raising Jude out of his pit. They sat him on a rattan chair that pinched his behind, in a room without windows. His captors had bulging waistcoats and soft baby hands. They worked in teams of four, with pipes in their mouths that stank of fruity tobacco. These were the fat sea lions the colonels had told him about. They laughed at Jude's accent, which they compared to a Spanish midwife blowing English syllables through a crack in her skull, and poked fun at his assumed name, calling him Andrew, Mr. Andrew, and Merry Andrew. "Well, well, Andrew my lad, how are things in Derbyshire?"

Jude mumbled a word or two about scones, since the English madness for tea had traveled to Ballenera more than a hundred years ago with the Duke of Wellington and his clerks. The sea lions weren't pleased with his mention of scones. They assaulted him from both sides of the chair.

"What's a toby? Quick now."

"Tell me the color of barley wine!"

"Do you fancy your 'courage' out of a bottle?"

Jude stayed mum in his chair while the sea lions sucked tobacco into their noses. "Speak up. What's that you say, Prince Jude?"

The boy (he was eighteen at the end of 1943) trembled, the tobacco reminding him of puke. His captors had unmasked him at the first interrogation with less than a full sentence out of him. He pitied the Hamburg colonels more than his own skin, for they had underrated the sea lions; they couldn't hope to beat cunning Englishmen with a deceptive bulge in their middle.

The sea lions spit in his ears. They promised to murder him if he didn't work for them. Thus began the slow, tortured process of turning Jude around. He might have withstood a steady burst of horrors, but the sea lions were fiendish with him. They starved the prince from Monday to Saturday, and fed him ice cream before church. They presented him with photographs that showed the effects of the hangman's noose on uncooperative German spies, then treated him to an afternoon of Cary Grant. This mixture of barbs and sweet poison confounded Jude, and enabled the sea lions to drive splinters into his natural reticence. They broke him in twenty-seven days, Jude walleyed with disgust for shaming the colonels who had nourished him as a spy and protected his life, but no longer having the will power to resist the sea lions' stratagems.

They took him out of the pit, gave him a new set of handlers and a London home. He had a housekeeper, Mrs. Simmons, who carried a snug Italian pistol in her apron pocket and called him "dearie" and "duck" with a malice he could hardly believe; then there was Rosie (short for Rosewall), an invalided sailor with crooked legs who became Jude's nurse, companion, and warder, and couldn't look at him without sneering. Officially Jude belonged to McDevit, his case officer, another pudgy sea lion with a pipe in his face, who provided him with ration books and clothes coupons and a new code name: Prince Hamlet. This name was bandied around with an element of sly humor in the boy's dossier and in conversations among the sea lions themselves. At a little house on Peel Street in Kensington he was known as Mr. Jude. Rosie and Mrs. Simmons had no use for subtle gamesmanship; they were good, blunt people with a spy on their hands.

McDevit appeared on those days of the week when Jude got on his Afu and communicated with the colonels in Hamburg. Familiar with the radio code Jude had divulged to his captors at the insane asylum, McDevit would feed messages to Prince Hamlet and scrutinize his "fist". The messages concerned troop movements and supply dumps that Jude had never seen. Tapping out the names Tilbury, Bournemouth, Maidstone, Brighton, Sheerness, Dover, and Gravesend, Jude would be gripped with a sadness that could gnarl his fingers and split the crease between his eyes. The messages that came over the wireless from the colonels depressed him all the more. They congratulated him for ferreting out invasion centers, quoted their favorite lines from Kleist, and sent the young prince wishes for his birthday. Jude seethed in his operator's chair, his body twisting with hate for the comforts of Peel Street, the Afu, his handlers, and himself.

McDevit wasn't ignorant of Jude's disorders and decline as a wireless operator. He brought a fresh sailor into the house, younger than Rosie, with straighter knees, and less of a sneer. This sailor, who went by the name of Toad, would stand over Jude watching him at the Afu with a hard, bitter eye. In under a week Toad had learned to simulate Jude's touch, and he took over the operator's chair. Jude was retired to the attic of the house, with the Afu locked in Mrs. Simmons' drawer.

As the prisoner of Peel Street Jude wasn't denied his vittles. Mrs. Simmons cooked him sausages for breakfast and buns alive with candied fruit and caraway seeds (McDevit gave her special provisions for "Prince Hamlet" that no Londoner could have gotten on her own), and a wrinkle at the top for burnt sugar. Jude couldn't cherish these buns in captivity; he had a hunger for Mrs. Simmons' imitation marmalade, sucking at the strips of cheesy rind in the jam and puzzling over Rosie's and Mrs. Simmons' speech.

"Don't brown me off now, Rosie. Didn't you hear the major, you silly cow?"

"I'll major him in a minute. I've had a basinful. Is the great man into his marmalade? Children starving for a bloody potato, and him licking sugar with his lip."

"Go on, eat your tay."

Jude would hear Rosie chomping, and wonder how anyone could "eat" his "tay". Mrs. Simmons never explained herself to him, and Rosie didn't have the patience to educate Jude. But he had to take the prince on walks, since "major" McDevit thought Jude would grow slothful without some exercise. "Move yourself, mate. It's time for a shuffle."

He would loop one end of a long piece of rope around Jude's wrist, grab the other end, and yank Jude over the doorsill and into Peel Street. The prince couldn't waver or pick directions; he kept to Rosie's leash. Rosie tugged him westward, into the deserted areas of Holland Park, because he didn't want a spy to see ruined houses or rubble in the streets.

But not even a nurse as diligent as Rosie could have hid all the markings of the London blitz. There were black-out curtains in the attic, blue hoods on the lamps outside Mrs. Simmons' front door, a bomb crater in the middle of Notting Hill Gate, a little north of Peel. Did Rosie consider Jude deaf and dumb? A bloody maniac could have heard the air-raid wardens' pipes, and the grinding jaws of the German heavy bombers. The house on Peel Street didn't have to shake or stink of smoke for Jude to tell the blitz was on. With the first blast of the sirens from Camden Town, Mrs. Simmons would arrive in the attic, usher Jude down the stairs with a paw in her apron, and lock him in her cellar, among the moldy potatoes and vacant cider pots. Jude sat out the bombings alone, his nose clogged with potato dust and the sweetened residue at the bottom of the pots. Mrs. Simmons, Rosie, and Toad would return from the shelter near Holland Park with soot on their faces and bits of glass lodged in their coats. Toad was the unlucky one; he seldom came through an all-clear without cuts on a hand or an eyebrow. They weren't in any mood to indulge a prince. Jude had to climb the attic in dusty clothes, without sympathy for his English handlers.

He amused himself in Holland Park. Captured at the wrist, with Rosie's instructions in mind, he couldn't stare at fences and walls, or beyond the roots of a tree. He had to be satisfied with seams in the ground until Rosie brought him to the edge of the grass. The prince, who had grown up with the skunkweed surrounding Wellington Schloss, was astonished by the wild grass of Holland Park; it had crisp blades, without scars or obvious nicks, that reached Jude's thighs with an absolute green color. "Want to go for your exercise then?" Rosie said, running Jude into the depths of the park. The prince stumbled, but he wasn't displeased. He had his look at the ducks who came out of a slimy pond with blue heads, and the thin, shaking figure of a pigeon with prominent ribs and skeleton wings.

At home on Peel Street Jude saw a little girl in the parlor. She was Mrs. Simmons' granddaughter escaped from a children's farm in Cornwall for London evacuees. The girl had dark scratches on her legs; she'd come in a tattered dress, and she bawled with or without cake in her mouth. Mrs. Simmons fed her the candied biscuits she'd prepared for Jude. There was no pistol in her apron now. She was an agonized granny, not a den mother to fallen spies. She didn't have time for Jude. He went upstairs on his own without hisses or prods from a gun. The girl stayed in the house for a week, hiding in a dress Mrs. Simmons had contrived for her from an old black-out curtain. Neither Mrs. Simmons, nor Rosie, nor Toad could lure her away from the attic. The girl sat with "Mr. Jude" at all hours. She had a tolerance for spies that went beyond the capacities of her granny or Jude's other keepers. She cracked biscuits for Jude and told him how her mother Gwen and her uncle Tom "was blitzed." He had no casualty stories to give back to her. "My country's out of the war," he said. The girl had never heard of Ballenera. "It's a tidy place," Jude confessed. "You could cross it on your tricycle in a morning and a half." The girl delighted over such information, and continued to scatter biscuit crumbs throughout the attic.

A man in a warden's hat came for the girl, carrying documents in a pouch. Jude began to deteriorate shortly after this. Rosie couldn't get him out for exercise, no matter how long he threatened to take Jude by the nose. McDevit arrived. "Major, he's lost his wig." McDevit stared at Jude, twisted his pipe apart, and then reassembled the pieces: that closed the interview. Jude was trundled off to the borough of Hammersmith, and the prison at Wormwood Scrubs.

Rosie said "Ta" with a nagging finger as he delivered "Prince Hamlet" over to the warders who'd come through the prison wall to collect their prize; the guard inside the checkpoint hut had a helmet that cut into the top of his brutal, leering head. A corner of the great prison door broke open like a wound in the wall; the warders had fists that could push a man through.

Yet Jude survived the Scrubs: he developed a different face in his isolation cell, wider, hairier, with blisters on the rims. He took kindly to his prison clothes. He belched dry air in that section of the main yard reserved for lunatics, saboteurs, and ordinary spies. He learned to sing, recalling the method and style of Matthew Inforgue:

> Henry, King Henry, where are you now?
> Did you lose a boy in Hammersmith?
> Or scatter him to the Yorkish Moors?
> He's a reconstructed Englishman
> With tea pissing out of his ears.

The warders, who figured Jude was repeating one of his spy codes, advised him to shut up. So he had four quiet years, with occasional attacks of shouting, which the warders would correct by stuffing handkerchiefs in his mouth.

He dreamed, ate enriched prison bread, rubbed up against the walls of his cell, squatted over the shitting hole with deep concentration, and was returned to Ballenera in the spring of 1948.

The citizens received their young prince, eight years gone, with a tumult that could be heard from Wellington Schloss to the gypsy caves in the outlying boroughs. Highborn and low, these folk had clean evidence of Jude's harrowing among the English; what other boy of twenty-two came home with such signs of damage on his cheeks? Scars and ruts, ratty beard, and a vile complexion. Most of them were struck by his new resemblance to the king. Father and son had broken teeth (from grinding their jaws too much), a wild growth of hair, and a similar stoop.

But Henry didn't rejoice over Jude's likeness to him; he kept clear of all the ceremonies for the prince. He scoffed at a war hero who arrived so late (sluggish homecomings meant nothing to him). He belittled the reputation of Wormwood Scrubs as a prison for incorrigibles and German spies. "It's a country club," King Harold claimed. "They kiss the boys over there, and bring in nannies to mend their socks." The king's own retainers disbelieved him: they were on the side of Jude.

King Harold wasn't the only person who smarted over the ceremonies for Jude: the prince hated adorations and crowds in the street. He chewed the buttons off his shirt and retched behind palace radiators in his misery. How could he tolerate a whole kingdom of worshippers, Arabs, gypsies, and aristocrats crashing into barricades and risking a boot in the cleft from Maxl's police for one look at him, when he'd had more curls and complications in his history than any Balleneran (including the king) could have imagined? He'd been a double agent, a dirty British spy, albeit for only a month and a half on Peel Street, before he was judged useless and thrown into Hammersmith. He longed to spit his secrets to the king, purge himself, but Harold already found him contemptible. Wretched in a prince's coat, Jude wanted to swim in his father's bile.

He couldn't locate the king. He visited the throne room, his father's apartments, the Cafe Grippe. The king had been forewarned of Jude's advances: he hid from his boy. Neither Emile nor Lazarus Grippe would come to Jude's assistance; they drove him out of the cafe with their arrogant smiles. Ultimately Jude trapped the king in one of the royal lavatories on a high floor of the Schloss. Harold was passing water with his trousers bunched around his ankles. The piss made tremendous steam in the cold room, fogging the small lavatory window. My father pees like a horse, Jude realized with a certain admiration. Harold turned his head away.

"Father," Jude said. "Please, can't we talk?" He couldn't tell whether the king was hissing or sobbing, or if it was just the stab of Henry's water against the urinal. Then the king unstuck his lips. "Prince Hamlet," he pushed through his teeth, and Jude went gray around the ears. The boy didn't lose his reason. He could feel his scalp tear over his eyebrows. The wind blew in and out of the dents in his skull. He understood how it was to have a broken head. Harold must have known all along about the crafty Britishers who had copied Jude's "fist". The boy left his father in peace. He never regained the pleasure of seeing Harold's smoky water rise above the urinal.

# THE CLEMENCY APPEALS
## A Dramatic Dialogue by Ethel Rosenberg and Dwight Eisenhower

*Robert Coover*

Bare stage. Dim figure of Justice in the background. Low distant hum of the world's ceaseless traffic. At no time during the dialogue does the PRESIDENT address the PRISONER, or even acknowledge her presence on the same stage. The PRISONER, aware of this, sometimes speaks to him directly, but more often seems to be trying to reach him by bouncing echoes off the Audience:

PRIS:   *(liturgically)* Petitioner respectfully
prays that she be granted
a pardon or commutation
for the following reasons:
FIRST . . .

PRES:   *(clearing his throat)* I have given earnest consideration . . .

PRIS:   *(insistently)* FIRST: that we are innocent.

PRES:   I have made a careful examination . . .

PRIS:   Innocent, as we have proclaimed and maintained from the time of our arrest.

PRES:   . . . Into this . . . case . . .

PRIS:   Innocent. This is the whole truth.

PRES:   And am satisfied . . .

PRIS:   Do not dishonor America, Mr. President, by considering as a consideration of our right to survive, the delivery of a confession of guilt of a crime we did not commit.

PRES: I am convinced . . .

PRIS: We told you the truth: we are innocent. The truth does not change.

PRES: There is no question in my mind . . .

PRIS: We have been told again and again, until we have become sick at heart . . .

PRES: No judge has ever expressed any doubt . . .

PRIS: . . . That our proud defense of our innocence is arrogant, not proud, and motivated . . .

PRES: The only conclusion to be drawn . . .

PRIS: . . . Not by a desire to maintain our integrity, but to achieve the questionable "glory" of some undefined "martyrdom."

PRES: . . . Is that the Rosenbergs have received the benefit of every safeguard . . .

PRIS: This is not so.

PRES: . . . Which American justice can provide.

PRIS: We are not martyrs or heroes, nor do we wish to be.

PRES: Every safeguard.

PRIS: We do not want to die. We are young, too young, for death.

PRES: Every opportunity . . .

PRIS: We wish to live. Yes, we wish to live . . .

PRES: The fullest measure of justice and due process of law . . .

PRIS: . . . But in the simple dignity that clothes only those who have been honest with themselves and their fellow men. Therefore, in honesty, we can only say that . . .

PRES: . . . Their full measure of justice.

PRIS: . . . We are *innocent* of this crime.

PRES: . . . In the time-honored tradition of American justice.

PRIS: SECOND: We understand, however, that the President considers himself bound by the verdict of guilty, although, on the evidence, a contrary conclusion may be admissible.

PRES: Now, when—

PRIS: But many times before there has been too unhesitating reliance on the verdict of the moment and regret for the death that closed the door to remedy when the truth, as it will, has risen.

PRES: *(firmly)* Now, when in their most solemn judgment the tribunals of the United States have adjudged them guilty and the sentence just, I will not intervene in this matter.

PRIS: You may not believe us, but the passage of even the few short months, since last we appealed to you, is confirming our prediction that, in the inexorable operation of time and conscience, the truth of our innocence would emerge.

PRES: *(flatly)* I will not intervene.

PRIS: *(after a moment's hesitation)* THIRD . . .

PRES: And I have determined that it is my duty . . .

PRIS: *(mustering strength)* THIRD: The Government's case . . .

PRES: . . . Not to set aside the verdict of their representatives.

PRIS: *(softly, to the President)* It is chiefly the death sentence I would entreat you to ponder.

PRES: *(as though to himself)* I must say that it goes against the grain to avoid interfering in the case where a woman is to receive capital punishment.

PRIS: *(gently)* At various intervals during the two long and bitter years I have spent in the Death House at Sing Sing, I have had the impulse to address myself to the President of the United States.

PRES: *(more firmly again)* Over against this, however, must be placed one or two facts that have great significance. The first of these . . .

PRIS: *(dreamily)* And Dwight D. Eisenhower was "Liberator" to millions before he was ever "President."

PRES: The first of these is that in this instance it is the woman who is the strong and recalcitrant character . . .

PRIS. Always, in the end, a certain innate shyness . . .

PRES. The man is the weak one.

PRIS: An embarrassment almost, comparable to that which the ordinary person feels in the presence of the great and the famous . . .

PRES: She has obviously been the leader in everything they did in the spy ring.

PRIS: *(sighing, turning away)* True, to date, you have not seen fit to spare our lives.

PRES: The second thing is that if there would be any commuting of the woman's sentence without the man's then from here on the Soviets would simply recruit their spies from among women.

PRIS: *(to the President, more firmly)* Be that as it may, it is my humble belief that the burdens of your office and the exigencies of the times have allowed of no genuine opportunity, as yet, for your more personal consideration.

PRES: The execution of two human beings is a grave matter.

PRIS: But now I ask this man, whose name is one with glory . . .

PRES: A grave matter . . .

PRIS: . . . What glory there is that is greater than an offering to God of a simple act of compassion!

PRES: But even graver is the thought of the millions of dead whose deaths may be directly attributable to what these spies have done.

PRIS: *(angrily)* No one, other than the trial judge, has even pretended that the atom-bomb material allegedly transmitted in the course of the instant conspiracy, was of any substantial value to the Soviet Union!

PRES: The nature of the crime for which they have been found guilty and sentenced far exceeds that of the taking of the life of another citizen; it involves the deliberate betrayal of the entire nation and could very well result in the death of many, many thousands of innocent citizens.

PRIS: Specifically, in relation to this case, the Government itself, after the trial, conceded that: "Greenglass's diagrams have a theatrical quality," and because he was not a scientist, "must have counted for little."

PRES: By immeasurably increasing the chance of atomic war, the Rosenbergs may have condemned to death tens of millions of innocent people all over the world.

PRIS: It is perfectly clear that such valueless information could have had little effectiveness "in putting into the hands of the Russians the A-bomb," even had they not possessed the "secret."

PRES: By their act these two individuals have in fact betrayed the cause of freedom for which free men are fighting and dying at this very hour.

PRIS: *(a bit desperately)* We submitted documentary evidence to show that David Greenglass, trapped by his own misdeeds, hysterical with fear for his own life and that of Ruth, his wife, fell back on his lifelong habit of lying, exploited by his shrewd-minded and equally guilty wife, to fabricate, bit by bit, a *monstrous* tale that has sent us, *his own flesh and blood,* down a long and terrible path toward death!

PRES: *(oblivious to this outburst)* When democracy's enemies—

PRIS: We ask you, Mr. President, the civilized head of a civilized nation to judge our plea with reason and humanity—and remember! *we are a father and a mother!*

PRES: *(pressing on)* When democracy's enemies have been judged guilty of a crime as horrible as that of which the Rosenbergs were convicted—

PRIS: *(rising to full power)* Our sentences violate truth and the instincts of civilized humanity! The compassion of men sees us as victims caught in the terrible interplay of clashing ideologies and feverish international enmities. As Commander-in-Chief of the European theatre, you had ample opportunity to witness the wanton and hideous tortures that such a policy of vengeance had wreaked upon vast multitudes of guiltless victims. Today, while these ghastly mass butchers, these obscene racists, are graciously receiving the benefits of mercy and in many instances being reinstated in public office, the great democratic United States is proposing the savage destruction of a small unoffending Jewish family, whose guilt is seriously doubted throughout the length and breadth of the civilized world! We appeal to your mind and conscience, Mr. President, to take counsel with the reasons of others and with the deepest human feelings that treasure life and shun its taking. *The facts of our case have touched the conscience of civilization!*

PRES: *(momentarily weakening)* My only concern is in the . . . area of statecraft. The *effect* of the action . . .

PRIS: *(seizing on this)* If you will not hear our voices, hear the voices of the world! Hear the great and humble for the sake of America!

VOICES: *(rolling in behind the PRISONER'S last speech, overlapping each other, slowly augmenting in volume, then diminishing as the PRESIDENT interrupts)* We the undersigned Rabbis and religious leaders of the Holy Land . . . Our committee is today comprised of men who you know, Mr. President, to be of the highest character . . . Will you express in my name the deep revulsion . . . I, an Orthodox Rabbi . . . I had the honor to fight with the American Army . . . spiritual and executive leaders in their respective denominations . . . Is it customary for spies to be paid in wrist watches and console tables? . . . utterly disproportionate to the offense for this couple with two young children to be put to . . . sinister threat of fascism and a new world war . . . Mr. President, all of us, as pastors . . . aggressive pressure of the anti-Semites, Negro-haters . . . hope thus to honor and render justice to the memory of my brother, Bartolomeo Vanzetti, who before dying said . . . indeed regrettable . . . profoundly moved by the death sentence pronounced on Ethel and . . . the extreme severity . . . a tragic event for all lovers of the . . . when conducted in a climate of fear and suspicion which breeds reckless and irresponsible action . . . I cannot but deplore . . . My conscience compels me . . . without precedent in the West . . . I pray the Lord and hope the cruel sentence passed . . . contemplate with horror . . . obtained during a period of mounting hysteria . . . never before imposed . . . Together with nearly 2,300 other clergymen . . . cruel, inhuman and barbaric in the extreme . . . in the name of God and the quality of mercy . . . your deep religious feeling and your awareness of the spirit of good within you . . . in the very name of our common ideal of justice and generosity which we derive from the Bible . . . political murder . . . to use the power which the Constitution of the United States gives you . . . urge you to commute . . . in the spirit of love which casts out fear . . . your prerogative of clemency . . . to reconsider your refusal . . . this savage verdict . . . would it not be embarrassing if, after the execution of the Rosenbergs, it could be shown that . . .

PRES: *(interrupting fiercely, VOICES fading)* I am not unmindful of the fact that this case has aroused grave concern both here and abroad in the minds of serious people.

PRIS: *(to the PRESIDENT, trying to hang on to the momentum)* The guilt in this case, if we die, will be America's! The shame, if we die, will dishonor this generation!

PRES: *(as though calling out to the vanished VOICES)* But what you did *not* suggest was the need for considering the known convictions of Communist leaders that free governments—and especially the American government—

PRIS: Mr. President—

PRES: —Are notoriously weak and fearful and that consequently subversive and other kinds of activities can be conducted against them with no real fear of dire punishment on the part of the perpetrator.

PRIS: *(urgently, almost amorously)* Take counsel with your good wife; of statesmen there are enough and to spare.

PRES: It is, of course, important to the Communists to have this contention sustained and justified.

PRIS: Take counsel with the mother of your only son; her heart which understands my grief so well and my longing to see my sons grown to manhood like her own . . .

PRES: In the present case, they have even stooped to dragging in young and innocent children in order to serve their own purpose!

PRIS: . . . With loving husband at my side even as you are at hers!

PRES: The action of these people has exposed to greater danger literally millions of our citizens.

PRIS: Her heart must plead my cause with grace and with felicity!

PRES: Within the last two days, the Supreme Court, convened in a special session, has again reviewed a further point which one of the Justices felt the Rosenbergs should have an opportunity to present.

PRIS: *(on her knees, pleading)* I approach you solely on the basis of mercy . . .

PRES: *(edging away)* This morning the Supreme Court ruled that there was no substance to this point.

PRIS: And earnestly beseech you to let this quality sway you rather than any narrow judicial concern, which is after all the province of the courts.

PRES: The legal processes of democracy have been marshalled to their maximum strength to protect the lives of convicted spies.

PRIS: It is rather the province of the affectionate grandfather . . .

PRES: Accordingly . . .

PRIS: . . . The sensitive artist, the devoutly religious man . . .

PRES: Accordingly, only the most extraordinary circumstances . . .

PRIS: . . . That I would enter. I ask this man . . .

PRES: Only the most extraordinary circumstances would warrant executive intervention in the case.

PRIS: I ask this man, himself no stranger to the humanities, what man there is that history has acclaimed great, whose greatness has not been measured in terms of his goodness? Truly . . .

PRES: If any other different situation arises that makes it look like a question of policy, of state policy, they can bring it back to me. As of now . . .

PRIS: Truly, the stories of Christ, of Moses, of Gandhi hold more sheer wonderment and spiritual treasure than all the conquests of Napoleon!

PRES: As of now, my decision was made purely on the basis of what the courts had found in all this long discussion.

PRIS: We do not want to die!

PRES: We are a nation under law and our affairs are governed by the just exercise of these laws.

PRIS: We are young, too young, for death. We wish to live!

PRES: The courts have done for these people everything possible.

PRIS: We told you the truth! We are innocent of this crime!

PRES: Have adjuged them guilty and the sentence just.

PRIS: *Innocent!*

PRES: Given them every right.

PRIS: Please—!

PRES: I will not intervene in this matter.

PRIS: *We do not want to die!*

PRES: I will not intervene.

# THE VOICE IN THE CLOSET

## Raymond Federman

here now again selectricstud makes me speak with its balls all balls
foutaise sam says in his closet upstairs but this time it's going to
be serious no more masturbating on the third floor escaping into the
trees no the trees were cut down liar it's winter now delays no more
false starts yesterday a rock flew through the windowpane voices and
all I see him from the corner of my eye no more playing some boys in
the street laughing up and down the pages en fourire goofing my life
it's a sign almost hit him in the face scared the hell out of him as
he waits for me to unfold upstairs perhaps the signal of a departure
in my own voice at last a beginning after so many detours relentless
false justifications in the margins more to come in my own words now
that I may speak say I the real story from the other side extricated
from inside roles reversed without further delay they pushed me into
the closet on the third floor I am speaking of us into a box beat me
black and blue question of perspective how it should have started in
my little boy's shorts I am speaking of me sssh it's summertime lies
again we must hide the boy sssh mother whispering in her tears hurts
to lose all the time in the courtyard bird blowing his brains out on

experimenting with the peripatetic search for love sex self or is it
real people america aside from what is said there is nothing silence
sam again what takes place in the closet is not said irrelevant here
if it were to be known one would know it my life began in a closet a
symbolic rebirth in retrospect as he shoves me in his stories whines
his radical laughter up and down pulverized pages with his balls mad
fizzling punctuation question of changing one's perspective view the
self from the inside from the point of view of its capacity its will
power federman achieve the vocation of your name beyond all forms of
anthropologism a positive child anthropomorphism rather than the sad
off-spring of a family giggling they pushed me into the closet among
empty skins and dusty hats my mother my father the soldiers they cut
little boys' hands old wife's tale send him into his life cut me now
from your voice not that I be what I was machines but what I will be
mother father quick downstairs already the boots same old problem he
tried oh how he tried of course imagining that the self must be made
remade caught from some retroactive present apprehended reinstated I
presume looking back how naive into the past my life began not again

whereas in fact my mother was crying softly as the door closes on me I'm beginning to see my shape only from the past from the reverse of farness looking to the present can one possibly into the future even create the true me invent you federman with your noodles gambling my life away double or nothing in your verbal delirium don't let anyone interfere with our project cancel our journey in my own words inside the real story again my father too coughing his tuberculosis as they locked him into the closet they cut little boys' hands alone waiting on his third floor crapping me on his paper what a joke the soldiers quick sssh and all the doors slammed shut the boots in the staircase where it should have started but not him no instead calmly he shoves the statue of liberty at us very symbolic over the girl's shoulder I tremble in his lies nothing he says about the past but I see it from the corner of my eye even tried to protest while the outside goes in then smiles among the beasts and writes one morning a bird flew into my head ah what insolence what about the yellow star on my chest yes what about it federman the truth to say where they kept old wrinkled clothes empty skins dusty hats and behind the newspapers stolen bags of sugar cubes how I crouched like a sphinx falling for his wordshit moinous but where were you tell me dancing when it all started where were you when the door closed on me shouting I ask you when I needed you the most letting me be erased in the dark at random in his words scattered nakedly telling me where to go how many times yes how many times must he foist his old voice on me his detours cancellations ah that's a good one lies lies me to tell now procrastinations I warned him deep into my designs refusing to say millions of words wasted to say the same old thing mere competence never getting it straight his repetitions what really happened ways to cancel my life digressively each space relating to nothing other than itself me inside his hands progress quickly discouraged saying that it was mad laughter to pass the time two boxes correspondence of space the right aggregate while he inflicts false names on me distorts our beginning but now I stoop on the newspapers groping to the walls for the dimensions of my body while he stares at his selectricstud humping paper each space within itself becoming the figure of our unreality scratched from words the designs twirl just enough for me to speak and I fall for his crap to with myself I threw sand in his eyes struck his back with a stick in his delirium whining like a wounded animal I squat on the newspapers unfolded here by shame to defecate my fear as he continues to scream multiplying voices within voices to silence me holding my penis away not to piss on my legs clumsily continues to fabricate his design in circles doodles me up and down his pages of insolence two closets on the third floor separate correspondence of birth in time seeking the right connection meaning of all meanings but from this angle never a primary phenomenon to end again reducible to nonsense excrement of a beginning in the dark I folded the paper into a neat package for the birds smelling my hands by reflex or to disintegrate years later but he ignores that too obsessed by fake images while sucking his pieces of stolen sugar on the roof by the ladder outside the glass door the moon tiptoed across the clouds curiosity drove me down the staircase but I stumbled on the twelfth step and fell now all the doors opened dumb eyes to stare at my nakedness among the beasts still hoping for survival my father mother sisters but already the trains are rolling in the night as I ran beneath the sky a yellow star struck my breast

and all the eyes turned away I told him tried to explain how it must
have started upstairs they grabbed me and locked me in a box dragged
me a hundred times over the earth in metaphorical disgrace while the
soldiers chased each other with stones in their hands and burned all
the stars in a furnace my survival a mistake he cannot accept forces
him to begin conditionally by another form of sequestration pretends
to lock himself in a room with the if of my existence the story told
in laughter but it resists and recites first the displacement of its
displacements leaving me on the threshold staring dumbfounded at the
statue of liberty over the girl's shoulder question of selecting the
proper beginning he claims then drags me into the subway to stare in
guilt again between a woman's legs at the triangular cunt of america
leads me down the corridor to masturbate his substitution instead of
giving me an original experience to deceive the absence of a woman's
hand makes believe that I am dead twelve years old when they left me
in the primordial closet moment upstairs on the third floor with the
old newspapers empty skins seeking unknown pleasure which is only an
amorphous substitution thinking that memory is innocent always tells

the truth while cheating the original experience the first gesture a hand reaching for the walls to find its proper place since he failed to generate the real story in vain situates me in the wrong abode as I turn in a void in his obligation to assign a beginning however sad it may be to my residence here before memory had a source so that it may unfold according to a temporal order a spatial displacement made of words inside his noodling complexities of plagiaristic form I was dead he thinks skips me but I am being given birth into death beyond the open door such is my condition the feet are clear already of the great cunt of existence backward my head will be last to come out on the paper spread your arms voices shout behind the walls I can't but the teller rants my story again and I am alive promising situation I am my beginning in this strange gestation I say I for the first time as he gesticulates in his room surrounded by his madness having once more succeeded in assembling single-handedly the carbon design of my life as I remember the first sound heard in this place when I said I to invent an origin for myself before crumbling into his nonsense on the edge of the precipice leaning against the wind after I placed my voices murmuring behind the doors refusing that which negates itself as it creates itself both recipient and dispatcher of a story teller told creature on my hands the smell of the package up on the roof to disintegrate in laughter divided I who speaks both the truth and the lie of my condition at the same time from the corner of its mouth to enclose the enunciation and denunciation of what he says in semantic fraudulence because I am untraceable in the dark again as I move now toward my birth out of the closet unable to become the correspondent of his illusions in his room where everything happens by duplication and repetition displacing the object he wants to apprehend with fake metaphors which bring together on the same level the incongruous the incompatible whereas in my paradox a split exists between the actual me wandering voiceless in temporary landscapes and the virtual being federman pretends to invent in his excremental packages of delusions a survivor who dissolves in verbal articulations unable to do what I had to do admit that his fictions can no longer match the reality of my past me blushing sphinx defecating the riddle of my birth instead he invents me playmates in his chaotic progress for his deficiencies

# P_____ : A CASE HISTORY

## B. H. Friedman

P_____ is middle aged, of medium height, neckless, bullet-headed, with features that are unrefined, almost blank. He has been stout but has been losing weight for no apparent reason. His skin fits loosely now.

He is in bed beside his wife—inches away, which might as well be miles. They have made love, and now she is asleep, breathing regularly, not as heavily as before, perhaps more contentedly. They are alone together, in their bed, in their room, in their apartment, a series of boxes within boxes, limitations within limitations.

P_____ can't sleep. He plays with himself, his penis still moist from his wife. He strokes it gently. Nothing happens. It is tired, this thing with a will, a life of its own, part of him and yet as separate as his wife, less than a foot away. He grips it more firmly, strokes it harder, teases the tip. Still nothing happens. He tries to shake it awake and alive. He doesn't want to admit that he (it) is getting old or, at least, with each passing minute, older, nearer to death.

He thinks of women at his office, secretaries, filing clerks, receptionists; women he has known; women on the street; women on the covers of magazines; women on the television and motion picture screen. They blur, become faceless, lose their identities in the single identity of their sex. P_____'s mind becomes one large collective cunt. He wishes he could possess it, fill it, this collective all with its core of emptiness. But for what? The same humiliating fiasco he would go through if now he awakened his wife, if he weren't so considerate. The irony is dark and dismal.

P_____ wishes that the act of love didn't pass so quickly, that he could sustain an erection for longer, for ever, that he could fuck every woman who goes through his mind, through his life, past and future. All this amounts to a single prayer: that God grant him a cock permanently rigid, always at the ready, a tool as tough as leather, as hard as horn, broad and solid as a man's thighbone—or that of a bull. He prays for a great crowing cock.

Images fly through his mind: winged Pompeian phalluses; Leda's long-necked swan; well-hung acrobatic Minoans; long pricks drawn on the walls of prehistoric caves, on scrolls of Egyptian papyrus and of Japanese silk; pricks painted on ancient terra cotta and baked for permanence; pricks illuminated by medieval monks; pricks carved in stone or wood; pricks cast in bronze and of precious metals; scrimshaw pricks made from whale teeth; pricks erected as monuments to the living and the dead; pricks worshipped, carried as amulets, used as dildos; pricks reproduced, illustrated, described throughout the history of art and literature; incunabulous pricks; photographic pricks; black-and-white motion picture pricks; blue-movie pricks; full-color pricks; off-color pricks; pricks wired for sound by Masters and Johnson; vibrating battery-driven pricks, sold in so-called drug- and so-called novelty-stores; pricks that can zoom to the moon . . .

Despite the loose-formation flying through P_____'s mind like so many birds, planes and rockets, all lofty, erect and goal-oriented; despite advances in technology and variations in symbolism; despite everything, the fact, the thing, the prick itself remains the same, unchanged after thousands of years, whimsical as his own, sometimes hard, sometimes soft and tender as his now. That is the reality; the other—the examples from art and architecture, engineering and technology, advertising and mass media—is the dream. And yet . . . And yet . . . As P_____ tells himself these things, he still fondles his prick, wishing it would fill his hand, both hands, both arms, and then soar altogether out of reach.

He removes his hand, wanting to sleep and forget this limp thing between his legs—and in his mind: there, a collective image as hollow as the cunt.

P_____ turns over. His prick is soft beneath his stomach. He is ready, finally, to settle for far less than a monumental prick of stone or for one that stretches ten feet across a scroll. He would settle for his youth, when he was able to masturbate five or six times a day; he would settle for the youth of classic Greece, a boy, with a perfectly ordinary hard-on, running perpetually around a vase. And yet . . . And yet, again, he does want it to be forever, to be eternal. He prays.

The clock rings. P_____ emerges from a world of snakes, swans, goats, bulls. His hand slithers from under the blanket, flies to the night table, butts the alarm switch, kills the sound. He is awake, quickly as always, precisely one hour from his desk at the office. Carefully, so as not to distrub his wife who has barely stirred at the sound of the alarm, he gets out of bed and shuts the window. A magnificent erection bulges out of his pajamas, and he regrets that it to will pass, die, like last night's, like those of all the other nights and days. Once again he wishes that it could last forever, that it could be as efficient and dependable as the rest of him which he presents at the office.

He tiptoes to the bathroom and quietly closes the door. In the mirror he hardly sees the tired, loose-skinned, lumpy image of himself. His eyes focus on his cock, erect as before, young, alive, and rosy. He tries to urinate but the erection won't let him. He presses his stomach, tickles his buttocks, turns on the water in the sink, concentrates as if in a doctor's office, fears that he may be late to work. As he becomes anxious, his prick relaxes slightly, asserting its own life. He tenses his stomach muscles, pressing, pressing. Painfully the urine forces its way out. The stream is thinner and longer-lasting than usual. It burns. In the toilet bowl, it seems to boil.

P_____ steps over to the sink and prepares to brush his teeth. He is surprised that his prick is as rigid as before pissing. He studies it more closely than his face. It intrudes as if to grab the toothpaste on the edge of the sink, as if to reach even farther up and take the brush from his hand. As he shaves, his prick is there, poised in the mirror, watching him, wanting to get in on the act, some act, perhaps wanting now to grab the razor. P_____ shaves mechanically, hardly looking at his face, aware mostly of his prick, still at attention in the mirror.

He starts to put on his underwear, first a T-shirt, then elasticized briefs which don't have the strength to hold his cock down. They bulge like a sail in the wind, a very still wind. He becomes anxious again, knows he can't go to the office like this. He remembers his wife, slips out of his underwear, joins her in bed, kisses her lightly on her closed eyelids, her ears, her neck, her breast; strokes her back, holds her close to him, makes her feel that great thing between his legs, between hers now.

She responds, opening her legs and mouth, saying, "You want me, you really want me, don't you?"

"Yes, yes," he replies, forcing his way into her. "I need you."

"What time is it?" she says, asking the sort of question that might another time have made him go limp.

He turns toward the clock and tells her.

"You'll be late."

He replies by driving the shaft of his prick as far into her as it will go. She writhes. Her pelvis churns. Her breath, slightly foul from sleep, comes in short hard gasps. Her juices begin to flow, reluctantly at first and then in rapid spurts. There is no stopping her. Her movement is relentless. She groans like a motor at maximum performance.

P_____ is pleased by her pleasure. She seems to be asking for more, more, more, as her hips hop beneath him. He rides her, wanting to give every drop, ounce, pint perhaps, in his balls, stating the message of their heavy content as they slap against her buttocks. We have so much to give, they say. But nothing is given. Ejaculation is as difficult now as pissing had been just a short while ago.

He pumps on, wanting not only the orgasm straining to be released within him, within her, but wanting also to get to work on time. His wife, churning beneath him, ceases to exist. He thinks about the orgasm which won't come, the breakfast he will miss, his tardy arrival at the office, his appearance there. He says new silent prayers, makes new pacts with ancient gods: If only this orgasm is granted, if only he can be released from the rigid prison in which he finds himself, he will never again ask for anything. The previous night and so many nights before, his wife had satisfied him. Now he can satisfy her but not himself.

He withdraws. She opens her eyes, smiles, says just one word, "Wow!", turns over and goes back to sleep.

His erection is harder, bigger, stiffer than ever. He can barely get his briefs on. They tug at his crotch. He takes them off again and gets an athletic supporter. This works better. It is stronger, more elasticized. He lifts his cock so that it rests close to his stomach, almost parallel to it rather than perpendicular. But still there is a great rock-like bulge straining at the jock. This is the best he can do, more comfortable, he's sure, than strapping or taping it to his leg the way studs do in pornographic novels, that world in which everything and everyone is controllable, that fantasy world.

He is late. As he finishes dressing, he wonders if he should call the office and tell them—what?—that something has come up. He smiles. That is just the sort of vague explanation his secretary gives. In his case it's precise, too precise. Never complain, never explain, he has been taught. But not complaining is difficult: he won't explain.

He hurries to work. With every step he is aware of the aggressive pressure in his jock. He is led, pointed to the office, by this leashed thing just an inch or so from his stomach, always that little bit ahead of him, impossible to overtake. Young girls, old girls, mature women come toward him, pass by quickly on the way to their jobs, noticing neither the bulge in his pants nor the need in his eyes, noticing nothing. This is both a relief and a disappointment, like having a pimple on his nose—huge to him, almost invisible to the world. But the analogy won't stand up (another joke, another smile); the scale of his present affliction is so much greater. He feels the hugeness of his cock, painfully pressing forward.

In the elevator he is thankful he is late. What would it have been like, at nine, pressed against all those bodies? How would he have explained his condition as some switchboard operator screamed "Rape!" or some male filing clerk yelled "Queer!"? As it is, with only four others in the car, he removes his hat and holds it over his crotch, still believing that everyone knows. At his floor he races past the receptionist and a corridor of secretaries, including his own. His greetings are perfunctory. He wants the protection of his desk.

There he gets through the morning, keeping the walnut top between himself and the world. But always beneath the correspondence, contracts, budgets, operating statements; beneath the words he dictates to his secretary and those he speaks at conferences and into the phone; beneath everything is his prick nagging at the jock and the jock nagging at him. That is the real problem, beneath, but also above, all the others. That needs attention, more than next year's prices, more than fluctuations in the value of the dollar.

Fortunately he doesn't have an appointment for lunch. When the executives who are free ask him to join them, he says he has work to catch up on. He buzzes his secretary and orders a sandwich and coffee to be sent in.

"Anything else? A slice of pie?" She waits, pencil poised over stenographic pad.

Hair pie, a nice juicy wedge of hair pie, P_____ thinks, imagining them going down on each other, as he says, "No thanks."

He watches her leave the office, studies the movement of her hips, wonders if—

What would The Secretary's Manual say? *Be cooperative at all times. At the executive level, you will be asked to perform personal chores such as addressing Christmas cards, minor shopping, the payment of bills, the sewing on of buttons, etc. These tasks should be done willingly. They contribute to the executive's efficiency, they free him for other work . . .*

What does that "etc." mean? How far does it go? How far would she go? She has done all the other things in the manual, all the other wife jobs, why not this? A little blowing to follow sewing, a job done easily, under the desk, during lunch hour. He could promise her a raise—

When she brings in his lunch, the executive area is empty. Again she asks, "Anything else?"

Well, yes—the words run silently through his mind—I'd like to discuss your salary with you. Please shut the door. I'm going to be requiring—

Still in his mind, he feels her out, himself in—with his tongue this time. And he imagines hers, moist and tender on his cock, licking it, soothing its painful throb.

The actual dialogue is as brief as before. He says only, "No, thanks." Again he watches her leave his office. Again he studies the movement of her hips. Until now he has never understood the psychology of rape. He begins to understand. And as he eats his lunch, he thinks of her eating hers and wishes she were eating him instead.

The coffee seems to drop right to his bladder. He goes to the executive john, chooses a stall rather than an open urinal, tries as hard as he had at home. The agony is more intense now. It burns like a licking flame, inside, out of reach. Even touching his penis is painful. He cannot aim it at the toilet bowl. It points straight ahead. He must bend his body to avoid splattering the wall. But that becomes academic. There is no splatter, no splash, not even a thin stream, not a single drop. There is only the pressing pain of urine trying to escape, the throbbing blood in his cock blocking that escape.

P‗‗‗‗‗‗ puts his cock back in its elastic halter, wondering if he is entirely responsible for his predicament, his pain. If he willed it up, why can't he will it down? If his past prayers were answered, why not the present ones? He imagines a computerized heaven in which prayers are answered in the order of their receipt. Perhaps the computer, like his prick, is jammed, jammed by all those other men wishing for perpetual hard-ons. The lucky ones, P‗‗‗‗‗‗ thinks, they don't know what they're missing.

From his office he calls his internist, who is as close to God as P‗‗‗‗‗‗ can get. He tells the nurse that this is an emergency. She She says she will fit him in. P‗‗‗‗‗‗ smiles. The world is filled with cruel jokes.


The nurse escorts him into the examination room.

"Undress and leave a urine specimen in the container in the washroom."

"That's the trouble. I can't."

"Oh! Well, the doctor will be with you in a few minutes. He'll fix you up."

Another joke, P‗‗‗‗‗‗ thinks as he undresses. It is a relief to take the jock off. His prick springs forward into a horizontal position, rigid as ever. He wonders what the nurse would think if she walked in now. Something like that had happened years before, when he was being shaved in preparation for an appendectomy. That nurse had given his erection a sharp tap with two fingers—a mini-karate chop—and it had subsided. He wishes that his present situation was as simple.

While he waits for the doctor, P‗‗‗‗‗‗ tries to urinate. He turns on the sink faucet. He flushes the toilet. He concentrates on the sound of the rushing water. Leaning over the toilet, with the container in one hand, he presses his bladder with the other. He tenses his stomach muscles. He tickles himself. Once again nothing helps. The container remains empty.

In this clinical atmosphere he examines himself—his prick, his painful prick—more carefully than before. Although the shaft is absolutely stiff, the tip is rather flaccid and insensitive, un-responsive to tickling or pressure. The pain seems to be at the base. He is still examining himself when the doctor enters.

P‗‗‗‗‗‗ forces a grin, somehow expecting a broader one in reply. Despite his pain, there is a comic side to the situation: he feels rather ridiculous, standing there with his hard-on, like a character in a dirty joke.

The doctor doesn't smile. The nurse has told him that P_____ can't urinate. He focuses immediately on P_____'s penis.

"How long have you had this?"

"All my life," P_____ replies, trying again to break the ice, to cut through the doctor's brusque clinical manner.

"This trouble, this erection."

The doctor's tone is urgent, he has no time for jokes. P_____ assumes that he is rushed because of squeezing in this unscheduled appointment.

"Since early this morning."

"How long since you urinated?"

"Then. With difficulty. Pain."

"What about sexual intercourse?"

"This morning too."

"Was it pleasurable?"

P_____ tries to remember. It seems long ago. "No. Mechanical. I thought it was a way of—you know—getting rid of it. What else does one do with an erection?" Again P_____ smiles. Again it is ignored. "I didn't come."

"Have you felt any sexual desire since?"

"Fantasies. My secretary blowing me. Even thought of rape, though seduction's more my style."

And once again P_____ smiles without response from the doctor. Instead there's yet another question:

"But don't you remember if there was real desire? Try to recall."

P_____ tries, puzzled by this line of questioning which is more like a psychiatric examination than a physical one. His prick hurts. It's what needs attention, not his mind. Finally he says:

"I don't think so. I guess I just wanted to use her. Like my wife . . . But for God's sake, I haven't been able to take a leak since this morning."

"I can take care of that. I'll catheterize you, but I'm afraid there are other things I'll have to do first."

"What?"

"Oh, some blood tests."

The doctor's casualness sounds forced. His "Oh" hangs in the air, like the smell of lysol.

"Do you know what I've got?"

"I know it's some kind of priapism. I don't know the cause. If I knew, you wouldn't need the tests."

P_____ is relieved. He has a vague idea that priapism is mental, a sort of male nymphomania. Now he understands the reason for all of the doctor's questions and the need to correct his own wishes and prayers. Yes, he will stop equating the life of his penis with his own life and with life itself. He will—But the doctor continues:

"What you have is very rare. I've never seen a case before. It may be common as a fantasy but not as a medical fact. There is usually a thrombosis—a clot blocking the passage of blood from the penis." He takes out a prescription pad and makes a quick sketch, including directional arrows, of an artery feeding what he calls "venous sinuses in the corpora cavernosa" and of veins removing the blood from them, finishes by drawing an X over the veins. "The clot," he says. "That's what we've got to find the cause of."

P_____ winces as the needle enters his arm. He watches the syringe fill with blood, identifying this blood with that in his penis and praying that it, clot and all, is being sucked out. He cannot yet realize that he is sick, physically sick, beyond blood-letting, beyond prayers, beyond magic, perhaps beyond hope.

The pain caused by the hypodermic is minor, no more than a bee sting, compared with the catheterization. P_____ can barely hold back his tears as the thin lubricated rubber tube is inserted and probes inward toward the bladder. He feels violated, tortured in a way that would make him admit to anything—things done or not done. After further probing, a stream of urine splashes noisily into the specimen jar. The removal of the tube is less painful than its insertion, but, though smooth and lubricated, it still feels like sandpaper—perhaps a finer grade now—being drawn across naked nerves.

The doctor continues the examination. "You've lost considerable weight."

"Yes, I've been working hard and playing a lot of squash."

"Trying to prove that you're getting younger?" the doctor asks rhetorically and rather gruffly. "I wish—" It is obvious that he is about to deliver a lecture, but he changes his mind and scribbles a prescription. "This is a mild sedative, in case you feel uncomfortable. I can't prescribe anything else until I get the results of the tests. I'll call then. Meanwhile, probably best that you rest in bed. Take as few liquids as possible."

P_____ returns to an empty apartment. He cannot rest. He

cannot concentrate on reading or television. He lies in bed on his back with his knees up protecting his penis from the slight pressure of the sheet and blanket. He looks at the clock, wishing it would move ahead faster; at the phone, wishing it would ring; at the clock again, still reading 3:22. He has had an erection for just over seven hours—maybe more—seven *waking* hours. This is as close to forever as he wants to get.

He listens for the sound of his wife's key in the door, wishes she would return, wants to talk to her but doesn't know what he wants to say, wants to talk to anyone but doesn't want to tie up the phone, realizes that the doctor can't possibly have received the results yet, thinks of calling his secretary but doesn't know what to tell her either. There's nothing to say, nothing to do but wait. It's 3:24.

P_____ tries to reconstruct the medical examination, to piece together the doctor's words, spoken and unspoken, his facial expressions and the lack of them. He is convinced that the doctor knows or suspects more than he lets on, masks the knowledge and suspicions with his professional manner, just as P_____ himself does when negotiating. P_____ knows now what he wants to say to his wife. He wants her to promise she will insist that the doctor tell him the truth or, if he will only tell *her,* that she in turn will tell him, that there be no censorship, no professional games.

And P_____ wants to tell his wife something else too, something that he has always found very hard to say. He wants to tell her that he loves her, that he has always loved her even when he was with other women. He wants to explain what it was like in hotel rooms in distant cities when the working day was over and he thought of her and the children (now grown) and knew no way to express his love except with his prick.

Another parade of women marches through his mind, not like last night's, not office acquaintances or movie and television stars, but only women with whom he has slept. Nevertheless, as much as the others, they are strangers and, more than the others, they are fuzzy and indistinct in P_____'s memory. Now as he tries to separate them, each becomes a different burden of guilt. He can feel their weight in bed.

The list is long, the weight crushing, but he cannot blame these women for his present painful punishment. Once again he blames himself. He lifts the top sheet and studies his prick, erect between his thighs, arrogant, willful, defiant, daring him to knock it down. He imagines the doctor's cool voice: "I'm afraid there's only one cure—amputation. You yourself said the only thing to do with an erection is get rid of it." "But not that way," P_____ screams in his mind. There is no smile now. He is as unresponsive to his humor as was the doctor an hour or so earlier. He has told a dirty joke to himself, or on himself, which fell flat.

Lightly he touches his penis, runs his fingers up and down its length, presses a little harder. As at the doctor's office, there is pain at the base and some softness at the tip. The rest, except for veins, is smooth and firm. P_____ feels no pleasure in his touch, no desire for a more masturbatory caress. He drops the sheet.

It is almost five, the hour at which ordinarily he would be going to play squash. He wonders if he will ever play again. How could he play in his present condition? How could he even go to the club? Undress? Shower? What could be more embarrassing? Only to have no prick at all, as in that fearful joke, that amputation fantasy. He lifts the sheet again, closes his thighs over his penis, sees only pubic moss or underbrush, misses that great tree which grew in the midst of it, hates its absence, parts his thighs, hates its presence, hates himself, hates his pain.

If his condition persists, there are other things he will no longer be able to do, summertime things, the things he likes best: walking on the beach, swimming in the ocean and riding waves to shore, playing tennis, sailing . . . As each of these past activities moves through his mind, he edits out the other participants, except for his wife. He and she are alone on the beach. They find an isolated stretch for swimming. They give up doubles (except perhaps with their children, to whom he will have to explain his condition). They sail alone (except, again, maybe with the children). P_____ feels close to his wife, closer than during intercourse last night, much closer than this morning. Again he wants to tell her how much he loves her. Where is she?

She doesn't arrive until close to six, 5:43 to be exact. But by then P_____ has gone through a long imaginary session with his tailor. How casually the man asks, "Which side do you dress on?" as if he had never asked before, as if P_____ had not been going there for years. "The left," P_____ replies, "but maybe you should leave some extra room up front." "I noticed." "It's some rare disease." "Such a disease we all want." "You don't. It's called priapism. You're not Greek, are you?" "Jewish." "I thought so. I'm not Greek either. Not as far as I know. Maybe some small part," P_____ says laughing mechanically, then continuing, "But this can happen to anyone." "You've lost weight." "Another symptom." "Not so bad either." P_____ feels that they are raving, that he himself is not making sense, not communicating, that the tailor is still envious. For a moment P_____ wishes the disease were contagious. Then he wonders how, if he can't communicate with this tailor who means nothing to him, he will ever be able to say what has to be said to his wife or children. He can't imagine talking about pain to anyone but a doctor.

Throughout the rest of the fitting P_____'s wife is there, where she has never been before, dimly reflected in the three-way mirror, murmuring the announcement of her presence—a preference for blue, a liking for slightly wider laps—beneath the conversation between P_____ and the tailor. But on a still deeper level of fantasy, beneath her whispered trivial comments, she is saying without words, that she knows he needs her, that that is why she is there in this forbidden territory, that she has heard him call, that she is waiting . . . And yet it takes so long for her to really appear—until 5:43, *really.*

"What's the matter?" she asks when she sees him in bed.

"Oh"—that casual, medical *Oh* again—"I seem to have something called priapism." P_____ lifts the bedding and shows her.

"I'll fix that."

"No, not this time. I'm waiting to hear from the doctor. He took some blood tests."

"He thinks it's serious?"

"Don't know Afraid so. That's something I wanted to talk to you about before he calls. *I want to know. I want him to tell me the truth.* And if he won't, I want you to. He was cagey at his office."

"Maybe he doesn't know what you have."

"He knows what I've got. He said he didn't know the cause, beyond there being a blood clot, but he knew."

"No point in imagining things. Are you allowed to have a drink?"

"I guess one would be all right. Trouble is I can't take a leak without being catheterized."

"Then we'll wait. We'll celebrate when the tests come in negative."

"You have a drink. Have one for both of us."

"I'll wait."

"Don't be a martyr."

She looks hurt. P_____ thinks that now may be the time to say he loves and appreciates her. "Sorry—" he begins, but even that one word is difficult to get out, and just then the phone rings. They both reach for it, but P_____ is closer.

"Fine, dear . . . You? . . . Yes, she's here but we're waiting for an important call. Can she call later? . . . Fine." He hangs up. "Fine. Everything's fine."

"There's nothing to be angry about. She didn't know you were waiting for a call."

"Sorry," P_____ says again, with effort. As if programmed to the word, another bell rings, the front door this time. "God, you're not expecting anyone, are you?"

"No. I'll get rid of whoever it is," she says, leaving the bedroom.

P_____ recognizes the doctor's voice as he greets her. That's enough. P_____ doesn't have to listen for the note of solemnity. The fact that the doctor came instead of calling says everything.

They are whispering now, but P_____ doesn't need to hear the words either. He knows that they mean the same thing as the doctor's visit. P_____'s impulse is to call them into the bedroom, but that can wait—the official professional word or words. He hopes only that his wife is doing what he asked, getting the truth. The whispering continues. It is not like other whispering he has heard in his life. Now they *have to* be talking about him, his prick. And they can't be saying anything good. Finally they enter.

"How's the patient?"

"You tell me."

The doctor hesitates. "I never know what to say at times like this. I've been talking to your wife. She says you want the truth. That's what most patients say. But I don't always believe them. A few really want the truth. Some want part of the truth. Most want only hope. Only hope. Of course that's a lot. But there *are* new drugs, better ones coming out all the time—"

"My wife told you what I want. I can tell you what I don't want. I don't want bullshit."

The doctor looks startled. "All right, the truth, then. But it's not pretty. And it's not funny," he adds pointedly.

"I want it anyway. Straight."

"The tests show that you have leukemia."

There is no misunderstanding this, no confusing it with a mental disease.

"I've reserved a room for you at the hospital. I want to have more tests taken. I want specialists to look at you. We'll do everything we can."

"How long?"

"It's difficult to say, almost impossible. Months, half a year, a year, maybe longer. It depends on so many things: how acute the leukemia is (the additional tests should show that), how you respond to medication, what new medication comes along—many things."

"Did you know all this when I saw you?"

"No. I was pretty sure, but—"

"What?"

"What good would it have done to know sooner?"

"No good."

P_____ is tested, examined by specialists, jabbed, probed, x-rayed. Fluids are removed from his body, others are injected into it. His responses to medication are continually measured by temperature, pulse rate, blood count. Something is always being put into his mouth, his arms, his urethra. A nurse or doctor is always touching him, "just trying to help," as they say when he becomes irritable.

Much of this irritability he saves for his wife, who sits hour after hour waiting for some word of hope. Though P_____ appreciates her devotion, he hates her pity, the solicitousness which oozes from her like tears. He wishes she would go away and not be there to witness his humiliation. But he can't put this into words. His eyes, dull and angry, say it. His silence says it. If, trying to make conversation, she asks petty questions, he looks at her as if she is stupid. If she asks the real questions, those that are on both their minds, he mutters, "Ask the doctor," usually no more than that. The facts, in answer to the real questions are: He feels neither better nor worse—well, perhaps a bit weaker from remaining in bed and eating little of the tasteless institutional food. Otherwise, there's nothing new. No change. His penis remains hard and painful. For three successive days he has had to be catheterized. "Am I supposed to say I feel great?"

His wife begins to spend more time in the waiting room. However, she is with P_____ when, on the fourth day, the internist tells him, "We've been afraid to use a conventional anticoagulant because of the risk of hemorrhage, but now that the case is fully diagnosed, we can give medication that should relieve the priapism."

P_____'s eyes become brighter. He can hardly wait for the medicine.

"What is the full diagnosis?"

"Acute leukemia—"

"But you said you can relieve it."

"The priapism. And that may recur. We have no cure for leukemia. You said you want the truth."

The doctor leads his wife out of the room. P_____ hears them talking as they start down the corridor. He imagines a still more complete diagnosis, a still more acute leukemia, a still more final word: *death,* the word, the fact his doctor must be telling her to prepare herself for. The phrase "acute leukemia" runs through his mind like blood. The addition of the adjective is a terrifying subtraction of time. And yet later the doctor tells him he can return home. That in itself sounds hopeful.

"What am I allowed to do?" P_____ asks.

"Almost anything you want. Just don't tire yourself unnecessarily. What do you want to do?"

"I was thinking of going to the office for a few hours a day."

"All right. But don't push yourself, don't feel you have to go. If you're tired, call and say you're not coming."

From the following Monday until the Wednesday ten days later, P_____ is at his office from ten till noon. He tells everyone that he has had some kind of blood infection but that it is clearing up. He is surprised that the short walk there is so tiring. He arrives as tired as he used to leave. He loses track of his dictation. Again and again he tells his secretary, "Please read that back." But as she does, his mind wanders. It is difficult to believe that not so long ago she interested him. Her hips are just lumps now, nothing that could give him pleasure. The words of contracts drift, float away. These, too, he must hear again as he repeats the words aloud to himself, trying like a child to seize them. The sound of the air-conditioning distracts him, works on his nerves, like a catheter. The chill penetrates, hums in. He is always cold.

On Wednesday an erection materializes on the way to the office. He thinks of returning home, but goes on, protected by a raincoat which he always carries now, even on the sunniest, warmest days. He reads and rereads a small pile of mail, recognizing that less and less is being directed to him. He dictates haltingly, remembers that the doctor has said not to push himself, and finally tells his secretary that he's not feeling well, that he may have one of those bugs that are going around.

The doctor seems to accept P_____'s diagnosis: "Yes,

probably that. These viruses attack when one is most vulnerable."

The medication is doubled. The erection departs. Without catheterization, it softens easily and painlessly. For the first time in weeks, P_____ makes a small joke. While fondling his penis, he calls it, "my measuring rod."

His wife winces, forces a laugh.

That is his last day at the office. He loses weight more rapidly and must go to the hospital for a transfusion. After that and returning home, he says for the last time that he would like to spend a few hours at business, but by the next day he feels too weak to go, the desire is dead, all desire is dead.

The bright wallpaper in the bedroom seems as drab as the walls in the hospital. His wife might as well be just another nurse. When he looks at her, he sees that she, too, is thinner, that she appears strained and forgotten. He forgets her.

She brings him his lunch and notices that he hasn't opened the newspaper.

"What have you been doing?" she asks.

"Just waiting."

"I had to fix it."

"I don't mean for lunch."

He eats one bite and pushes the tray away. The food tastes bad, but in fact it is not the food he tastes but something persistent, like lead in his mouth, some base metal. She takes the tray and eats a little of what's left before throwing the rest away.

There are more transfusions, almost commutational visits to the hospital. P_____ lives off the blood of others. His existence is a passive cycle of blood drained and replaced, of clots and priapisms formed and dissolved, of drugs taken and evacuated. He is half his former weight. He can no longer bear to look at himself in the mirror or at his penis, too frequently rigid, swollen with bad blood. Now his only prayers are for death.

Several times he thinks of speaking to his wife, of saying what he has to say, words dimly remembered. At last, feebly, he calls her to his bedside, takes her hand without the strength to really grip it. Rather he feels her gripping him, her warmth surrounding him.

"Sorry," he begins. But can't go on. There is no strength left, no other word left. He dies with the erection he had wanted for so long, for ever, never having told his wife all he had to say.

# BO AND BE

*Thomas Glynn*

Be watched him buy the tokens.

Bo would buy two.

Be, her right leg, calf, swathed in bandages, nodded her head and bounced an aluminum cane on the cement.

Bo, smiling, wondering if they would sell him the tokens.

One dollar. Five dimes, four nickels, one quarter, five pennies.

The place where you put the money in and got the tokens back was like an upturned hand, cupped. Wood shaped by hands.

Be had white hair, hand soft, a crew cut.

Bo was shaped like a question mark, head bent forward to one side, supported by a huge mushroom neck inches thicker than his skull.

Be gathered her shopping bag. Bo pushed the tokens in the slot.

They both turned the heavy blades of the turnstile.

Cautiously going down the steps.

This is where the muggers liked to hit you. Bash you on the concrete, grab your change.

Bo went first, Be behind.

Be had glasses, heavy lenses, thick frames. Be had old lady tits hanging like flour sacks above her waist.

Bo. Where was Bo? Inside his blue army coat, with optimistic double-breasted shoulders that airplane-hangered his own inside.

Be holding her shopping bag—*I'm a Princess, I shop at Mintz's.*

Bo, baseball cap, army officer shoes, white socks, green Lee work pants too big at the crotch.

At the bottom of the steps, Bo walks ahead to the front of the platform, turns around, watches Be, this struggling sack of flesh, still stair huffing down.

Was this his bed, riding so many nights, his saddle to her moon?

"Come on," he said, a little boy, impatient with his mother.

Bo smiled, indulgent, "Come on," he said. His waddling rhinoceros bride.

On the platform they stood behind the girder. Be bounced her cane on the cement. When the muggers came you bounced it off their skulls. Bo's ribs were taped, his back had scars, they knew.

Bo smiled. Why? They had escaped. Butterflies in hell.

Older than any two people have a right to be.

Be looked at Bo.

She knew this old man, spoon fed him pablum, knew his flappy old prick (he wasn't even circumcised). He still tried to climb on her.

A child, my boy, always my boy.

Who had seen their children? Where had they gone?

The subway came, they got in, sat near the middle, searched for the subway guard, looked out for pr's.

Be's flesh against his. Spreading hip, like grain in a sack. *Oh, they had substituted her for his wife. He knew. That wasn't her. He smiled. No, his wife was not so fat, didn't wear a mask like this one and gave him things he wanted to eat. This creature here, not his Be.*

Turning to talk to her, smiling, pretend she is his wife. Remember? Oh no, don't remember, that coat worn out years ago, he had to throw that away. Married, young, a butcher working in a Polish Pork Shop, bought bobka on Sundays, they slept next to an air shaft where they could smell the man who lived two apartments below who hung himself for a week from the ceiling.

Bo noticed mail in his mailbox. Writing to the dead.

*Who was this woman sitting next to him? Why did she torment him so? No right, absolutely no right.*

"Do you have your cards?" Be asked.

"What cards?" Bo asked.

"They need the cards for the forms," Be said.

Cards, well he played cards. Drank beer too.

Be blew her nose.

She rattled around in her shopping bag. Brought the old man's diapers? Yes, here. He used to be all muscle, now his bones collapsed, packed in wet cotton.

"Watch, another one of them just got on."

"Where's the guard?"

Alone, down here, they didn't belong. The young hated them, they knew. Be thought about acid, wanted to pour it all over their smooth faces. Let them lap that up, walk in pain, bones glued together, stomach and heart scotch-taped in place. Let them try it with that.

*The one that just got on, was he looking at them?*

She elbowed Bo. He was smiling, dreaming, dancing in his seat. He's off this time, off for good, I'll have to clean his pants. She always had to take care of him, taught him how to love, coaxed, made him move, buy his own shop, got him into a trade, what did that lunk know anyway, nothing but beer muscle, would still be picking coal if she hadn't let his hands roam one night. Cooked, fed his gut, satisfied his prick, suckled his babies, scrubbed his back.

*Look at him now! A baby.*

Her scabs were bleeding again. Snotnose kid doctors and their snotnose bandages messed it up. She had veins like anchor rope, her leg was tied with them.

She wanted to pee. Harder to hold it in.

Bo was flying. He had opened his army coat and discovered an airline ticket pinned to the inside lapel and it said fly so he held his coat open and started to fly.

Subway stations flew past, girders, old tile, strings of light bulbs, Bo was flying. He would leave that old sack sitting next to him, leave those dumpy potato legs.

*Where was Be? Where had she gone?*

Black hair tied in knots, she used olive oil on her face and smelled of vinegar after she douched. Long fingers held his hands, Be's fingers, and she licked his nose.

Bo sniffled, reaching into his pocket for an old white rag he used to wipe his nose. Old nose, upturned nose, it looked like part of his back, like part of his shoulder blades. Where was he going, they had to go some place. He turned to ask Be.

"Where are we going?"

She didn't hear. Look at her. All fat wrinkles. Have to walk up and down steps for her, feed her milk. Used a cane, didn't need a cane, sucked on wint-o-greens.

Bo took a stale Cheeze-Whiz from his pocket and stuck it in his ear.

He looked around. Was it their apartment? Had they been kicked out? Were they looking for another apartment?

"We looking again, Be?"

She tapped the can and looked over at him.

"All we need is the cards. Cards for the aid, cards for the stamps."

He scratched the Cheeze-Whiz in his ear. You got to play your cards close to your vest. You got to hold 'em tight. He never let no one see his cards. Where the hell was she?

Bo's hands, heavy, knuckle thick, full of slow blood and tight muscle, teaspoon fingernails too long. His arms, now spaghetti, empty in this huge coat. *Not for me, this arm. Used to be I sang of strength on Sunday, lifed bricks, see those hods I carried on my back?*

*Seen 'em come in.* "Be, you see 'em?" *Seen three come in.*

They sat in the seat opposite Bo and Be. They looked at Be's shopping bag and looked at Bo's army coat and pants too short for his legs.

Be looked around for the Transit Patrol. Come quick and smash those heads, knock 'em off those heels.

Be started tapping her cane. The subway jiggled and jounced, Be's flesh danced, the metal straps overhead swooned from side to side.

Look at old Bo, don't even know where we're going. She scratched her leg. The bleeding stopped. She scowled at the three sitting opposite them, a toothless gummy scowl with lips in a vacant mouth drawn over crusty gums.

They passed a section of track that made the lights dim, all of them going out except three.

"Oh!" Bo said.

"What?" said Be.

"I thought we were at a party," Bo said, "where they turn out all the lights and you have to find things. I thought it was a party."

Be thought, he can still walk, even run, but that other part on his head, that cauliflower, is going soft, moulding, like peat moss, like scraps of vegetables thrown in damp earth. Everything's sinking down into his neck. Got a big thick neck he does. Me, I got tomatoes for legs. Can't walk to speak of. But I can think. Should take his body and my head and scrap the rest, junk it, garbage. It's all extra baggage.

She felt the smoothness of her hair. Her hand was soft, like old dandelions. Please don't hit me there she thought. Not the head.

They would bash my head and cut my skin just for the pennies in my purse. They like to cut and stomp, specially old jelly like me.

Like to see them hurt, badly. Subway train take off an arm, let them howl, muggers de-armed.

*(Oh my God, too old, how did I ever grow so old? Ashamed to tell anyone I'm so old. What happens when they discover me and Bo roaming around like this with the cards, sleeping in parked cars, poking in supermarket alleys.)*

She sifted a pattern in her mind.

Old Bo, too old to think for himself, a little boy, should go back to school. A giggler too, wash his mouth out with soap, Fels Naptha.

"We getting off here, Be?" Bo asked.

"Tell you when," Be said. "Said I'd tell you when."

"Well too soon can't be enough for me."

"Hope you got the cards."

Bo patted his pocket. These days you need cards. You need a card for everything. They had all the cards so that's why they could be so old.

Bo pulled his baseball cap down on his forehead. He tilted up his small head on his enormous neck and looked around the car, eyes fluttering like a gondolier's.

"There's money to be made in underwear," Bo said.

He'd read that somewhere. He nodded his head, laughing. When you tried to stop people from understanding they'd understand anyway. Wasn't nothing you could do to prevent knowledge, 'cept take a pill, and even then. Oh yes, even then. He gave the Masonic secret signal.

Bo thought, where are we going? How did we escape? Why is everybody so young?

Bo thought again. Why do those young people chase us? What makes them so young? What makes us so old?

*Be, if we're so old, if so, why? And how?*

Inbetween thoughts, his mind paused, as if to catch its breath, a smile between the brain and tongue, a clotting of the tube when the lips were thick and heavy like fat fingers swollen with arthritis. Stopped, the mind flying, a blank, a jump between patterns, a leap between memories and that terrible space that separates the two, a black, timeless hole.

Bo watched his eyes, a glazed greyness, a seared cornea of memory transplants. First he was a butcher, then he carried bricks. Worked a permanent curve in his fingers, a claw, his long, doglike fingernails. Skin stiff with lime. Meat greasy. A heavy steel blade hacked through meat and flesh and bone, spattered his glasses with blood, and while he was learning chopped the tip of his finger off and they found the tip, wrapped in some lamb chops, and took him to the hospital where he had it sewn back on. Didn't have all the sensations, couldn't join all the nerves, and in cold, damp weather it was a different color than the rest of his hand. A pale grey. A sign, Bo thought.

*During my sleep, Bo thinking, they came and took my Be away and left this terrible hulking piece of flesh. This waddling sack of farts. This pee stained bag of fat. This grease ball.*

Bo thinking, he thought.

It is her, and why, and if so, how, when we don't know it's happening and it comes upon us like a slow tide, this sea of old skin.

He started to cry.

One of the men opposite them got up and walked over to Bo.

"Hey," he said, "Old man."

Bo looked up, crying, smiling.

"You got the time, old man?"

Bo looked at him. What time? What time was that?

"I asked you, you got the time?"

Not much, Bo thought. I had a lot of it, but it's all gone. He looked up at the man, feeling wiggly, wanting to laugh, thinking he could open his mouth and speak some words if his lips weren't so heavy and wanting to say this too but his lips were weighted down. Didn't they know that?

"Hey, old man, what's the time?"

There is no time. It's all here, right now, all the time there was or will be is right here.

"You jivin' me, man?"

Bo could feel himself being picked up under the armpits, strong arms finding his weak arms inside his coat and using them to pull him up. He felt like a rag doll, all joint-loose, floppy at the neck and knees. Maybe they would shake him around. He giggled. Strong men knew how to shake and they did it too when you couldn't move your lips. He laughed, and it was at them because they thought he had the answers and they always thought that because he couldn't bring himself to tell them he didn't.

Be got up, on her cane, leaving her shopping bag on the seat.

"He don't do nothing to you," she said.

The man holding Bo looked at her as if she were some fat, smelly spider.

"You got money, lady? Give me some money."

He dropped Bo, who sank slowly along the back of the subway seat and then into the seat itself.

Be shook inside. Her stomach shook and rolled and her guts twisted and turned like an angry snake. She shook outside too. Her legs and her arms and the heavy sacks of fat that hung under her arms jittered like jelly. She looked up angry, toothless, bulldog tough.

"My money . . ." she began.

Yes, what about your money? *(We'll get money with the cards).* But what about your money now? *(My money is my business).* No, how much do you have now? *(That's my business).* Tell him you don't have nothing. *(I got money, just you wait).* No you don't, nothing, not a penny, everything went for the tokens.

"Give me five dollars, lady."

"My money . . ." she began again.

He had on a knit cap and an army jacket with a private stripe sewn on the sleeve. He looked like a hitter.

Look at how young he is, Be began. He's so young and he wants my money. He'll take it. I bet he's a rapist. Likes to bash heads. His face torn apart, that's what I'd like to see.

Be grabbed her shopping bag and held it to her chest. It was stuffed with rags and the rags were important to her and she held her arms around the sides near the top so none of the rags would fall out.

"Go on, get out," she said, "Get out of here, I want you to get out of here."

She swung her cane around as if she were summoning an invisible chorus.

The man laughed, taking a step closer.

He needed a shave, wore a mustache, had a dirty t-shirt. Be kept waving her cane around, an errant propeller.

The subway train pulled to a stop and the young man mysteriously sat down in his seat opposite them.

Be eyed him, her yellow goggle eyes full of hate.

Bo thought, will he pick me up again? Will he hold me?

Doors open, pause, shut, train rushing off like a metal waterfall.

Be had lost track of the stops. Was that their stop? Was it the next one? She looked around, her neck thumping, veins in panic.

The subway map, where was the subway map?

She reached in her shopping bag and brought it out, frayed and seam-ripped. She opened it up and traced their stop with her finger and looked at the stop before and then remembered she didn't know what that last stop was. She started to shake. There was nothing she could do about it. If they got off at the wrong stop they could always get a train forwards or back so there was no need to worry, but she couldn't stop shaking. Mustn't let Bo see, he'll get upset. Shaking, she grabbed ahold of her cane and tried to grind it into the floor, twisting and turning her teeth. It was like this, like something let loose inside her body, something scampering through her veins shaking old china and crockery as it ran and she tried to find it and choke it with her hand but she didn't know where it was, it was running too fast getting everything upset, ruining the stillness and the sluggishness of the blood that pumped through her with such great regularity. Her eyes roamed, loose moons searching for the sun. Get off at the next stop, no matter what. Get off at the next stop.

The train pulled into the next stop and Be, standing like a Prussian General, jerked Bo to his feet. She motioned towards the door and started waddling for it, tank-wide in the rear. Bo shuffled along, quickly, almost hopping, hoping to beat her to the door. Shoulder to shoulder they raced, squeezing through the door together. On the platform Be turned around quickly to face where they came from. The men sitting opposite them were laughing. One of them held something in his hands. It was Bo's hat. The man with the hat finger-gestured at Bea. She spit at the door, shaking in fury. Cut their cocks off, she thought. Hack them off with a meat cleaver.

They started walking along the platform.

It was long and dirty, full of hazy subway air. Stained tiles curved up the walls and disappeared in the neon dusk at the ceiling. They shuffled along, Be plodding, Bo hopping, turning around to prod Be on, smiling because this was his game, this was the game he got to play.

They came to the stairway. Bo looked up. It was the first of many.

"Three more, Be," he said.

She started up. He was now at the top of the landing. He watched her huffing up, face down, back bent, clutching at the railing, head almost on the steps.

"It's all right, Be," he said, "they end here." He pointed to the top step. She was too tired to look up.

She rested at the landing, looking around.

Bo giggled, dribbling from the mouth.

He should offer to take the bag, she thought. Why doesn't he do that? She started to cry. He'd lose the bag. He'd forget he was carrying it. She had to carry it. She stopped crying before the tears had even reached her eyes.

They started up the second landing.

Pull, step, huff. Pull, step, huff.

At the second landing, looking around, wondering why they did this to us.

At the third landing, daylight.

And a strange sun.

Be, grabbing a trash basket for support, looked around for familiar buildings. All the shapes looked foreign, the windows leaner, the bricks dirtier, the signs duller.

Bo danced. Someone looked at him. He smiled.

Which way, Be thought. She looked at faces. They won't, she knew, give directions.

She pulled out the slip of paper with the address on it and looked up at the street numbers and looked for a block sign. The lamppost on the corner had no sign. Where were they?

She started to walk.

"I like this place, Be," Bo said.

She ignored him. She plodded towards a street corner. There was a sign. It wasn't the kind of sign she was used to reading. The letters seemed to be spelled different in the words. These letters were very sharp. She was used to letters with curves and hooks on them. She looked up, and then down at her address. They weren't the same. "Where is . . .," she started to ask someone, stopping when they walked past. That name on the sign, it was no name she could remember.

"Are we there yet, Be?"

*But where was there?*

She reached in her shopping bag and took out a street map and located the street they were on and then found the street they wanted. They were far apart. They would have to go down in the subway again. No tokens, no money. Take a cab.

She waved at cabs, saw herself a foolish old lady shaking her cane at those that didn't stop. They rolled up the windows and locked the doors and looked straight ahead when she banged on their roofs.

Bo waved at them with his hand, saying goodby.

"They look happy," he said.

He started to flap his hands. He wanted to fly.

"Look, Be," he said, "I'm flying."

He was smiling, teeth in the sun, stepping up on the balls of his feet. He opened his mouth and walked off the curb.

"By, Be."

Out into the street, cars honking, swerving, Bo flying.

Be waddled after him. Her shopping bag bumped against her hip and her cane accompanied her leg. She stood with Bo in the middle of the street. There was a frenzy of honking and swerving, one car jammed on his brakes and stopped inches short of Bo.

The driver got out and Bo tipped his hat.

Be pulled him back to the sidewalk.

"You can't do that, Bo, they'll hit you. They'll hurt you bad."

"Oh no, Be," he said.

"They don't know you, Bo."

"They're nice, Be. They're real nice."

"Drivers kill, Bo. That's their job."

"Is it good pay, Be?"

Be thought, he's going to need his pants changed soon. He's getting too excited. He'll want to know about the beach. He'll think we're there. I'll turn my back and he'll take off his clothes and look for some sand and start digging and I'll have to get him back inside somewhere and get him to put his clothes on without people watching us.

She looked at him. His brain is rotting. It's getting too hard. Get him somewhere where you can put him in a chair and tie him down to keep him from flying. Watch his teeth, he'll gnaw the ropes. He's a kid now. He keeps going backward. He'll end up inside his mother.

She started to wave at cabs again and this time one stopped.

They got in and Be handed him the address through a swivel change holder at the bottom of a scarred plastic partition. There was a sign in the cab that said, "Thank you for not smoking. I have asthma."

"I don't smoke," Be said.

The driver turned around to look at her, jumping a red light. At the next stoplight Be looked for a rag in her shopping bag and looking up, found Bo gone. She looked along the street, searching for a dancing cap, a performing bear, an imp, an urchin. She reached for the door handle, thinking to get out, wondering which way he went. But she couldn't find the handle and she tried to think of the last thing Bo had said. That she couldn't remember either and she tried to get a picture of Bo in her mind, got it hard and clear and went around inside her head to make sure it stayed that way and when she walked all around inside her head noticed the picture was getting fuzzy up at the top and sand was running out from the top of his head, colored sand, his colors, and she ran around inside her head trying to get a bucket and knew she was going to lose him.

# AU MILIEU INTÉRIEUR

*Richard Grayson*

What is a dream?

He was in the city, but it was his own block. And she was in his house. Outside she pointed to his car in the driveway; two other cars had parked too close to the yellow lines on the sidewalk, and it would be difficult for him to remove his car. He was afraid, but he got into the car, and she showed him that he had plenty of room. Suddenly she began to point out an airplane that was coming in for a landing, and he became annoyed with her for distracting him during such a difficult maneuver. Yet somehow he managed to get the car out of the driveway even while watching the airplane land. And then she disappeared, so apparently he would be able to go home.

What is a dream?

He was driving, and had to urinate. So when the pressure on his bladder became unbearable, he stopped off at a carnival to look for a bathroom. But when he got out of the car, he discovered that it had been a false alarm, merely the pressure of the car's seat belt on his groin. At the carnival, a clown was entertaining scads of small children. The clown kept blowing up a balloon, bigger and bigger. He would say, "Shall I do it more?" after each blow; the children were delighted. "More! More!" they squealed. Eventually, of course, the balloon burst.

He had been expecting it, yet the loud noise startled him anyway.

On the way out of the carnival, he ran into his uncle, who had gotten so much older.

How does it feel to be a man?

When he was ten years old and sitting poolside at a San Juan hotel, he called a woman an adulteress. She was a redhaired secretary from Cleveland, sunning herself in a brown bikini. She told him that one day someone would punch him in the nose. He felt strange when she said that, and he protested that he assumed an adulteress was merely a female adult, just as a poetess was merely a female poet. But he knew it went beyond that; how far, he wasn't sure. He was scared of the pink flamingos which chased him across the hotel grounds, and he was even more terrified by the naked children shouting, "Americano! Americano!" as his parents threw pennies from the taxi. And in El Morro castle, he was worried that he might fall through one of the holes in the floor. The guide had said that Ponce de Leon once fell through one of the holes and thus discovered Florida.

What is an anxiety attack?

One evening, while baking carrot cake, he realized that he always cringed inwardly when his mother approached, knowing that there was something he was doing wrong: either sitting down incorrectly so that he was damaging the back of the car, or getting powder in the cracks of the tiles of the bathroom floor, or else getting a stain on the carpeting, a stain invisible to everyone but his mother. His mother, as well as his father (by his silent acquiescence), had believed in a sterilized world and an antiseptic, well-thought-out life, and for a long time he believed that it was the only kind of life available to him.

Once he found out differently, he was furious for what he had missed. And while it made him doubt his own reality, he learned after awhile to appreciate the possibilities. Eventually he stopped listening to his mother. When she talked about something, he would imagine her an inmate in a mental institution, screaming out insane, irrational things from behind bars. In the long run, it made things easier.

Why do people have to die?

In the 1950's there was a television serial he watched when he came home from school for peanut butter and jelly. The show was called "Love of Life." Every day, the program would begin with a deep-voiced announcer announcing " 'Love of Life': Vanessa Dale's Search for Human Dignity."

He wondered if it had become impossible to live with dignity. There were long lines everywhere: at the movies, in banks, at gasoline stations. On the subways people were cattle, herded from one malfunctioning train to another by transit cowboys disguised as policemen. All over the West Side, he was treated like a messenger, and hence as less than human. Behind all those precise, lower-case graphics and shag carpeting and Danish modern glass partitions there was a machine, a machine with people for parts. At five o'clock the machine became a monster and vomited up the day's food. He was quite nearly a part of that vomit.

What is a dream?

For years he was obsessed with vomiting. While nobody he knew thought the process was charming, no one but he seemed to realize the extent of its horror. Every day he would become nauseated to the point of vomiting. Every day he would sit and sweat and put things in his mouth and write out secret codes on notebook loose-leaf paper. "NNN" meant "No Nausea Now." "LMBOK" stood for "Let Me Be Okay." "DGPNVT" was shorthand for "Dear God Please No Vomiting Today."

Once he came very close to vomiting. It was in high school, in a Social Studies class. He sat next to a girl whose eyes bulged out of their sockets; he assumed she had some kind of condition, but her eyes were robin's-egg blue and the overall effect was not un-attractive. When the teacher told the class that President Harding had had VD, the girl wanted to know what VD was, and she almost seemed to believe the teacher's smiling explanation that the initials stood for Valentine's Day. But that day he could stand the onrushing wave of nausea no longer, and involuntarily he moaned, "Oh, I'm gonna throw up . . ." The girl with the bulging eyes became agitated and jumped up from her seat (they sat in the middle two rows and their seats were attached) and she cried out to the class: "He's sick! He's sick!"

Three years later, when he was able to use public transportation again, he saw the girl on a bus. Evidently she had married, for she carried a baby in her arms.

How can people live like that?

On the back of the photograph she had written in a small, neat handwriting: "Well, we went through a lot together, but I think we finally understand each other. I know I'll always remember you and what we went through together. I hope you will, too, and whenever you look at this picture, you'll remember only the good times."

Where does it hurt?

He called her, crying hysterically, great heaving sobs. She told him she could not make out the words and that he should calm down and try to tell her exactly what had happened. He took deep breaths and finally related the story of the unprotected eggs and the muttered obscenities and the hollering and the lost appetite and the threats and the mess and the scorned tears and the cry, "But I love you!" going unheard. He knew he was powerless, he said. When he finished the story, she told him, "You need to know someone cares." He agreed, but said he needed to know more; he needed to know he was not crazy. She told him there must be a reason why he was so affected, and he, being rational—before she could say it—said, "The telephone is not the best place to discuss these things. I'll see you at the usual time on Tuesday." And he hung up the receiver, looked in the mirror, watched himself sob, his face and eyes red and swollen, his stomach rebelling, and he thought: Well, at least I've cleaned out my sinuses.

How does it feel to be alone?

He was almost surprised that he had survived the night. It had hardly bothered him at all, having only himself for company. He drank jasmine tea and dipped into Proust, and after a while, he looked up from his book and the digital clock read 11:47. So he put on the flannel bathrobe and went to the kitchen and watched the poor fools in Times Square and the older, more affluent fools dancing to Guy Lombardo's grey hotel music. To him it was absurd: cheering a new year, applauding the passage of time. One might just as well celebrate the movement of a glacier.

He settled down to sleep at about 1 a.m., only to awaken two hours later when the telephone rang. No one spoke, so he just said, "Happy New Year," and he hung up the receiver. Within five minutes he was asleep again.

What should a person do?

On the way to her house, he felt nauseated. When he realized that the nausea was anger, he found himself becoming furious. He walked in and immediately proceeded to tell her how damned sick he was of her controlling his life, of his jumping at her every command. He had fantasies of torturing her, he said, using the toilet seat.

She was silent. Then she asked, "Why?"

"Damn you," he said. "I'm angry because you're so fucking important to me."

He gave her a very hard time, waiting for her to become angry, waiting for her to become hurt. But he knew he was afraid to hurt her, because he had made her a goddess, and if she cried because of him, his image of her would be shattered. Then there would be no order in the galaxy.

Afterwards he felt ashamed.


How does it feel to be a man?

For a long time he wanted a black eye. The thought of physical violence excited him only when it would result in his getting a black eye. He kept hoping to get into a fight, a fight in which a stronger opponent would punch him squarely and surely in the eye. Although he took to hanging out in tough neighborhoods, and though he sometimes shoved people in the street, he never did meet anyone who would fight with him, and he was sorely disappointed. He had to resort to artificial black eyes, those made from carbon paper or mascara or India ink.

Eventually he became close enough to another person to ask for a black eye. But almost as soon as he got the words out, the desire had disappeared. A black eye was no longer necessary.


What should a person do?

He was taught that one way to relieve tension was to have a knock-down, drag-out argument at home so that he could appear calm in public, in society. So it was natural, perhaps, that when he first began to see her, he would pick a quarrel before he went out. Yet when he had the presence of mind to ask another if something was bothering them, he got a look of almost pitying puzzlement. Why, they wondered, would he bring up *feelings* when someone's cuff links were missing? He remembered his father telling the first psychiatrist that the best thing to do sometimes was to repress a thing that upset you. It was a not untypical reaction from an American male with ulcers.

What is a dream?

Coming over the bridge in the evening, he saw the moon directly between two cables. It was a mustard-colored moon, partially covered by low-hanging grey-blue clouds.

What should a person do?

He was told, "The world, after all, is a large place . . ." And he grudgingly admitted that perhaps he wanted to know her intimately, that he wanted to know all facets of her. He was told that he was interested in knowing people and experiencing them in many ways. Why, then, she asked, did he limit himself to one person, and at that, a person who would not be completely his. He protested, "Do you mean that it's not really *love?*" and she said that it was not necessary to assume she was taking away the anchors from his life; she was merely raising questions. Bitterly, he said, "Well, excuse me, I thought that I was enjoying myself on Saturday. Now tell me I was mistaken." She did not respond to his challenge, but said instead:

"You want to be a baby, neither a man nor a woman. You have a fear of losing control during orgasm. You are scared of losing some part of you, a vital creative essence, along with the loss of semen. Even though others acknowledge your manhood, even though it comes from the person from whom you want it most, this does not satisfy you. For it does not come from within."

He said that it scared him to even think about it. She smiled.

"That's a different problem," she said.

When do people become happy?

Someone told him: "You may think that you're unstable and fragile and insecure, but I'll tell you, kid, when it comes to other people you're a brick."

He was a brick.

How does it feel to be with someone?

He was desperate. Finally he said into the receiver, "It's just that you get into the habit of loving."

"But is that love?" she asked. And before he could respond, she excused herself from the telephone. It was very characteristic of her;

she said that her brother had been calling her.

Years later, at parties, she would tell people that they had been together for two years. He would laugh and correct her and say, "It was only a year, eleven months, two weeks and three days." And she would laugh, and look at him, and take his hand, an old friend's hand.


Why do people have to die?

He was reading the sports section of the newspaper. A story about a football game. The quarterback had to leave the game at half-time; he received a telephone call saying that his father had died. The team was defeated, 21-16. The coach of the team was quoted, in speaking of the quarterback, "His loss was greater than ours."

He put down the newspaper, wondering what to do next.


What should a person do?

He was called in as a consultant on a very difficult, very similar case. A ten-year-old boy who was afraid to go to a basketball game in Madison Square Garden. The boy was afraid he would get sick there.

The father asked him for advice. He told the father, "Force him to go. Otherwise it will only become worse in the future. He will avoid going places until finally he won't go out at all." He was sure of his diagnosis.

When he went in, he found the boy in a familiar state: pacing, crying, overbreathing. "I'm having a nervous breakdown," the ten-year-old said.

He told the boy that one must do the things that were frightening. The boy still cried, and the father slapped the boy, saying, "Listen to this man! He's the voice of experience."

He told the boy that he really wanted to go out, that he loved basketball. He said it would be hell and then asked, "Who ever said it was going to be easy?"

After half an hour of talking, he convinced the boy to go. The father was very grateful; he called the next day to say that all had gone well, that they were only sorry that the home team had lost.

It was the satisfaction he needed, the confirmation of what he had just begun to suspect: that he was a success.

What is a dream?

He was half-asleep when the telephone rang. "Are you awake?" the caller asked.

"No, I'm a funeral," he said, smiling dreamily.

And then there were widowers. Widowers flying everywhere.

# ASHES: a fragment from a novel in the making

## *Marianne Hauser*

—But tell me this, my dear: what happened to his ashes? my mother-in-law asked the day after my cremation. And Gwen, I am amused to report, did not know what to say. Dumbfounded, she stared at the giant cactus alongside the Steinway, a concert grand I had talked her into buying before the wedding. None of us played. But in those days she was in love with me. And I was in love with the idea of grandeur.

—His ashes? God! I haven't the faintest notion . . . Her sleeve brushed the lid of the instrument, its polished black surface reflecting no face or mask. She slowly shook her head at nothing. And then she broke down and cried.

She wouldn't be crying for grief over me, I am certain. The grief on which she had fed through the years had already worn thin during my lifetime. No one can mourn a failure endlessly. A failure: that's how she saw me and that's what I was. A fuckup, in my own words.

Dear Gwen. My frequent absences from home had drained her and left her lethargic. The parlor had been shrouded in silences. But my unexpected quietus had brought her back to life. She had functioned tremendously, staging for my sake or hers the perfect last act. And now my ashes were missing. That was what appalled her and brought the tears to her eyes: she had bungled the epilogue of my demise.

Every other detail had thanks to her foresight come off without embarrassment to anyone. No queers or winos living it up in the pantry. No party crashers falling off balconies. Nor had I chosen to rise from the dead and mortify her with one of my notorious, preposterous scenes—a blow for which she may indeed have been prepared, despite her stern rejection of superstitions.

However, the fact remains: my ashes were gone. How could a sensible mind like Gwen's cope with that reality, unless, of course, she put the blame on me? Each object in the house had its fixed place, and what seemed to be missing was only hiding. Yes, I'm convinced she would have liked to point a finger at me. But I was dead and therefore blameless. For Gwen does not believe in ghosts, except perhaps in her own ghost during those gray areas of night between two dreams.

—His ashes . . . It almost sounds like one of his insane jokes . . . Ah, she *was* pointing a finger, as though I were standing right there in the flesh in the sunlit parlor where she was pacing restlessly, head down. Where was the urn which the white-gloved mortician had handed her with an exaggerated bow, exposing the big shiny seat of his custom-made pants to her mother? An ugly urn, fake silver, with a tiny angel about to jump off the lid, she said, shuddering in the warm sunlight.

( . . . again my sympathies, Gwen . . . at least your husband departed from us in his sleep . . . here is my private, unlisted number in case of a sudden . . .)

Bastard. He beat me. At poker. But that's irrelevant. The urn with my ashes was missing, and she couldn't, she confessed to her smiling, undaunted mother, recall for the life of her where she had stored the vulgar item—a temporary abode for my scant remains. She had meant to pour me sooner or later into an antique silver urn. But now that gesture of respect was washed away, down the drain by accident, she may have thought (or, as I strongly suspect, by one of my innumerable enemies).

Poor Gwen. The lost evidence of my death was the one defect in an otherwise flawless last curtain. She had worked out a perfect send-off for me, now that I was unable to spoil her show. And her show it was. As soon as my body was found at a cheap rooming house in Brooklyn, the engraved invitations went into the mail. She must have ordered them ahead of my final exit, as she would order her Christmas cards ahead of Good Friday—always in bulk, you understand. It's cheaper, and leftover Christmas cards can be used the following season when our lord is born again. But a repeat performance of my death is highly improbable, even for a character like myself who (haven't you guessed?) is l'acteur manqué par excellence.

Leftover death. I almost feel pity as I imagine her stuck with a carton full of conspicuous waste when she had simply meant to economize—a not uncommon paradox among the rich. Come to think of it, the bash she threw for me in her private brownstone, silk-stocking district, was a deplorable waste. Yet with what vigor she prepared for it, hanging on the phone for hours, the Yellow Pages flipping back and forth from *F* to *F*. Flags, Frozen Foods. Fuel, Fumigators, Freighters & Funerals. She had made notes on a legal pad, comparing prices. —Any package deals this month? Sorry to shock you, but let me remind you, sir, that we, the bereaved, are your only consumers.

Good old Gwen. She was not easily intimidated, and if she found herself overcharged, it wasn't because she failed to bargain. She haggled so much and so long, she talked herself out of a bargain. The long distance calls alone might have paid for my wake.

Well, we get what we shouldn't have paid for to start with—I am quoting her mother—and the function went off as planned. Gwen disposed of me with dignity, and with her social conscience intact. *Instead of flowers, please send donations to Alcoholics Anonymous,* a group which, incidentally, she had implored me to join, as though I were a chronic case when I only drank to brave the leap across the flooded sewer from her world to mine. The night I passed over, I had already passed out, having made off with a bottle of Gwen's choice cognac, Napoleon's favorite, supposedly. He's on the gift box among gold laurels, the old con man with an emperor's wreath around the corporal's face. My ass. The bottle was empty when they found me on the floor of that fleabag flophouse amid lesser, smashed bottles, beer cans, trampled sandwiches and overturned chairs and ashes. I died alone. Or did one naked torso, brown and anonymous, lie asleep on my chest?

—No flowers. They are a waste, Gwen reasoned. But in a moment she changed her mind (and did you ever observe those methodical minds, through what chaos they float or stagger?) and she phoned the undertaker to engulf me in flowers, to stuff my coffin with them. As if she had forgotten my allergy! Lilies-of-the-valley. Snapdragons. Roses. Gardenias. Was I to be killed all over at my own funeral? My ghost breaks into sneezing fits at the mere thought of her assault on me.

Of course when the guests had with feigned sorrow filed past my coffin and proceeded to the house for the feast, the flowers were dispatched at once to pester the living dead in mental institutions and other prisons. Thank heaven, no flowers went into the fire with me. For that I am grateful. But I profoundly resent her insensitivity to my allergies which, as I had warned her a thousand times, included her large family and her equally obnoxious friends.

Each single guest she invited was my sworn enemy; while she rudely ignored the few friends I had left. Scum, perverts, she'd call them into my face. Poor devils, she might add to herself with a sigh. In any case, the security men she had hired for the affair wouldn't have let them through, she insisted—those drinking pals of mine whose clothes were too sharp or too ragged. They couldn't be trusted with the silverware, especially not with knives. Ah, if I had been less hostile toward her exercises in charity, less cynical, she reflected, she might have made them over into responsible citizens as she had hoped to make me over, like an old coat. However, the old coat—and that truth Gwen never would fathom—had been beyond repair long ago.

But my cremation: there I had my will. There I won out. I put it in writing, had it witnessed and notarized. I still wonder why I took the trouble. Earth or fire—what difference does it make? Both elements fill me with secret dread. But I may have been anxious to thwart her scheme that my corpse be turned over for medical research. She herself had years ago, on our first wedding anniversary, I remember, signed over every part of her body for the good of humanity.

The hideous prospect that I might be carved up by a bungling student was worse than death.

## I WILL MY BODY TO THE FIRE

One line. A simple testament. I had nothing else to will. Not even the shoes I wore on my feet were my own.

There was nothing we could do. I still haven't got over it. The barrel was full of tiny, delicately carved ivory elephants. Some of them were still alive, and when they saw us they climbed over the backs of the dead ones and marched around the rim of the barrel like their big counterparts in the circus. Naturally my dog went crazy when he saw the creatures. He treated them like rats, crushing their delicate, hollow ivory skulls in his big jaws. The only way I could stop him was by clubbing him with the tire iron. He was finished, and it's a shame. In every other way he was a nice dog. Dead or alive those elephants were worth a mint. The three of us looked at each other. We didn't dare say it, but we felt like profiteers. And we were rich ones. We closed the barrel and slowly pushed it up the bank to our Chevy. Each of those elephants weighed only a few ounces, but I wouldn't want to estimate the weight of a whole barrelful. One time the barrel rolled back on my son. His legs and pelvis were crushed, but we got it up the bank, and into the Chevy, and deciding that discretion was the better part of valor we left in a hurry, not bothering to even pick up our tent and camping gear. We headed home with our find. When we were stopped at a light a colored man approached and started to engage us in conversation. I didn't catch everything he said, but something to the effect of, "Hey, jive turkey, you peckerwood toejam motherfucker," was the gist of it. "If you want to get anywhere in this life," I suggested to him, "You'll have to improve your English. Take this, my good man." I gave him one of the elephants my pooch had crushed. "Hey, motherfuck," he said, as our Chevy pulled away. "I'm gonna motherfuck you motherfuckin' motherfuckers." I had completely forgotten about my wounded foot. It wasn't until after we got the living elephants into the birdcages at home that I tried to treat it. By then it was too late. I lost the leg, and decided on a peg leg instead of a prosthesis, because it seemed appropriate. We sold the elephants, got four hundred apiece for the dead ones, eleven hundred fop those still moving. Now we've got lots of things. Traded the Chevy for a Caddy. Bought this yacht. My wife grins all the time. She wears a veil, but lifts it when she sucks on my peg. We have more fun now, even as a family. I had a wheelchair made for my son out of the staves of the very barrel our fortune came in. We have three little elephants left. One whistles like a canary. The other two are lovers. What I enjoy now is things like when I put a rollerskate on my good foot and stick my peg into one of the holes on the deck of our yacht. Then my son comes along in his wheelchair and pushes me around.

I spin like a top. It's better than working. Or my wife attaches some muslin wings from my arms to my belt and I turn like radar in the wind. I did that for them at Gibraltar and they loved it. We love it too.

## II.
## NEED

There's the sea. Finally. You'll have to do without a beach chair and a boat because you're the one who spent money on that little white elephant you bought from that black man. Sure he was well-groomed and polite and sensitive and poor, but I still say he was too damned expensive. Anyway there's the sea. We can't go any further in this direction. If we turn around it's back to the mountains, and what can you do there besides swing from the trees? If you have a feeling for it you can go back, honey; I'm going to stay here and watch that there old raven peckin' at the spume. Look at his buddy try to coax him away, swoopin' up and down, but my old raven figures that these big waves are bound to wash in something good. Waves always seem to be ready to wash in some good stuff. Let's wait right here till we get something. Snore. What? Wait a second. What's that riding in on that big wave? There goes the raven. Whatever it is, he don't want it. I think it's comin' in for us, honey. Let's climb down this bank and get it. Wait a second. Look at here. Just what we need. It looks like a great big penis and riding on that penis is a lovely mermaid. Put away your elephant, honey. You take the penis and I've got the mermaid. Now I bet you're glad we came to the ocean. See you later. Hello, miss. Pucker up and I'll kiss you if you promise not to slap me with your tail. Ouch. Those scales scratch. Let's just talk. You must get lonesome riding around on a penis. No, listen, don't be offended, and don't prick me with your fin again. What I mean is, a penis doesn't make a man. And a man doesn't make a penis, either. Sure them tits are nice, but I need the rest of the anatomy to get roused up. If you've got a sister at home who's got the bottom half bring her along next time. Honey, you about through with that penis? Wait. Good God. Miss, your penis has jaws, and he just ate my wife. That's not fair. Now my wife is gone. You get out of here, and take your penis before anything else happens. There she goes, the damned mermaid on the penis that swallowed my wife. But I'm not going to cry. Mermaids aren't all they're cracked up to be, and neither are giant penises. I still say the seashore is better than the mountains, but it's just not satisfying, and now I'm alone. Hey, what's this coming in now? It looks like a bed. It is. It's a waterbed. Too late. Thanks a lot. Now we've lost each other and now I've got this waterbed. Hello raven, whatcha cravin? What the hell. Have an elephant. No? Okay. See you later. Fly away. Can anyone believe what has happened to me on my vacation? Now all that's left for me to do is sing my Schwanz song.

Hello.
My name is Steve Katz.
Have pity on me. A giant
Penis ate my wife, and now
I'm left alone, with a tiny
Ivory elephant, and a waterbed
On the beach.

# THE MISPLACED TROUT

*Bruce Kleinman*

There was once a recipe, published in the periodical "Chefs of 3 Continents"—an esoteric gourmet-cooking journal—and this recipe was for a French dish, I forget the name, which consisted of a fresh, broiled trout served over "a steaming, swelling bed of firm, ripe, round mushrooms and rice, simply wallowing in its own special deep, succulent, wine sauce." In this recipe, however, or rather in its printing, there had been made a very minor omission, so that the word "trout" in the line "lay trout upon steaming, swelling bed of firm, ripe, round, etc. . . ." had been deleted, with the obvious result. I must conjecture, incidentally, since these small-circulating publications are generally edited with a precision greatly out-weighing their impact on the world at large, that this error was not actually accidental at all, but the deliberate prank of some one of the staff, who wished to see his little joke in print, especially inasmuch as no one could possibly mistake the true meaning of the line in question.

When the issue of the journal containing this recipe was delivered to its small but eager band of subscribers, many were tempted by the luscious-sounding dish and tried preparing it themselves, with generally good results, for most of these people were already fairly good cooks; some were even professional chefs. But there was one certain woman who, when she reached the line with the misplaced "trout", decided, the peculiarity of the instructions notwith-standing, that the journal did have a good reputation and was trusted implicitly by even the best of French-cooking enthusiasts, and that it would be best to do exactly as it said. Thus when Bill, Nancy's husband (since this was the woman's name, Nancy) got home, he found his wife lying back rather uncomfortably in a huge casserole which sat on the kitchen floor; she was smothered in mushrooms and rice, and was contriving to prop the recipe up so that she could read it from where she lay, and find out what to do next. Her husband, a sensible man, quickly checked the recipe and discovered immediately the error.

"But Nancy," he said, "it seems so very obvious . . ."

"I made a mistake," she said. "People do make mistakes."

"Well sure they do . . . but *this* . . ."—he waved vaguely at the kitchen—"by the way, where did you put the trout?"

"The trout? Why, it must be here, somewhere . . ."

"Well it didn't just *walk* away, did it?"

"I don't know!" she cried, and bolted from the kitchen. Bill, who could never stand, really, to see his wife cry, ran right after her to apologize; he begged her forgiveness, offered to take her out to dinner, and told her to wash up. When she had gotten out of the shower and come back into the bedroom to dress, she found Bill there waiting, a little uncertain.

"Darling," he said, drawing her to him, "I'm sorry I lost my temper."

"Oh, Bill," Nancy sighed, "and I'm so sorry I lost the trout."

"Oh, but it's not *lost*, exactly," he consoled her. "I mean it'll turn up . . . they always do . . ." She settled snugly into his arms.

"Where shall we eat?" he asked.

*　*　*

They decided to eat in a little Italian place nearby, they knew it well, and they walked right over; they were hungry, but still not sure of what to order.

"Would you like cocktails in the meantime?" the waiter asked; Nancy ordered a Bloody Mary, while Bill, after some thought, decided he wanted a Martini.

"And what will you have in your Martini, sir?" asked the waiter.

"Surprise me," smiled Bill, and he looked affectionately over at his wife. She touched his cheek, and was about to kiss him when the waiter brought the drinks. The couple beamed at each other, proposed a toast to themselves, lifted their glasses.

"Waiter!" Bill cried, rising. "Waiter! Waiter!"

"Bill, you're making a *scene.*"

"Waiter!" he called. The waiter came. "There's a . . . a *fish* in my drink!"

"He is a trout, sir. It is the specialty of the house."

"I don't give a damn! Look at the size of that thing! And he's grinning at me—Good Lord, he's got teeth!"

The waiter looked at Bill in bewilderment, and said slowly to him, as he might to a stubborn child, "But look at him, sir. He has such an honest face. I am certain . . ."

"Then *you* drink him!" Bill yelled, and grabbed his wife and left. On their way out the door Bill looked back, and he saw a grey cat jump up on the table; he was poking his paw into the glass, which was still there, and wagging his tail slowly, as they walked out.

*  *  *

"Where shall we go?" asked Bill, and Nancy said, "Why don't we just walk around and go wherever it looks good?" And so they walked several blocks, looking in at various places with names like "Dino's" and "Clyde's" and "Leon's" and even "Harold's", but none of these really suited them. They turned in finally at one which had no name at all on the window, but which I happen to know is called "Freddie's", after the proprietor's cat. They asked for a table, and were told there would be a small wait; ravenous as they were, they were still too tired to look for another restaurant, and so they decided to wait at the bar, which was in the next room.

"Oh my God!" cried Nancy upon walking in the door.

"The trout!" said Bill.

Surely enough, it was indeed the trout, standing behind the counter in a bartender's white cap and apron, surrounded by rows of glasses and big bottles.

"It's amazing," Nancy was saying, "it's just like you said."

Bill was nonchalant, and said simply, "Well that's . . . I mean this, er . . . is nothing unusual, really . . . I mean they always do, you know."

They walked over and ordered drinks, but said nothing else to the trout, nothing of a personal nature which would show that they recognized him. The service was very slow, and a few of the customers were making a scene over it—they were loud and abusive, made all sorts of nasty remarks about the trout, and even about his family. One man in particular, he apparently thought himself something of a wit, kept cruising past the bar in front of the trout with his nose all crinkled up and sniffing, repeating ". . . something *fishy* going on around here, something awfully *fishy* . . ."—at this the whole line at the bar would burst out laughing, and fling fresh insults at the hapless trout. He turned to Bill with a worn face and said, "I don't see why they can't just be a little more patient, you know. After all, I haven't had much experience at this sort of thing."

Bill watched the trout work for a while; it was true, he was inexperienced, but he was also further handicapped in that, having no hands or even arms, he had to lift each glass with his teeth, and pour from each bottle in the same way, and so on. Making change was particularly difficult.

"They *are* awful," Nancy whispered to her husband.

"I'm not really sympathetic," said Bill, although his face plainly belied his words, "and they *are* right about these drinks—mine is terrible."

"Let *me* taste it," Nancy said.

The trout leaned over the counter and spoke so that only Bill could hear. "I really got lucky landing this job," he confided. "I just walked in this morning, right off the street, and the guy hires me, just like that!" He was positive this was because of his honest face. Bill looked dubiously at the trout's face; it was certainly *honest* enough, but each time he smiled, Bill saw, the trout would reveal a full set of the largest, whitest, sharpest teeth Bill had ever seen on a fish. In fact, this discovery so unnerved him that he took his wife under the arm and led her away to a spot by the juke box.

"Did you see the teeth on that trout?" he asked; but she hadn't noticed, really. A man walking by, though, overheard this remark and came over to them. He was very conservatively dressed, in a very dark suit and thin tie, and he spoke to them in a smooth, conspiratorial tone.

"He *is* an ugly beast, isn't he?" said the man. "I can't imagine how *he* got in here in the first place, can't imagine."

"He has an honest face."

"But those teeth—you noticed the teeth? Horrible. And then he *is* a fish, you know. Bass, I think."

"Trout," said Bill.

"Trout, then."

"I think," asserted Bill, "that he has as much right as any of us to be here, even to work here, if that's what he wants to do. I mean, he *is* a natural resource."

"But look here friend . . . I mean he's just so out of . . . so out of . . ."

"Misplaced," put in Nancy. "He is misplaced."

"Nancy! How could you!" Bill cried.

"You see, even the little woman here agrees, friend—misplaced. That's the very word, misplaced."

But Bill didn't hear any of this, he was still so shocked and angry at Nancy's outburst.

"But you said so yourself, Bill. You said so before."

"I said no such thing!" Bill shouted. "And I should think you'd have a little . . . a little loyalty! I mean he is our trout, isn't he?"

"Your trout?" the man in the suit laughed. "You say it's *your* trout?" He turned, laughing loudly, and called back to the crowd at the bar, "Hey boys, the man here says this here is *his* trout! The man can't even keep his own trout at home!" All of them broke up laughing, and Bill, angry beyond words, took his wife by the arm and virtually dragged her out of the bar.

"We're going home!" he said, and as they left, he could see the trout, stubbornly doing his job, mixing drinks, making change, as best he could. The voices of the customers died slowly in the distance as Bill and Nancy strode away.

\* \* \*

They had walked several blocks without speaking.

"Bill, I don't think we're ever going to get to eat tonight."

"What a night!" said Bill. "Well, there must be something in the house."

"We always have each other," said Nancy.

They came upon a large crowd at the next corner; it looked as if there had been an accident, and they went over to look. There was a big grey cat lying dead on the curb, and a man was pushing his way through the crowd.

"I am a doctor," he was saying, "let me through." He examined the cat closely for a few minutes, then pried its mouth open and pulled a long skeleton out from within. The bones were picked absolutely clean, but it clearly had been a large trout. The crowd gasped, and the doctor laid it back on the sidewalk, next to the cat.

"Poor fellow," he said, wiping his glasses, "he never should have eaten such a big one."

Bill felt a little sick, and Nancy said, "Oh Bill, let's go home."

* * *

By the time they reached home, both were feeling a little better, and had even begun making little jokes about their evening; they even felt that, like all disasters, it had probably only brought them closer together, and to seal their agreement, they stood in the darkened kitchen for a few moments and embraced, before turning on the lights. They found the casserole just as they had left it, on the floor, filled with mushrooms and rice and sauce, still with the imprint of Nancy's body. They could not stop laughing for several minutes.

"I *knew* it *seemed* a little peculiar like that," Nancy pouted.

"Rather," Bill said. "But don't fret, I'm sure we'll find something or other to do with it tomorrow.

"Or tonight," said Nancy.

"I *am* hungry . . ." Bill said.

They made love that night, and both agreed in the morning that they were certainly well-seasoned lovers, and that they were, furthermore, quite to each other's tastes.

new. We were warned not to go there so we went. We went to all those bars full of skinny Irish sailors with small hard buttocks and pimpled faces. They were so glad to see us too and curious because we came from somewhere else—belonged to another place. And we were so newbreasted. They stared at those points and laughed and whispered to each other. God, my eyes were still half-closed! They pressed so close to us when we danced—breath smelling from sour beer. Harder. We didn't know what to do after a while when those penises got so hard and tried to press right in through our tight white pants. I laughed. She did. We ran. Away. We ran laughing up the damp boardwalk through the saltnight under the glare of light from those tall lampposts. Hello. We passed old limping Jewish couples with white shoes and fat ankles. They smiled innocently— our mothers and our fathers everywhere. Up further on 118th Street those Jewish boys stood in groups watching our bellies and thighs and inbetween, letting out their breath in whistles as we passed. I was only thirteen or fourteen feeling that hot sun on my back and his leg hard and hairy pressed close to mine so the first sweetness ran clear through my body. (It was it is a golden shock of joy.) And with it the first hurts. That was when someone who always sat next to me making that glorious glowing in the movie theater switched his seat. Suddenly. Something in a word or a sentence was misunderstood. Oh. That was to happen all my life and I didn't know it—all those comings and goings of the men. I never understood those crazy comings and goings in my life and all the looking looking and flying back and forth to find the best ones and the right *one*. Where is my precious manrose, manbird, manfish, man of stars and light and ocean kisses. Where? That in itself—all that searching in itself being fun and a game, but getting all mixed up and tired out if you put too much into only one. That was always a mistake I made—even back then—putting too much feeling into one like he was God of the Whole Ocean. Why do that when all the others were and are lined up right there, hidden around corners, in certain bars, lying bronzed on beaches—Everywhere! Had I known then that it was to go on for so long, always the same with my eyes moving seeking their eyes, I might have stopped. (You could kiss the hands they have hanging from their warm hairy arms.) It was a painful thing then, and now still the same—that sudden moving into a traincar or bus. IS IT HE? His hands are beautifully carved. I see those veins pumping blood right through. Shoulders so . . . those hairs must be alive curling through . . . hard thighs . . . I want to . . . And his greenfire eyes question into mine seeming for me and me only, seeming not ever forgettable. COME. Abruptly he gets up from his seat and stamps down the bus steps. OH DON'T! I watch, sometimes even getting off and following but mostly not— mostly sitting as his eyes look into mine once more through the window. He disappears. Come back. Oh. There is only one chance and never again will I see you in my entire life! Even if we searched we wouldn't. This sadness was no different when I was fifteen or twenty-four or now. And I *did* forget. And I have made such terrible errors I could scream and was even given second chances sometimes by that Creator of Men. He gave me so many . . . six years ago walking down a street that black-haired concert pianist stopped me with his eyes and his Hungarian accent. I want YOU. He said, "Please stay with me . . . you are exactly . . ." It was there in that ordinary coffee shop on 66th Street. And I don't know why—ever—could never know why I ran out, away, as though he was an Irish sailor trying to push inside me. I ran so quickly and was so sorry. NEVER NEVER any way to find him, no name and he has long forgotten. Why did I run? (Perhaps something final is not what I really want.) Stay please stay. I would have to give up the hunt, the excitement of not knowing who is coming next—what form of speech or mind or touch—because some of those men planted right here on this earth can touch my skin like Gods. Some can stroke in the most magical way. You would hardly believe it on this planet right here where I am spinning around like a crazy lunatic. It is always new and someone always does something better than the last memory. Oh, how is it possible to stop? How is it possible to stop wanting to search even if that search is so lonely and never comes to anything but goodby. If YOU knew how hard I have always been looking—for *you.* God, some of them make a mess of it, cannot touch or pinch and punch instead and miss the slow spiraling rhythm completely. Where were *you?* The way you touch me . . . it is . . . I never dreamed . . . that it could actually be . . . I mean here in this world . . . are we . . . your movement is so . . . exactly . . . it is happening to me . . . He had such deep eyes and a dark voice singing that poetry, caressing Aphrodite's marble buttocks in the museum you wouldn't dream that his fingers would scrape my skin. He turned my flesh to sandpaper, deadened my nipples and back—oh don't do that when so much is possible. Please don't run away when we have barely begun. Don't die now! "I don't feel anything anymore," he said.

"Maybe I'm afraid to get involved again. I was once, you know," he said. "I don't know what I want. I thought. It wasn't meant to hurt you. You are so beautiful," he said. "Nice breasts. I need to meet more women, or men even," he said. "How else will I find out if I. I'm sorry," he said. Please don't run away when we have barely begun. Don't die now. Everything dying breaking ending again and again since it first began—these men with their eyes and minds. WHY ARE YOU LEAVING? Why? I never understand how to go on or what it was for. HOW CAN YOU LEAVE THESE PLEASURES SO EASILY I WILL NEVER UNDERSTAND. I want to cry, to slash my wrists and lie nude in the bathtub like a female Christ until you find me. You'll be sorry. I admit it—that even that sorrow curls up and disappears (after death and destruction of course). But it does, it disappears when a man smiles. Who are you? Hair like thick rope, moustache singing. Promise of pleasure in the eyes. See? There is someone somewhere once again. Everywhere is someone and many. Don't look behind. Stop him. Stop him. But he is walking on—turns back a moment, hesitates and walks on—Stupid Fool. You won't remember me in a day even if I *did* make my wrists bleed foolishly. Don't you do it. Hear? The point, don't you see, is that they exist—and will—and don't ever forget it. Lilies of the field: long straight cocks, short stubby ones, small sad thin ones, some crooked—twisted slightly to the right or to the left and those the size of half a pinky. All over the place. Blossomings. There is no logic to it, no way to know since it has nothing to do with height or weight. There could be nothing there or something monstrously huge. It is a surprise and a secret like the way they think or touch or when they leave. Lose one, find another quickly. No waiting. No waiting. That phone won't ring anyhow and even if it should it is much better not to be there waiting for anyone ever, I have learned. Go to the church—long line of cocks and minds waiting to pay four dollars to meet me. Name tags on their chests, hairy or pale. The big church is full of them—all sizes all ages—just beginning, flown from wives or set free. There they are. Look. It is like a feast. One over there redshirted graying beard bright eyes, name tag MICHAEL. I remember YOU. Another with thinning blond hair straight nose, hawked cock, spectacled, JIM. Walk around and examine them all—the various flowers growing all over the world. Too young. Too old. Not intelligent. Too fat. Too handsome. Mean. That one. I want that one. A blue balloon. He is talking to someone else. Oh-oh. Look who is coming toward

me—baldheaded midget with wrinkled cock. Poor Flower. Don't
hurt him. How to get away. Don't take it seriously. There are those.
And others. Keep looking and trying which is the only way. Look.
There's one over there with a kind . . . do it . . . go over to
him . . . he looks so . . . Life happens only once. Why don't
YOU understand? Too many, almost. How to tell which one
is . . . Hello. He walked away. That's alright. I do the same thing.
Quick. Move. Here comes one I don't want . . . with so many in
the world why should I . . . hide behind the pillar . . .O.K.
. . . come out . . . another one . . . stand next to him to see if
he . . . someone else got there first, seems engrossed—no darting
eyes . . . that one doesn't look too bad . . . you really never can
tell . . . give him a chance. I mean the thing to do is to never give
up. But I miss HIM. Forget him he didn't want to he'll be sorry
when I who does he think he is I didn't think he would not a sign
there are others—THE SPLENDOR OF IT ALL—even after all
those hurts given and received and all those nights and years of
searching. Oh. I think I have found someone wonderful who wants
to stay. Alleluia! Hair on chest . . . the neck . . . the fingers
. . . Pain? Yes, I understand. And it is as though I have also been
waiting for you. Always. Don't go away. No. Look how beautiful
the stars are. Mostly because of being here with you. Whirling
planets, if we could move closer to them and the movement of the
stream. Currents. Like your heartbeating. It is pumping your blood
all over. Listen. I have always wanted something like this. We can
make something growing and alive like the night trees. Your hand
and the veins and the way it touches mine. I know. Soft. Hard. We
are so lucky to have found each other. Ever. We can do. We can. It
can be healed. And saved. I won't get tired of it. Never. It isn't like
that. How I love the tides. And the sand dunes. The strange
formations under the sea. Birth. And death too. I never forget it for
one day. For one minute. What else is life for? Hold me like this.
The fish. Yes, rainbows. Things all have tides and currents like the
blood and the ocean. I understand. No one else does. When you are
inside me. It is our own. Secret. Doesn't have to be perfect. No.
How lucky I am that you have beautiful shoulders and arms with
hair and buttocks. I like the way your back feels. And your eyes. I
could lie here touching you in the sun forever. It goes too fast. I hate
when we have to sleep. That is separate. Even if it only lasts a few
months it was beautiful when it was. But it is over now. No sun. No
hands. The planets used to be shining. All the time, all those years, I

# SHOES

*Laura Kramer*

It was just after lunch one day in Camp. I know that it was lunch
and not supper because I remember hours of bad feeling afterwards
that corrupted the sweet country air. It was towards the end of the
summer and I was a young girl—I was no longer a child but barely
had breasts—and had only begun bleeding the winter before. I had
attitudes. I was caustic and too tender, and the part in my hair was
vague and erratic.

The weather was changing. I can remember that quality of
August light, still warm and piercing, but less than the day before,
each day more diffuse than the day before. I was changing, and the
leaves were changing, but they did it so easily, turned green to
yellow to red, folded, fell. The afternoons faded earlier and I walked
about most of the time with an inward ache, it never really let up, it
moved around from breast to groin to temples but I never had a
moment without some awareness that I did not fit. Sometimes all I
wanted was invisibility or mediocrity. It was around this time too
that I began writing "Laurie will be Queen of the World" on
buildings and bathroom stalls and the roof of my bunk.

Here it was then, a warm mid-day in late August, and I can see it
leaf for leaf and second by second. My summer camp had a green
rolling main area, with an infirmary, belltower, dining room and
social hall set among old New York trees and imbedded boulders. I
knew every piece of ground, every half-buried root and pebble of
the place, I'd been there five summers and would walk there in my
head in the winters. (After eight years I would be able to climb a

twisting wooded hill at midnight, barefoot and half naked, with no bruises.)

It was lunchtime, and a kitchen boy was ringing the last bell, his body arching into each swing of the clapper, then tensing as the shuddering moved down his long brown arm. The wooden bell tower was painted dark green, an airy trapezoid of four by fours and six by sixes, with a tree stump inside on the ground. Even the tallest had to stand on the stump to reach the clapper. I'd rung the bell once, had stood on the stump, braced my feet, grabbed the worn brass and banged it against the inside of the bell. I learned after one gong that you didn't hold fast, just set it going and guided it, or the sound wouldn't be true and you'd vibrate for minutes. I had tried to aim the clapper against unused parts of the bell's lip, wanting to disperse the corroded gilt.

There was no waiting list for ringing the bell, and no one to suck up to for the privilege. One just tried to be in the right place at the right time. The day I'd been allowed to do it was a fine one for me; watching the kitchen boy's face and back I had to grin, remembering my own forced nonchalance, how I ducked unnecessarily to get inside the structure (the lowest crossbeam was two feet above my head), how I looked at no one and nothing but the lovely metal dimness of the bell. But perhaps the kitchen boy really was nonchalant, he did it almost every day; maybe one had to look nowhere and smile crookedly when there's a good chance everyone nearby is watching you burst your ears and swing your body into those sounds.

I was sitting on the porch outside the dining room as people went through the screen doors, and the big room was filled with laughing and the sounds of shoes on worn wood floors and steamy lunch smells. I went to my table and ate and then it was rest hour. Counselors and campers, filled with well-made Army surplus food, went slowly back to the bunks. We'd had fresh plums for dessert and I sat again on the porch eating the plum. It was dark purple, sweet-skinned and more sour toward the pit. It was somewhat irregular not to go right to rest hour so I'd prepared a story about wanting to throw the pit into a nearby butt-can, but I wouldn't have needed a story anyway. I was a good camper, I did not smoke in the privy or make out, I wrote skits and responded and was most likely a joy to write reports about. And I probably knew this somewhere behind that constant ache, probably knew the interracial/non-sectarian/non-profit power structure liked and respected me and so this small infraction—slowly eating a plum in the early afternoon instead of resting—was no big deal, and easily absorbed.

I moved to the porch railing and leaned back against the weathered door, breathing in the smells of warmed paint and creosote. My left foot was on the railing, bringing my knee to my chest, and my right foot scraped against the porch floor. I was wearing an old pair of dark green shorts, the legs wabbed out, and I could feel heat in the hollows of the insides of my thighs.

My eyes were shut against the sun and I was concentrating on pulling the plum skin off with my teeth so didn't know anyone was near till I heard footsteps on the porch. I looked down and saw a pair of battered work boots, dark brown and creased across the toes, the leather changing color near the ankle knob and heel. There were two different laces, one striped grey and blue, the other a piece of knotted jute. Loose khaki pants just overlapped the tops of the boots; a slim white man, his hipbones and pelvic muscles pressed against the waistband and thin cotton shirt.

I was not anxious about his becoming authoritative, or asking me why I was here and not there, he wouldn't have cared: he was a hippy, a Digger, a streetperson, a beatnick roughly adapting to a wilder way of difference. He was a clever and snotty man, his fine drawn lips curling easily, one eyebrow often up, if he cared even to express that much. Brown hair flew uncombed around his lean face and he smelled of strong tobacco and he had a motorcycle. He was not my counselor but had been seen in bed with a counselor who was a family friend, so I felt obscurely and illicitly related to him. I also felt in his presence a need to be terse and sharp-tongued. I *did* like his boots, I loved those boots, something about their age and brokenness touched something in me, they were Van Gogh boots, rounded toes and resoled, and were as another skin to his small feet.

"Hi."

"Hi."

Nothing about Rest Hour or plums. I realized as he stood there that he hadn't been to lunch, he looked as though he'd just woken up, and I wondered who would yell at *him*.

"You weren't at lunch."

"Nope." The last few campers were going off through the trees and up the hills to read their mail. My chest got tight then, and then huge and empty, and it was very quiet there in the sun, with the smell of paint and creosote. I could feel splinters from the porch railing working through my old shorts and my underwear.

Something was shining in his hand.

"Look what I've got here."

It was a spoon from the dining room and he was bending the handle slowly upward. My thoughts ran together, throwing pits on the ground and stealing spoons, and I watched the small muscles move across the backs of his hands while he bent the spoon. The tendons on the inner side of his right arm stood out and I wanted to touch them. I took the plum pit out of my mouth and held it, held it till the shreds of flesh squeezed through my fingers. I looked full into his eyes, blue against brown, wide open against radiating corner lines. Laurie will be Queen of the World. I looked away and again at his boots. How had I never seen those boots before?

"Do you know what you can do with this spoon?"

I looked up then, and breathed once through my mouth. I looked at the spoon, the handle almost touching the bowl, he widened the angle a little, he smiled at me. I thought of worms and dry mustard, of tight shoes, of plums. The trees were still.

"Do you know what you can do with this spoon?"

"No."

"You can eat shit with it."

I cried as if I'd been smacked in the mouth, I said "What's the matter with you? Why did you say that to me?", and his smile shook for a moment and his eyebrows drew together, and then that passed too.

He put the spoon in my hand and went away; I heard him walk away, heard leather against wood and then some pebbles crunching but I cannot say I saw anything at that time but the spoon and the plum pit and my own hands.

After a while I got off the porch railing and went to the bell tower and sat inside on the stump. Above me dark green four by fours and six by sixes, I felt the bell above my head and thought about living inside the bell, being little enough to live in a hammock out of the clapper's way, leaping down to the tree stump at dawn, spinning webs between the beams, to be that little and made of sound. My wrists were pressed against my knees and it slowly came to me that the afternoon was moving along and I was still, too still.

One Saturday morning in the Spring I was cleaning my father's room. I hated doing it and I loved doing it. I hated doing it because it was dusty and filled with underwear and orange peels in saucers and old cups of tea. There was no place to put anything, the closet was full of camping equipment and water-skis and empty cleaner bags on their hangers, and dust. It was a small room with one courtyard window and the furniture was too big. The dresser was brown and massive with a tilting mirror, and the double bed and bedboard he'd shared with my mother almost reached the length of the room. The bedboard overlapped on one side and from time to time I tried to remember if that was always so. It didn't seem likely that she would have had an arrangement like that. Perhaps it was a different mattress, one without body memories. I could not recall. My father used the overlap part at his night table. It was there that I found the greatest concentration of orange peels and nutshells, books interlaced with scraps of paper noting quotes and thoughts for theses and class discussions. It was not the Aegean Stables, but enough like Sisyphus' hill. The dust always rolled back and the orange peels reblossomed.

But I loved doing it for him, for that excited few minutes before he came home from work, and no one would say a word, my sisters and I would not say a word, or "pretend we're sleeping!", and he'd open his door, adjusting his eyes so's not to see the dirt, and he'd see instead a smooth big bed, his shoes in line, dresser cleared, floor vacuumed. And he'd cry out and come into the living room tripping over the dog and I'd watch him reject the mock-angry bit and thank us instead. And we'd all four hug. Or if it had only been *me* in there with the filth and the memories, my sisters would say "Lau did it" and so I'd get further in, my own hug, and tell him it was the last time . . .

But here it was another time, and I moved through his things carefully, trying not to look at them, just making order. Once I'd been putting away clean laundry and had found some papers with familiar writing. I had sat down in the narrow space between the bed and dresser and taken out the papers. I hadn't felt in any way out of line, he knew his drawers had to be opened if his socks were to get in, he never said not to. Perhaps I had seen it as a form of payment, some privilege of sight. (Once I'd found an old poem of mine, written when I was nine, folded till the ink had disappeared at the folds. It was a good poem, an Ode to Spring.) I had taken out these papers, knowing my mother's handwriting. I set limits: I would not read love letters.

So, I sat there with my elbow on his bed and my knees under the dresser and read my mother's last will and testament, a rough copy (the only copy) in longhand, written with a fountain pen on the same newsprint my father brought home for me to draw on. It was actually a letter to him and from the date I knew she'd been in the hospital, sometime in April six years before. The ink was fresh and the writing was firm. She'd left her drawings and paintings to me and her clothes to my older sister. Nothing specific was said about the baby. I'd felt bad sitting there, reading that, not because I'd pried but because it was creepy to read a bequest. I'd put the papers back and said nothing.

So on this morning I was careful not to look for anything, I just vacuumed and cursed and got dirty. I moved across his bed on my knees to open the window, and sat for a while with the back of my head against the bottom of the window frame, and the sill against my back. I had never seen the room from this angle before, it changed subtly somehow, grew larger. This is what the room looks like to a fly on the windowsill, I thought, and then thought about how small and neat rooms look when you are outside on the fire escape washing the windows. A slow wind lifted the hairs on my neck and forehead.

It was time to line up his shoes, that was the job I saved for last, a decisive order-making. I had before me one pair of cordovans, one pair of canvas deckshoes I'd never seen before, his new brown dress shoes, a worn down pair of moccasins that he used as slippers (and in a few years how I tensed and grew to hate their whapping sounds against the floor) and one odd black shoe. My father has, and has given to me, bony and knobby feet, with incurling toes and strong calloused heels. As his shoes get older they take on more and more strongly the bumps near the big and little toes. I was always somehow relieved when there was a new pair of shoes, unmolded, sleek, and not looking like a foot.

There was one odd black shoe. I looked in the closet and under the dresser and then, there, at the furthest corner under the bed where I hadn't vacuumed, I saw a shoe and poked it out.

I held the shoe and pushed off grey fluff. I didn't think I'd ever seen this one before either. It might have been the odd one's mate, but if so, living under the bed had changed it too much. It was black or brown or grey, a tie shoe with no laces. The light in the room shifted suddenly, rushing out of the corners and doorknobs and into the shoe. I stared at it, the eyelets blind, the upper flaps ineffectual, tongue rippled and hanging lost in the empty shoe.

(At some point in that summer day I had walked dreamlike into a counselor's bunk and stood there with the spoon and the pit and told my story and she took me into the woods and I threw them away. Somebody spoke to him and we never spoke again. But I had not cried again, only right after, in the surprise of sudden pain.)

I held this shoe and it all came back to me, the porch railing, and the lovely boots, my hands filled with obscenities, that time of silence and stillness in the bell tower, my rage, my rage.

# from INLET

*Clarence Major*

I see blood here I am in myself.

There's a woman down there in the river scrubbing two small children. She runs her fingers deep into their ears, cleaning them. The mud at the bottom of the river is warm and it feels good to her feet it has sucked her in a little. It keeps sucking her down.

The girl in the department store is counting the underwear and dresses these things people will slide into and feel warm, safe. Deep inside clothes there is a sense of privacy. It's dark like an underground city.

The woman who was sick in bed had her husband throw out the medicine. The dog sleeping at the foot kept whimpering in its sleep. The pot-chair in the corner smells awful. The windows and doors are locked. There is no fresh air. She is groaning.

A beautiful young brown woman steps lightly across cool rocks in the surf stopping to collect bright stones. Her bare feet are pink and gray like the stones. In her womb she feels the separate life moving giving expression to itself.

I wrestle gently with abstract news items: people by the thousands are taking to the streets of the cities dancing and fighting teasing wrestling and loving each other. Many are drunk and giant insects and large birds and fish out of water have joined in. There is nothing large enough to contain their excitement. A giant bird with a container clamped in its beak tried this but it didn't work.

Altar flowers. *Do you hear voices.* I offer mass for the dead. You don't say. My grandparents helped build the thresholds of this city. The post office. The general store. The supermarket. The bank. My great grandfather was the only man successful in altering the conflict between Catholics and Protestants. That's why this place ain't a ghost town today. What's today?

A woman's belly is protruding she sits half dressed. The room is small and dingy. A well-dressed man of fifty sits in a chair by the window smoking a thick, expensive cigar. The woman's hair is rolled up to keep from having to untangle it after a romp. Her pubic hair is thick and black, veins in her ass along her thighs large varicose veins purple in the lamplight. The man looks out the oriel window a slight yellow glimmer of sunrise along the skyline. He takes off his jacket his suspenders are pale red with gold stripes. He strokes his moustache. The woman slaps her naked belly and laughs. Gotta lose weight.

That same group of young women three black and one yellow two white one red, stand close together, just like before, smelling each other's breath. They blow then they cover their mouths and laugh. They're together under a large loose veil. An owl, with large yellow eyes, flies suddenly into them saying hoo hoo hoo. One screams my god what is that!

The body has caved in on itself yet the person in it goes on seeing and understanding certain facts about the trees outside.

The only way to get out of this is to keep going all the way into inlet blues into inlet doings where they dress in children clothes and wear white gloves with bright sparkling smiles while doing filthy housework like this look at it it's a mess and it keeps everybody hustling Mrs. S's daughters the kids the yoyos who hangout on the block everybody. They are the cleanest kids on the block a soap company filmed the family for a TV commercial for six months everybody went apeshit just watching these kids! You wouldn't believe your eyes!

Right now a drunk woman sits at a drunk table with two drunk men. A fly is crawling into the woman's open mouth.

They arrested Mrs. T. who was guilty of violating the threshold law ninety-nine times. But her husband was *more* guilty because that meant that he had not protected her from her violations. This is a news item. It is six o'clock yet? The judge . . .

The arrest took place . . . The reason has not been released.

The crowd booed and heckled him threw rocks bottles at him and he said I have no sacraments no creeds. "I simply took my wife's hand when we got married. I carried her across the threshold she was not heavy, *I swear* to you she was light! . . ."

She reaches deep into the torn muscles where the heart was still beating. She eats it.

Thousands of students at the university are running naked across the grass. "My name," says one who stops long enough to talk to a reporter, "is Marlene. I always wanted to be a famous sexy bitchy movie star. In London, naughty boys like me are called delinquent. We do not necessarily represent the middle class. By the way, Rod Stewart is a friend of mine and I'm going to dedicate this next song to him and to my favorite movie star, Miss Marlene Dietrich! *Yeeeeeeeeee!"*

Blackness hugs her till she releases herself. Inside it is dark. A throbbing sensation around around me and her. We are closed in this area forever. Warm wet acid burning liquid walls suck our faces our arms our thighs all our tender areas.

Sluggish men stumble in dim lights. Thresholds all around them.

He cuts into the nerve bed, eats the liver, the kidney then wipes his hand on the pelt then sleeps and dreams he's dead underground.

Smoking cigars and fingering the women the men in the back office fart and belch when they are drunk. They forget to lock the doors.

A hammock swings between two trees. A man and a woman resting in it legs dangling facing each other eyes closed not sleeping. Inside the nearby house the doorbell rings telephone rings dog barks the children yell. The man opens one eye the one opens her mouth. Twitch. Wiggles one toe.

Two young women were found pissing on a diamond-studded threshold in City Hall. The woman police who arrested them said they did not resist arrest.

Old women in black selling lace, woven and knitted things. They sit patiently on low stools along the giant walls of government buildings. Their faces pink red. Hair iron gray. Hands thick knotted fingers. Tight mouths. Blank eyes. One with a large square straw basket balanced on her head moves urgently along the sidewalk toward the open door of the public toilet for women.

Old men here marry young women. They stand in the gardens looking worried. The women are cute, well-dressed (they wear evening gowns before noon) and the men wear turtle neck sweaters and jeans. They look younger than they are. The leaves sparkle in the rain water. The women have tiny breasts have wear rings on all their fingers. They like to slide their fingers in and out of the rings.

I parked the car on the road went down to say hello to thirty cows eating grass they all came to the fence to greet me. I cut the fence and they stepped across the threshold into the ditch followed me up to the car we went down to the local beer pub and got smashed. The bartender was so delighted he set us up twice. Said all we have to do is vote for his man. I can't remember the guy's name.

The young woman is playing with the ring on her finger. She watches the finger ease up to the opening then she plunges the finger through the ring. She pulls it out with just as much ceremony. It's fun she says her husband continues to look worried it's the same expression he has when he smells something bad like rotten onions.

The woman washed her back with a brush. The spam grew from the table filling the apartment and when it reached the bathroom where she was washing her back it consumed her and clogged the water pipes. She never even made it to the door.

You finish washing your body and lock the bathroom door. You break down the wall that separates your apartment from the one next to yours. A family is there gathered around a table eating summer. You dance for them then take up a collection for your services. Under the table surrounded by their feet you sleep dreaming of being lost in one of Goya's paintings.

My teeth are broken my words they are in another language I am a stranger here unable to speak.

A fat man in undershirt making pots sticks his hands into my mouth to try to help me find my way his fingers touch the inner darkness and his shoe strings fall off his shoes a cigarette stuck at the top of his right ear vanishes.

The church bell rings it is in the bell tower across the street gothic windows with ribs and bars. He opens his bottle of beer and says it's six o'clock forget about language have a drink.

I take him up on his offer as the children from the school bus wave at us getting drunk and happy.

Elegant Madison Avenue type Black women in long peasant dresses are coming through the open doorway to join the party. Dudes in expensive jumpsuits and short leather jackets. They all talk long distance talk. They stand in corridors and whisper cliches and drop words straight out of the pocket thesaurus. When something hits their funnybone their beautiful laughter echoes across the threshold throughout the building from the basement mopcloset to the beachchairs on the roof!

He was on the beach wandering around. The sand was still damp from the storm during the night. Debris: rotten oranges cigarette butts egg shells pop bottles candy wrappers. The sun was pink coming up a dead hawk stuck in the sand, its head rammed into a soggy grapefruit rind. He ran his naked toe into the earth and felt its juices. At this hour in the morning the ocean was calm the sky was calm the house back there was quiet everybody still sleeping. The sun suddenly stopped. It began to melt. He couldn't believe his eyes. The hawk at his feet began to shake itself. The sun suddenly disappeared that's when the rain came and he ran toward the house with the sound of the bird crying for help.

"The door to the oven is hot. I open it. I take one side my wife the other. Together we lift the stuffed onions out. Smells good. Are you coming to dinner?"

A French sailor is visiting. He's in the park and pigeons are eating peanuts from his hand. The name of his ship, *Portail,* is printed on the band of his cap. You ask him where he's from he says, *Seuil.* His method of returning: *battage.*

The buildings have all fallen in on each other. Years ago opposing groups of experts warned against this. Windows doors doormats and eyes mouths thresholds all rubble piles of structure, form, and across the street Edward sits in a restaurant with his back to it all even the people out here in the rain carrying umbrellas. His brother is in the hospital he cut off his finger. He won't talk to me keeps whispering to himself. I take a train to the all-night café to see if I can dig up somebody who cares about what is happening. The lighted backroom shows through the open doorway. A man at the edge of town is whistling on a bridge watching a boat arrive. I can't stand the lack of concern so I go south to watch people from the open window built in 1905 to show the beach and the ocean.

I pushed the furniture against the door piled the logs against the furniture. What ever it was it was still out there. I refuse to be dragged out or fed or loved or tortured. I push the people, the short fat man the tall skinny girl the wide flat woman the thin ugly girl, against the whole pile of stuff. I think I'm safe in here. No one is strong enough to move all this stuff, all these people. I take the bear by his ear and throw him on the pile. He groans. The door is no longer visible . . .

A family—man woman and child—is exploring the mountains nearby. Camping equipment attached to their backs. Clouds move swiftly overhead.

During the summer I see from the streets of New York people in windows looking down on other people. Boys sitting in doorways. In one window only the tip of a face. An elbow. An arm. A leg. A small portion of somebody's back. Each summer I go back.

Small raggedy Indian children are chasing a drunk man on the beach. They're barefoot it's fun. The drunk stumbles and falls and rolls in the sand laughing. The kids climb on his chest and walk up and down. They can't stop giggling they stuff shells and pebbles into his mouth. Seaweed sprouts from his ears.

"She is speeding along an isolated country road in a light blue Dodge, current model. Pavement hot grey. I'm watching her. Trees grass bushes a thick dark green splash of earth on the far side. She is going upstate to . . . at the gas station she stops, asks the attendant, how do you . . ."

Robot Repair Shops, Inc., have sprang up all over town. A chain of them owned by two brothers who live in Florida. Business is fantastic robots break down more often than cars.

# THE GHOSTS OF LEAVES ON WINTER TREES

*Ursule Molinaro*

The beautiful girl stands looking into the store window.

At 2 beautiful female figures that are striding toward each other, aggressively, right arm thrust forward, left hand on the left hip, behind 4 tall red letters S A L E which stand like red tree trunks on paper snow.

The figure on the right has earlobe-long blond hair, the figure on the left has dark short curls, like a lamb's. The bright red mouths are smiling triumphantly, as though preparing to bite each other.

Both figures are dressed in short wrap-around skirts glossy electric blue for the blonde, glossy avocado green for the curly brunette which their striding step causes to fall open at the knees. & in see-through tops lavender for the blonde, chartreuse for the brunette which expose the midriff, & contrast absurdly with the winter weather in the street. One feels colder, looking at them.

The beautiful girl is considered beautiful because she has an "in" face that is considered commercial by casting directors of advertising agencies. She is the type of girl one sees on colorful glossy pages in midwinter magazines, striding about the ruins of Yucatan, or riding a bicycle in Barbados, in a wrap-around skirt & a see-through top. With a bare midriff.

The skirts have been marked down from $85.-to $55.-, the tops from $35.-to $15.-

On a Siamese connection standpipe in a recess between the store window & the store entrance sits a woman of undefinable shape &

undefinable age, surrounded by shopping bags.

Her face is bright red, probably from the cold, unless it is the reflection of the bright-red earmuffs which she is wearing over a baseball cap, from which protrude long narrow strands of yellowing hair that look like strips of yellowing felt, the kind used for winter window insulation. Or perhaps she has been drinking.

The woman's shoulders & bust are wrapped in a blue blanket which glistens when she moves her hands. Which seem to be holding her breasts, under the blanket.

Her rump & legs are wrapped in a second dark green blanket, from which protrude large electrician's boots. From which protrude one green sock, on the right foot, & one blue sock on the left foot.

Across from the woman on the standpipe, on the opposite side of the street, is a small park. 4 tree trunks & several bare branches are reflected in the door of the store, where the glass has been made opaque by another S A L E sign. They sway & disappear when the store door is opened. It opens into the shop.

The beautiful girl has $20.- in her coat pocket. Perhaps she should buy herself one of the see-through tops. The lavender one, perhaps, since she is a long-haired blonde.

As a reward. Because she has just telephoned her mother in Riverdale. Who has told her that she is still young, & has a face that is considered commercial, & should have little trouble finding a job. After all, she has only herself to be responsible for.

She certainly can't blame Tony for not wanting to see her any more after running out on him, to go off to India, her mother has told her. She can't expect a man to wait around forever, for her to come back.

Tony telephoned her mother in Riverdale, the day she left for India, her mother has told her. He sounded very upset, & said that he felt she was running away from herself & from him to India, but that he felt he had no right to stop her if he could have stopped her; nobody could stop her once she'd set her mind on something in case her religion craze was for real.

Tony had asked her mother if there was maybe another man in the picture who was maybe an advertising executive or a dentist or a doctor, who was not a writer & was earning regular money, who was maybe going to India with her & was maybe paying for the trip. A question her mother had not been in a position to answer since her mother always was the last person to know what her daughter was doing. Her mother hadn't even known that her daughter was leaving for India until her daughter called from the airport to say that she was leaving for India. Her mother hoped the trip had been worth it. Had she found what she'd been looking for?

She is a lot better off than her mother had been at her age, her mother has told her. 29, a month away from 30, when her mother had just become a mother, shortly after having become a widow, when her father had died totally unexpectedly; absurdly, from a bee sting in his upper lip, right under the nose.

Her mother had had to go out & find a job immediately, to take care of her little daughter. Any job her mother had ended up being a saleswoman in a clothing store since her mother's face hadn't been considered "in", commerical, when her mother was still young. Whereas she had only herself to take care of. But she is welcome to come out to Riverdale & stay for a while, until she finds something suitable to do, & a suitable place to live. If she can manage not to turn on her stepfather.

The woman on the standpipe in the recess between the store window & the store entrance asks the beautiful girl for a cigarette. A Camel, maybe, or a Pall Mall, an honest cigarette, preferably without a filter, although one can always break that off. Maybe the beautiful girl smokes those dark French ones, Gauloises. She looks the type that might be smoking Gauloises.

The woman pronounces the French name with an easy precision that contrasts with her imprecise bulk & her position on the standpipe.

The beautiful girl shakes her head and smiles apologetically. She doesn't smoke.

Preserving yourself, so that you can be unhappy longer: says the woman on the standpipe.

The beautiful girl has $20.- in her coat pocket. She offers to go & buy a pack of Gauloises for the woman. But the woman doesn't want a whole pack. She doesn't like to commit herself that far ahead.

The 4 reflected tree trunks & several bare branches sway & disappear as the beautiful girl opens the door to the store. She thinks she will buy herself one of the 2 see-through tops.

As a reward. Because she had just telephoned the casting director at the advertising agency who had almost given her a job before she left for India.

The casting director has remembered her name. & has asked if she has finally had her hair cut as she had been asked to have it cut before she disappeared.—How long has she been away? 8 months; has it been that long?—& has told her that there is no shortage of girls between 17 &—how old *are* you, dear? 29! . . . Twenty-nii—iine!!!—with commercial faces who are willing to cut their hair according to job specification, & that she, the casting director, does not allow her girls to wear wigs unless it's wigs they're advertising. & has told her not to call her again before she's had her hair cut. To earlobe length, dear, that's the current style.

Which the beautiful girl resents. Because the casting director doesn't realize—perhaps she does—that her hair is babyfine. & would blow uncommercially in the slightest breeze, if she cuts it to earlobe length. Unless she sets it every night, & sleeps in rollers, which a girl can do only if she sleeps alone.

She did cut her hair once. In a rage, after she broke up with Marc. & gave up acting. When she had spent the month of July in Riverdale, in her mother's & her stepfather's house in Riverdale. When she had given herself a crew cut after her mother said that she certainly couldn't blame Marc who always looked so well-groomed for not wishing to walk around with a girl who wore a finger-thin ponytail drooping down to her waist. One can also look too natural: her mother had said.

Before she had lent her one of her wigs to hide the crew cut, after a dinner during which her stepfather had remarked that she now looked like a high-school boy playing Joan of Arc. Something middle-aged men might pick up in a hotel washroom, on a business trip to New York.

She has never understood why her stepfather married her mother. Or her mother her stepfather. She would rather not go to Riverdale.

A middle-aged saleswoman with steel blue earlobe-long hair has climbed into the store window from the inside. She stands in stocking feet, with slightly bulging stomach, carefully peeling the lavender see-through top off the blond figure on the right. She folds the top over her left arm, but does not immediately step back down into the store.

Did you see the old woman out there? she asks the beautiful girl who is standing below her in the store, expectantly smiling up at the lavender top over the saleswoman's arm. She *lives* in that spot, the saleswoman says. She's there in the morning, when I open up, & she's there at night when I close. It's bad for business. People feel guilty to come in & buy something nice for themselves with her sitting there, looking the way she looks. I've complained to the police, but all they can do is nudge her once in a while. & I haven't the heart to drive her off with a broom.

The middle-aged saleswoman probably is the owner of the store. & she is probably wearing an earlobe-long steel blue wig.

The beautiful girl smiles commiseratingly. Her right hand has been reaching for the lavender top. She receives it, finally, & disappears with it behind a floor-long blue curtain under a FITTING ROOM sign.

An invisible radio is playing a nostalgic song: Like ghosts of leaves on winter trees . . . small gestures of the love I lost . . . keep rustling in my mind . . . I *love* that song! says the middle-aged probably wigged saleswoman who probably owns the store in the direction of the curtain.

From behind which the beautiful girl emerges, wearing the lavender see-through top. She walks over to a narrow floor-length mirror next to the counter & scrutinizes herself. Questioningly, with pursed lips.

It looks gorgeous on you: says the middle-aged probably wigged saleswoman or storeowner from behind the counter where she has gone to sit on a barstool. Just gorgeous.

She is staring at the beautiful girl's bare midriff, above the beautiful girl's jeans. The beautiful girl thinks the saleswoman or storeowner is probably a Lesbian.

The beautiful girl goes back behind the curtain. From behind which her voice asks if she may also try on the other see-through top in the window, the chartreuse one.

Sure dear, says the middle-aged probably wigged saleswoman/ storeowner/Lesbian; with a sigh. She removes her shoes, climbs down from the barstool behind the counter, pads to the window in stocking feet, preceded by a slightly bulging stomach. She climbs into the window & carefully peels the chartreuse top off the brunette figure on the left, half-looking toward the woman who is still sitting in the same spot. Steps back down into the store, pads to the curtain. Here, dear: she sighs.

The beautiful girl's right hand has reached out. It pulls in the chartreuse top.

Chartreuse might look good with blond hair too. Less obvious with blond hair than lavender. & therefore more striking. Tony would probably prefer the lavender top on her. But then, Tony won't see the lavender top on her or the chartreuse top since he won't see her any more.

She has gone to Tony's apartment, directly from the airport. But he hasn't let her in. Has she found what she went looking for in India, he has asked her through the door. He has refused to open his door & let her come in. He knows he can't give her enlightenment, hand it to her on a silver platter the way she'd like to have it handed to her, he has said, & he can't go through any more of her experiments in saintliness. Which have more often than not landed her in someone's bed. He is tired of promiscuity as a path toward universal love. He has his book to finish.

But I love you, she has told him through the door.

& he has asked, through the door, if she's through with whomever she went to India with. Or if whoever is through with her.

Are you living with another woman? she has asked him. Is that why you won't let me come in?

& he has repeated that he has his book to finish, & can't go through any more of her . . .

But I have no place to stay, she has told him.

& he has told her to go to Riverdale, to stay with her mother & her stepfather until she finds an apartment, & a job, or some new man.

But I have no money left—I haven't even enough to get to Riverdale, she has told him.

There has been a silence. & the sound of Tony's feet walking away. & coming back. & then a $20.-bill has slowly come out under the door. At the same moment 2 young men have come up the stairs, & have looked at her questioningly, & said a tentative: Hi! & she has put her foot on the money & stood on it until they've continued to the floor above & she has heard them unlock & relock a door. She has rung Tony's bell once more. But he hasn't answered. She has called: Tony . . . Tony? . . . a number of times. Finally she has said: Thank you, Tony, & has slipped the money into her coat pocket & walked down the stairs.

The beautiful girl comes out from behind the floor-long blue curtain under the FITTING ROOM sign. She is wearing the chartreuse see-through top. She walks over to the narrow floor-length mirror next to the counter & scrutinizes herself. Questioningly, with pursed lips.

Chartreuse looks gorgeous on you, too, says the middle-aged

probably wigged saleswoman/storeowner/Lesbian from behind the counter where she is again sitting on the barstool. Everything looks gorgeous on *you*. Just gorgeous. She is staring at the beautiful girl's bare midriff above the beautiful girl's jeans.

The beautiful girl goes back behind the curtain.

The woman of undefinable shape & undefinable age is still sitting on the Siamese connection standpipe in the recess between the store window & the store entrance.

How old do you think I am? she asks the beautiful girl who is coming out of the store.

The beautiful girl raises her right shoulder & smiles apologetically. She has no idea.

I bet you think I'm at least 50! says the woman. Well, I'm not. I'm not even 40 yet! I'm 39, a month away from 40. Another month, & I'll be celebrating my 10th year in the streets. She sounds triumphant.

The 2 beautiful half-naked female figures in the store window look like topless barmaids, preparing to fight over a customer. The beautiful girl feels cold, looking at them.

# THE BROAD BACK OF THE ANGEL

*Leon Rooke*

What more can we do to ourselves? Is this the question that keeps lights burning in this house through till morning? One might think so; I do myself. We make a clean target. But is this appreciated?

Having tired of the blue umbrella, Gore now elects to have a silver ring inserted in his lower lip. Matila complains.

"Gore, Gore, I don't want metals on your face!"

Gore is himself uneasy; he goes out, he returns. He's up, he's down: a man in my condition notes the uneasy play of limbs. Here he comes again, his eyes bloodshot, his lip hanging low. The finish is silver, but anyone can see there's lead inside. For the expression, he says. Just the right lip for my day and age. I like it fine, he says. Play a song, Sam, for me.

Ta-dum, ta-dum. Who reaps the harvest of this merry-go-round? Is anything so cheap—and yet so expensive—as this way we live.

"Ah, friend," he says, "—you're not fooling me!"

What can the poor bastard mean?

Weeks go by. Months. No one in this house is sure. But this we know: the ring interferes, it affects whatever we do. Gore pines for soft foods, to mention one: for those that do not require the grip and churn of his lower lip. To appease our hunger we are obliged to take furtive walks in the cold night. In this neighborhood? We remark to each other: how many others have you seen? Are those human—or inhuman—shapes? And these uphill routes are hard on a man in a wheelchair. I prefer to remain inside, gnawing on the forbidden thumb.

And Gore?—what a tease! Last night he stabbed the fork into his
nose. For the expression, he said. Is not my countenance much
improved? He can't eat—but puts on weight, even so. Look now
how he drags the floor, how the boards creak and bend! You would
think his feet were carved from this very wood. "I like it fine," he
says. "My, how I pity yours!" His motion arrested, how he drools!
Saliva thickens on his chest, but is that a grin? My wife thinks it is.

"Get rid of it," Matila pleads. "Do!"

She commands, she entreats. Her desires have no effect and soon
she is adding to the moment with her tears.

"Mrruff-mrruff," Gore remarks, his lower lip having stretched.
"Mrruff-mrruff!" What is the man saying? Better he should say
nothing, or go out and barter with neighboring dogs. His voice is a
throaty mutter that Matila hears in her sleep. My wife confesses:
"Oh, Sam, I hear it too!"

Yet he continues to sing when he bathes, and I notice a glint of
logic in his eyes not evident before.

We meet at the dining table and Matila holds aloft her fork—
"What need have we for these?"

You would think our lives had no form but for this scheduled
food.

But why am I telling you? My past life was more elegant, but was
it more refined? I ask you now: how was yours?

Matila whines. Each new emergency ushers in the familiar notes.
"Do-re-me . . . !" My wife marvels: "Are your ears so condemned? She's in agony! Can't you project at least a friendly smile?"

The fact is I proffer what I can. I listen, but who am I to intrude?
Indeed, it's Matila whining—but is hers not the voice which
brought me to this chair? The voice that keeps me here?

Whose screaming bullets are these that ignite my groin? Is it me—
or Matila—on the receiving end?

But oh how she howls. "I won't put up with this! Metals on his
face! I'll sue for a divorce! Why should I suffer these mad
extremes?"

And from some place in all this a practical—a reasonable?—
voice is heard. "On what grounds?" It is my wife speaking, and her
words reach me as if through a tube. Is it Matila, or myself, whom
she addresses now?

Later, bedroomed, I can put this question to her face. "Oh," she
says, "I am soft and patient with Matila's moods. I am with her, in
her skin. I love her for her temper. For her moods. I find nothing

objectionable in her whines."

And I am asked whether I share these views. "It is Gore," she says, "whom I find too miserable to contemplate."

Me? I take no sides. Though a love for Gore engulfs me even as she speaks. I too would have metals on my face. I poke out my lip and am disconcerted at finding nothing there. "Oh Gore!"—that's the one sentiment my mind reveres. "Gore! Never mind that he's a fool! Never mind that he's the product of what he wears! That what he wears is what most wears at him!" This chair, I think, would fit him almost as well as me.

Delirium has its pause. I have not served in seven wars without learning something from them. A tolerance for the other side.

My wife is unmoved. "You cripples!" she says.

And thus am I wheeled again into the dark. "Think this issue through," she says to me. "I'm sure you will come to your senses soon."

And here in this darkness, what are the thoughts that occur to me? That women are unpredictable. That women pursue where nothing leads. That wives willingly betray whoever first betrayed them. That for a friend they would forsake either the gallant or hideous dead. That breasts and legs and man's imagined lust combine to create some holy orifice. That nothing eludes them like sweet sympathy. That no womb, empty or full, is worth the smallest sacrifice. That men are perhaps different after all. That the same darkness which greets me here drove her to drive me to its dingy embrace. Or that it is sleep which finally captures all.

Thus I nod.

How curious it is that in my black dream sweethearts continue to promenade in pairs. A hand inserts itself in mine—warm, fragile, a mysterious hand. We walk and walk and no one speaks. We never tire. But after a while our footsteps pass on in front of us.

When I was a boy . . . but how distant I seem to myself. Was there ever a moment when I was not this clunking bull? When these two wheels did not frame my eyes and my raw hands did not shove these knobs? Yet a boy's vision endures. There was magic in those innocent coils between heart and brain. Its presence makes me shudder in embarrassment now, looking back.

This obnoxious spasm in my legs! I slap cruelly at my thighs, at my dancing knees. My wife sighs irritably in her sleep. My feet clatter loudly against the steel shoes which support my legs. I continue to box at these limbs, squirming high in my sweaty seat.

This monstrous chair knows the disgust I feel.

My friend Arturo, dead now, had a story he liked to tell. "There was this poor man," he would say, "who owned nothing except one sorry mule. And the beast cost more to feed than he brought in. 'If I could teach this brute not to eat,' the poor man one day decided, 'my situation might gradually improve.' "

Here Arturo always paused. "You must understand," he would say, "the significance this story has for me." And his lidded eyes would make their appeal. I would strut here and there, no doubt uncorking and pouring wine or slapping down yet another drink. I had no patience for Arturo's stories. He took life much too seriously, in my view. "So," I would finally say, "—so, did this poor man teach his animal to go without food?"

Arturo's melancholy face would draw nearer. His hands would clutch my arm. "Yes, yes!" he'd say, greatly excited. "The mule learned to go without food! Took to it without complaint! But then the sonofbitch up and died!"

Morning. I have passed another night in this chair. It occurs to me, wheeling myself past an open window, that this was a story I told Arturo. Still, it was his hands that left bloodprints on my arm: "Impossible! How people can be such fools!" Poor Arturo.

My wife sleeps soundly now. She is bedded under a spangle of white daisies and yellow butterflies. My trembling limbs can make her toss, but Matila's rage bothers her not at all. Matila is fiery at daybreak, a person back from desperate frontiers.

"I want a divorce!" she screams. "I can't live like this another day!"

Gore stumbles by, in one hand his razor, in the other scissors for close work about his hidden chin. His lip ring flashes brilliantly, but it is his silent tread that ignites my wife: "What is it?" she exclaims, on her elbows—"What's happening here?" She settles back, contented, secure, as Matila starts up again.

"I hate it! Hate metals on your face!"

We are guests here, I remind my wife. Offer comfort, yes—but on no account should we interfere. I go on speaking while garments are flung down. My wife at night is tented under seven folds; in the day flimsy playthings decorate her flesh. "You kept me awake," she says, "with your groans. Arturo's dead mule story, I suppose." But then she's gone.

My wife is a committed woman. She is committed to these people. Her life, she would say, is wrapped up with theirs. Some measure of concern is due them, to be sure. They have provided us with a home. Elevator and washtubs have been installed. They do not deny us their food, such as it is. They would even give up their best bed did we not constantly refuse. Yet I am puzzled each time I labor to change my clothes: was I crippled when I arrived here?

Once again I wheel myself into their midst. Gore sees me and his eyelids fall. "On what grounds?" my wife is asking them. "You people have always been peculiar and extreme. You have always been somewhat ridiculous, as you know." Matila nods. Gore weaves his head from side to side. "Mruff-mruff," he appears to say, "—I like my expression fine." Matila groans. "There!" she says. "You can see how impossible he is!"

I have no opinion on this. One outrage is so much like another, and in any event no one thinks to inquire about my view.

"There are," my wife is saying, "your children to be considered."

And that completes it for this hour. We leave on our separate missions with bowed heads.

Weeks pass. Months. How much time who can tell? Can more be done to ourselves? Through many of these days my chair is positioned dead into the corner walls. My neck aches. The condition worsens. So much wanton checking of activity at my rear. The furrows in my brow would indicate that life is no picnic here. Yet what can I say for myself? I speak of Gore, of Matila, of my wife, I make passing reference to this chair—although nothing is further from my mind than these. I stare at my hands but it isn't these deformed knots I see. The eye is wretchedly endowed: images form prematurely along the optic nerve, introducing mystery patterns on the eye's darker side. It is this which gives rise to the sensation often felt: that we are retreating even as our bodies move ahead. It explains too why dogs at times chase each other's tails.

We meet at the dining table and I find myself asking: Who are these people? what curious forces unite us here? My wife shoves me to the toaster. I am invalid but someone must perform these chores. With his new lip Gore can not eat toast. He shoves soft bread into his mouth and groans.

"My new lip," he announces, "is catching on." Mruff-mruff.

He speaks the truth. Earlier today the postman rang the bell, wanting to display the polished ring he wears. Next week we may expect his wife to appear with her breasts exposed, drinking champagne through silver straws, wearing a hat cut for donkey ears. What lengths we won't go to transmogrify these tiny lives!

When Arturo was a boy he had wanted a dog. The dog died, run over by a car while Arturo stood in the pastry shop buying a loaf of bread to support his mother's stingy meal. *"My dog, my dog!"* he cried, and stood out on the pavement, ruined, holding the mangled dog in his arms: stopping traffic, stopping pedestrians who were properly horrified. *"Little boy, don't you know? . . . Little boy, you! . . . Little boy, don't you know you'll get blood all over your clothes! . . . Little boy! . . ."*

In the meantime . . . well, it's always in the meantime, every moment that we breathe . . . in the meantime the dog's guts have spilled out over the boy Arturo's arms, the blood flows in a puddle around him, and Arturo—striken!—what could he do except cry out in the most profound and absurd grief: *"No no no no you can't take him this dog is mine!"* And, weeping, squeeze the sopping beast more tightly to his chest.

Finally someone shows some sense—we are not total morons after all—someone says to someone else, "This boy is in a state, can't you see he is? This boy needs looking after!" And someone else has roughly the same idea and eventually the boy is approached! "Little boy, what's your name, where do you live, little boy? Your parents! . . ." And so on, though of course the boy is perplexed with grief, oh you should have seen the tears wash over him. Even so, he intends to fulfill his purpose here, he's got the loaf of bread still in his arms, mixing with the dog to the extent that no one can tell which is which. It requires three people to pry the dog from the boy's arms and three more to restrain him as he attempts to get the dead burden back. "Little boy, can't you see! . . . Little boy! . . . And all the time the boy is screaming, yanking dog fur and guts back to his embrace: *"my dog my dog my dog my dog my dog my dog my dog . . . !"*

My wife wheels me out into the yard. "Stop muttering," she says. "What is it now? Your dead dog story?" She abandons me to the open sky. Had one the vision, I think, one could see through it and beyond. The weather contents me, although it was in this very spot that yesterday a rock struck my chair. Thrown by the small child who lives next door. The fence is high, I could hear his labored breathing as he climbed. And his father's quiet encouraging voice: "Did you *get* him? Did you hit him *hard?*"

We are intelligent, we have emotions, we have will. We have strength. Power innate and much of it at our fingertips. We have all this but we are helpless in every way.

Gore, for instance, makes a rare appearance beside my chair. "Our wives," he mutters, "are looking distinctly odd. I prophesy there soon will be trouble in this neighborhood." Mruff-mruff. My wife arrives, elbowing him aside. "I am sorry," she tells me, "I have let you remain too long in the sun. Your poor face is on fire, do you hurt?"

She administers a white salve and I find myself marveling anew at our pathetic efforts to cajole love out of where it hides. The salve worms under my skin, she delivers bromides, anodynes: tears wet my cheeks in gratitude and, pardon me, I nap.

When I was a boy . . .

When Arturo . . .

The boy's mother was telephoned. She came running over, found no one there, the street empty of traffic—no evidence of madness except for this puddle of blood in front of the pastry shop. She goes running back to her own house, and as she bursts through the front door she sees half-a-dozen people she's never seen before, and hears one of them saying, "He's dead." He's dead, he's dead.

He's dead.

She rushes forward screaming, lamenting, wailing, pulling her hair, shoving everyone. Grief vanishes the moment she sees her boy standing in the room with the dead dog dripping from his arms. She hurls herself against the boy, shakes him, slaps him, twists and pulls at him, all the time screaming I TOLD YOU TOLD YOU I TOLD YOU DIDN'T I TELL YOU I WELL MARK MY WORDS YOU WILL NEVER NEVER HAVE ANOTHER NEVER ANOTHER DOG! DIDN'T I DIDN'T I WARN YOU TELL YOU SO! She tears at the boy's ears, chops his head, pushes him, shakes the dog out of his arms onto the floor and stays there herself kicking at the dead thing, screaming at it, and now shoving the boy into the bathroom, ripping off his clothes, while the boy shouts back at her *my dog! my dog! my dog! my dog! my dog! my dog! my dog! my dog!* . . . on and on.

I awake in my chair in the familiar corner, shivering, a grey blanket over my legs. I stare at my hands and for a long time cannot make my fingers move. Behind me Matila is weeping. She and my wife, like twins born only for such emergencies, are pacing the floor. Matila strides a short distance, my wife chases after her. Matila whirls, comes back again. My wife remains at her heels. Each time the distance shortens. Finally they are face to face. They exchange expressions of surprise, they cry out, and fall wounded into each other's arms.

"What can I do now?" moans Matila. "What now? It's no good telling me this is my own fault!"

"It's our fault," my wife replies, "for being here. You could have slept in our bed."

"I couldn't stand it if you were not here," sobs Matila. "What was I thinking of? I must have lost my mind!" Her voice rises, levels off, follows an unchartered route filled with groans, demented appeal for compassion which she cannot grant herself. "At night it's different! That ring! his lip! in the dark!" Tears burst forth anew with this declaration, her neck thickens. "I'm so ashamed!" Her body folds, and my wife leads her to a chair. She sits and for an instant the grief recedes, Matila's body goes erect, she glares menacingly and shakes a fist at the vast wrongs done to her: "Another *baby!* The last thing this marriage needs! Now it will be months before I can divorce the prick!"

My wife pulls up another chair, sits so that their knees are touching now: "I don't know," she asserts. "Perhaps the responsibility will bring your husband to his senses. I've never felt that Gore was a hopeless case." She smiles, sends it crashing to where I sit. I respond with the simple movement of a single hand, which motion suddenly arouses my stick legs. Lifeless, they thrash away in their hideous dance.

Days go by. Weeks. Lamps know all the wrong hours in this house. Matila's stomach swells, her belly is as immense as her new pride. She smiles and the gleam is on us all.

"I have been neglecting you," my wife remarks. She brings hot water in an enamel bowl, plops herself on a cushion in front of me. Sponges my legs.

Gore moves from room to room, distracted, muttering to himself. "A child's perceptions are limited," he explains. "All the same a man would be a fool to take unnecessary chances." He has the ring removed, wears a black cloth over his chin, is never seen now without the walking stick slung over his left arm. "The snow," he says. "I fell, bruised my knee." Snow? Was it not yesterday I sat out under a high sun, sipping juice through a tube, recalling Arturo's dog? Arturo—afterwards, the next day, that very night perhaps— out in the backyard burying his dog, going at the earth with a splash of grunts, throwing soil the length of the yard, going down deep, throwing it up hard: *"My* dog! *My* dog! *My* dog . . ."

Snow is indeed packing us in. To my mind we are stuffed here like souring Judases in a crate. Gore limps from window to window, tap-tap advances his cane. He halts beside Matila, takes her fingers to his lips: "And how's my little girl?" Matila blushes, bows her head: she is capable only of whispered speech. Gore moves on to my wife whose hand likewise gracefully awaits. Her face, tinted, with its softened eyes, with its shadowy cheeks—do I recognize it from someplace? Yes, like features imperfectly chiseled at the center of some clouded moon, viewed through my own foggy telescope. These quarters, from where I sit, are cast in aphotic gloom, much as if Mary Magdalen has come in out of two thousand lonely years of mud and snow to express herself through their wistful eyes. As if she has come in to say: "The life He gave me is not all He promised it would be." To be forgiven is a dubious gain; to forgive is to ripen into fulsome pain. Gore, too, by his affectations, by his doleful show of warmth, so perceives. Yet I envy him. Once I too must have limped, employed sticks, with some alacrity and conviction could lift and tease a woman's hand. Now these doorknobs I call hands crawl upward from my lap and scratch to recognize whatever growth exists above or below the skin: this circle of raised or indented dots, these fuming pools I call eyes, nose and mouth.

Arturo, before he died, spoke of giving birth to a dozen perfect beasts . . . but before that buried his dog and pitched a tent for half a year in his back yard. His mother nightly stationed herself at the nearest door, shouting her restless warnings into the cruelest darkness she had ever seen: I TOLD YOU TOLD YOU DIDN'T I TELL YOU WHAT WOULD HAPPEN IF YOU GOT A DOG?

Come out here, Arturo replied, and I'll bury all of us.

Seasons flush us from these careful holes in which we hibernate. Witness Matila flushed from hers. Arturo's photo removed from the mantleplace. His mother forming wings or horns for whatever is to be her brief afterlife. Arturo and Matila, Matila and Gore: marriage is whatever our best locket holds. Our lives before we attain them come wrapped in dust. Arturo, brother and friend: in his family and in mine we arrived condemned. My bones are last to survive these wicked, privileged hours. Dust is all-knowing, all-powerful. It appropriates, even engenders where nothing else will. It has the weight of a thousand pennies over my eyes.

"But you must eat something!" insists my wife. "You're snake-thin, you're not getting enough nourishment to keep a frog alive!" She snaps her head away, startled by the note of triumph her voice can't conceal. The words, too, discomfort her: this frog shape is mine . . . this sack of snakes, dormant always, which forms my body from neck to thighs. My head twists up, I allow an arm its furtive crawl—my wife recoils, finds escape in the busy arrangement of silverware, while I acknowledge with found indifference that vanity thrives under the most obscene of conditions. Gore laughs. I look to find his face at the usual chair and for a moment can discern nothing in that space. Only a swirl of dust on the other side of some milky field. Gore goes on laughing. "I've got his number," he says. "Old Sam is not fooling me!" My hand twitches back to hide again under the grey blanket which supposedly dignifies me. "Look," someone says, "he's crying!" "Oh look!" another says, "what a rush of tears!"

My eyes are indeed aswim. But whose voices are these? How is it that strangers come to be seated here? Has someone invited them? Do I know those voices from somewhere? My wife is making the easy excuse for me: "Don't let him disturb you. He's probably thinking of Arturo's buried dog."

"Arturo?" One of these newcomers speaks Arturo's name.

"A previous occupant of this house." It is Matila bringing dishes, speaking with a festive air.

"Ah, Arturo," responds Gore, "—whatever happened to him?" He lifts his cane, pokes its tip to that space where I breathe.

"Everyone dig in," Matila says. Her apron falls casually over my knee.

"Eat, eat!" encourages my wife. "God knows how he lives," she murmurs to them.

I get enough. I get, in fact, more than my share. I get hers, I get Matila's, and Gore's. I get Arturo's too. I get whatever portion his dead mule most enjoyed.

These newcomers are ravenous. They can't remember when they've dined better or imagine how soon they're likely to have it so well again. Yet while juices drip from their lips they are already recalling the simplicity and beauty of life where they come from. What a glorious future, they assert, one may have there! My wife scoffs, but is too devious to ask why, if so, they have come here. Matila and Gore hold hands, speaking delicately of their tender hopes. "One child, a single child," Matila maintains, "may change the world!"

When I . . .

"Arturo's dog—" I begin to say . . . but my wife's laughter

drowns me out. "Mruff-mruff!" she barks. "Mruff-mruff," Gore rejoinders, and their laughter spreads around the table and orbits there. My knees quiver, my legs thrash under cover. This weeping does nothing to extricate me. Snakes snooze contentedly in the warmth of my groin. This frog tongue thickens when it greets air. This blanket is dead earth borrowed from a grave. I speak of my wife, of Arturo, of Matila and Gore, I make passing reference to mules, dogs, and this chair—yet nothing is further from my mind.

I remember a large house, panoramic grounds. The solemn expressions of ancestors in oval frames. The abiding sovereignty of one massive glass chandelier. My mother in her ghostly . . .

But someone's hand is resting lightly on my shoulder now. I look up into the face of one of our dinner guests. She has red hair, I notice, and a small pretty space between two front teeth. "I'm so tired," she says to me. Behind her other guests are expressing this mutual exhaustion. Her hand tightens on my flesh. "We are new to the neighborhood," she confesses. "Will you consent to walking us home?"

The moment is awkward. My wife is stacking dishes, Matila and Gore sit as though dazed, staring at their wine glasses. So it is that I volunteer. I rise without difficulty from my chair; the woman smiles and wraps a hand over my arm. I glance back to see my wife's head cocked, her mouth rounded in mute surprise.

I lead our guests out the door, I advance with them along the sidewalk that led them here. I walk with the woman's arm light upon mine. The night has no scent; it has neither color nor size nor substance of any kind, yet there is nothing I do not recognize. We reach a certain corner and their footsteps pass on ahead.

I see them and marvel at the broad backs they have.

Once Arturo, in passing, spoke of his mother: "She advances, with pail and mop and broom, to clean up battlefields."

I return to find my wife crying, tears plopping into the white beauty of her half-consumed dessert. "How humiliating this is for me!" she says. "I'm worn out from all he's put me through!" Gore lifts one drunken eye to her: "I told you," he says. "He wasn't fooling me!"

Matila rocks, arms joined over her breasts as if she is holding there a child. "It was Arturo," she moans. "He would never forgive me for leaving him."

They return to their despondent watch of my empty chair.

The elevator chugs, it rattles, but it delivers me to this room.

Matila's bed is perfectly satisfying. Far more comforting is it than the other in that adjacent room.

I like it better, to tell the truth.

It has the scent of talcum and fresh earth. It has Arturo's handprints on every wall. He and I: we were born and raised in rooms such as this. What has become of those oval portraits which were here? Whatever became of our glass chandelier? It cried—we all said it did—whenever anyone moved in rooms above or below. And someone, where I lived, was moving all the time.

"It's weeping," my mother would say, "for all the children you shall have."

What is the hurry? The question is immaterial now, yet it is one which engages me.

In our family we were discreet: we mapped out our paths of solitude, and then we fled.

We followed wind gusts—always with an eye alert for the old family trails. "You go far," she'd say, "but you do come home."

Matila is first to enter. Her shrouded face, in this light, seems rouged. She too has been crying and now her face further distorts. She wimpers, drawing up a chair. In a moment she will tell me that Arturo was no better than other men. That she could not live with him. That no woman could. She bends nearer, fixing her eyes on mine; the depths which open to me are incalculable—it becomes clear that Arturo has no existence anymore. She sees only what fronts her here.

"It's your fault!" she says. "You would not share yourself! Don't expect me to grieve! I feel nothing! Nothing! And Arturo would say the same!"

Of course she lies. I tell her this, through she pretends to hear nothing. She bites her lip and her hands seize and clutch each other as if she imagines their warmth could give life to some tiny thing which would otherwise die. "You deserve this!" she cries. "Deserved it all!"

*My* dog! *my* dog! *my* dog!

I am the mirror of her enraged eyes. We would both sweep me up like some long dead fly, poke me with sticks until I am driven to the most remote garbage pile. A person's eye is monstrous, it sees around and beyond the woman in this room. It sees the space that is missing here. It sees space tumbling in upon space, the rubble of waves where nothing upright moves. The ear expands. It asks the value of this daily sacrifice. Defending one's self in the last indignity. The ear is magic: it listens to nothing. Yet these bones continue to annoint themselves. The longest war is one of nerves. Love bends to its pleasure as it flees towards another transient ache.

The eye widens.

"Oh Sam, Sam, you've done it at last!"

My wife's form shivers between these high posts at the foot of the bed. Her finger spins a meaningless insignia, while her nostrils flare with a poison old in her.

Incantations are aswirl throughout this house.

What have we done to our lives? What brings us to this mad rapture we call remorse? Snakes crawl out from my guts and I feel little more than a tingle in that cavity where they were. My own remorse is waiting to crawl inside. I lament these times. The dreadful vigor of seasons, the shove of year into year.

I can recall a large house, panoramic grounds. During his last years my father slowly cruising the fenced-off yard in his motorized chair. Myself at a high window watching him.

My wife claws at the bedposts. "Why? Why?" Who am I to say which of us in haunted more?

The moon's pull is stronger than my own. These people by size are lifelike. They walk, they speak, they will go on doing so. I will reappear among the dust motes and give the kiss to their hands.

But now . . .

When I . . .

My face takes the oval frame. Nothing is obscured. I see back all the way.

I rise, and return to my chair.

"This is madness!" the two women shout. "Why does he do this to us!"

What have we done to our women to so incline them now to these accusations? To this loyalty? To this melodrama? What have we done to ourselves that induces us to notice?

The single eye of the swivelfish, confronting phenomena, enlarges. The eye becomes all.

All that is outside will now come in.

Say no more, I tell myself.

Reveal nothing.

By morning no trace shall remain.

# WHOLE

*Steven Schrader*

The first morning I slipped off the ladder of my loft bed and landed on my ass. I cried. I cursed my ex-wife. Then I laughed. I flexed my ankles and stood up. My ass didn't fall off. I was whole.

I joined the block association to meet girls. They were all afraid of getting raped and mugged. A police captain came to the meeting and handed out whistles so the victim could blow it and summon neighbors. The girls collected money for brighter lights.

My wife missed me and we started sleeping together. It was just like a new girl friend. I left early before my son got up, so as not to confuse him.

It was a mild winter with many sunny, springlike days. Time didn't seem to pass. I was separated but I was still sleeping with my wife so I stopped. I needed change. I started sleeping with a girl in Riverdale. She was heavy and couldn't assume some of the athletic positions I was used to. On the other hand, I didn't have the warmth of Bernie, her previous boyfriend. We had awkward breakfasts on Sunday mornings. I wanted to rush away to visit my son, but I chewed toast and grinned. She smoked.

There was always snow on the ground in Riverdale. It never seemed to melt or get cleared away. People could ski. It was a resort area. I left and never returned. We spoke on the phone and became friends. You call me. I'll call you. Lose some weight. Develop some warmth.

I went to a party and fell in love. She was quiet and serene, the way my wife had been before she got angry. This girl had a boyfriend, though. Forget him, I told her. I'll show you a good time. Call me in a few weeks, she said. I'm tied up. I waited celibately. Almost. Just my wife a couple of times. She was there. It was convenient. My son saw me leave one morning and I said hello guiltily.

I cleaned my new place, bought some lamps and dishes and a rug. Never again with my wife.

I called the girl I loved but she was still tied up. You're not in love with him, I told her. You're too quiet. I could turn you on, perk you up. Theater, movies, and dance, songs and jokes. I'm terrific. She told me to call in a few months.

I bought colored sneakers and went to parties and danced for hours. I tried to connect. But the beautiful girls were all taken. And I hated the imperfect ones. One breast smaller than the other. Or else braces. I wanted a beautiful white smile. Now. I didn't want to wait two years for someone's bite to be corrected.

I went back to sleeping with my wife. In the morning my son came in and played on the bed and asked if I was moving back.

Spring came and I had to have extensive dental work. My teeth were okay but the gums had to go. I felt older. My body sagged. I was eating french fries too much, so I started cooking home. Lettuce and tomatoes. I learned macrobiotic cooking. I went to exercise class and took up yoga. My muscle tone changed. I was lean and wiry.

I fell in love with a young, beautiful girl back from England. She told me I had lovely muscles in my arms, a thick chest, flared nostrils, and distinguished features. We ran our bodies gently over our hands. I don't sleep with a man right away, she told me. Fine, take your time. A couple of years, decades, even. I can wait.

She broke the next date. I'm in love with someone else, she said.

I slept with my wife again.

What are you doing here, my son asked.

I fell in love with a girl who taught history in college. I want a relationship, I told her. Not just fucking. Communication. I'll try, she said. But I'm busy. I went to protests with her. Marched in the rain. Read the News of the Week in Review with her till three in the morning and fell asleep with a hard-on.

I answered a personal ad in a magazine, a mineralogist who wanted to meet people outside her field. She had nice breasts and a horrible twitch which distorted one side of her face. I started twitching, too.

Are you making fun of me?

No, I'm sorry. I can't help it.

We climbed up to my bed and made love on top of the sheets, in time to our twitches. At the end her twitch had stopped. She thanked me profusely.

I began answering lots of ads. None of those sensitive, nubile, whimsical, esthetic, artistic, and warm ladies mentioned their twitches or problems in the ads. But I discovered them right away. I laid my hand on their foreheads and took away birth marks. I cured stammers and club feet.

By summer I was tired. My apartment was steamy. My wife called and begged me to come over. I refused. I had my last personal to respond to. I was with a girl who wanted to kill her baby and I helped her throw it in the river.

That night I dreamed my wife had bought a gun and shot me. I woke with a pain in my stomach, the sheets red, and realized I was dying.

# from THE MEATRACK

## R. D. Skillings

### PRIORITIES

I was down on the wharf, I saw this beautiful girl, I sidled over, you know, we got talking and she says You know a cheap place I could stay tonight? I said Yeah, you know, You can stay with me. For Free. She said No. I didn't show any disappointment, I just went on talking like I didn't care. We walked a while and then she got in her car and left.

I saw her driving around later. She said, you know, Get in. I said Huh, all right. We drove around and I gave her the old line, you know, Come on home and see my etchings. It's hard to keep a straight face when you've got a houseful of etchings. So we wound up at my studio. I was lucky, I haven't had that beautiful a girl in a long time, never, I never had a woman like that.

I had a dinner invitation the next day, I didn't want to break it, you know, I said I'd come. We were lying in bed and I had to tell her. I said I'll only be gone a couple of hours. Come and go as you please, make yourself at home. When I got back she was gone. I never saw her again. I guess I should've stayed right where I was.

### BRAVERY

You hear how bad it is in New York, you hear how bad it is in St. Thomas, it's worse right in my own back yard. This guy came right into my house. I was just sitting down to dinner, I had daffodils on the table. I'm a married woman I said I just got done watching my husband die four months, what d'you want with me? He grabbed my arm and dragged me from room to room. I've had my eye on you for years he said. Well you must need glasses I said I'm an old woman. I looked better than I do now, at least I had my hair up. He kept coming back, he terrorized me a whole month. He lives right in town here, he's got a black beard. I went to the police but they said they couldn't do anything unless I signed a warrant, they wouldn't even go talk to him. He's a married man, he's got kids, I didn't want to get him in trouble. I met him on the street one day, I saw him coming, I didn't know what to do, run or what, but I was mad, I went right up to him, I looked him right in the eye and I said I'm not trembling, I'm not shaking, I'm not even afraid of you, but if you're going to make trouble for me in a public place you'll be sorry, I'll see to it, that's a promise. You know what he said? He said No hard feelings? I said No and he never bothered me again. Was I brave or what? You got to stand up to the bastards.


## SEE

Pals? Me and Suzie Speed, are you kidding? She's no pal of mine, I'm going to do her in, I'm going to make her a nice drink some day, next time she comes over. She sold me some pills, little yellow pills, for money too. I said What are they? She said You'll see. I said They ups, downs, what? She said You'll see.

So Hoodoo and I took one, all of a sudden it was like your head hit the moon, my body felt like a cloud of dust, all my nerves were dead, I couldn't move, these little motes were streaming through my brain.

I got scared, so did Hoodoo, I thought if this guy's scared I should really be scared, he takes everything, he's never straight. I says What's in the stuff, strychnine? He says I don't know Man, nothing like this ever happened before.

Actually it was quite a trip, I wouldn't want to do it again though. I would've gone to the Drop-in Center but I couldn't face that, this 35 year old you know freaking out on drugs. There'd be some 14 year old chick on duty, she'd say Uh-huh, uh-huh.

Hoodoo put the pills in an envelope on the top shelf of the medicine cabinet for stuff you shouldn't take under any circumstances. Some day Suzie Speed's going to come by for a drink. I'm going to grind up the rest of those pills, there's about 10 left, and put them in it. She'll say What's this? I'll say You'll see.

## DREAMS OF AN ITALIAN HAIRDRESSER

They say if you dream on Thursday it'll come true, I don't know, the younger generation don't believe in those superstitions any more, still you start to wonder sometimes. My aunt dreamed my brother was playing ball and the ball went over a fence around some high frequency wires and he climbed over after it and in turn he was electrocuted. My uncle kept saying Don't worry about it, don't worry about it. My brother was supposed to come for supper so when he didn't come she called the police but they didn't know anything. So after we ate my uncle said Well pack your bags, it's true, he's over in Hoboken. He didn't want to spoil her supper.

Another aunt dreamed a black child came to her in a vision and said Who'd you rather have die, your mother or your father, if one of them had to and you had to choose? So she said I'd rather my father didn't die, we have a big family, we need someone to support the children. And her mother was dead in a month.

It's stupid but it happened in Provincetown because that's where I met him, it wasn't too recently ago. I was going out with this guy down here. One of my customers back in Hoboken had a dream, I don't know if it was a Thursday, she said that her boyfriend, he was a divorced man like mine, said to her We have nothing, my wife and I at least have our children. She came in a week later and said he'd married his wife again. The same thing happened to me. Could be a coincidence but it seemed weird. I wouldn't want to live here all the time, you never meet anyone in the winter.

# THE HERMETIC WHORE

*Peter Spielberg*

## I.

In 1569 A.D., the anatomist Realdus Columbus discovered the clitoris or, as it is commonly called, the spinster's button. Some four hundred years later, American social workers, with the cooperation of freethinking psychiatrists, launched a campaign to legitimize the utilization of this button for the achievement of better mental health.

I cite the above facts by way of introduction. And I add a corrective: I am not, in principle or practice, concerned with clitoral masturbation. Penile self-gratification—primarily for the aged—is my special field of interest. Rightly so, since I am a man (though not aged) and it would be presumptuous of me to attempt to speak for women on this matter.

The Department of Social Services for which I work agrees and, accordingly, appointed two of us, one female, the second male (me), as co-directors of Project FULL LIFE—a flippant (in my opinion) imitation of military jargon whose acronymous origin is mercifully unknown to most participants: Full Utilization of Lingering Libidos for Longlived Inmates of Federal Enclaves.

"Self-abuse is self-*use*" is the way one of our publicists put it. I'm sure you've seen the message on subway billboards. Space donated by the Greater Metropolitan Advertising Council.

The impetus for our project came from an unlikely source: the passenger wing of the Interstate Commerce Commission. It seems that the ICC was embarrassed by a series of articles printed in a national weekly dealing with the take-over of bus terminal waiting rooms by the elderly. As I recall, it was one particular installment describing the condition of New York City's Port Authority Terminal, beginning with a poetically heartrending understatement "—a few are waiting for buses; most are waiting for death—" that got under the collar of the Commissioner.

Since public sympathy had been stirred and the bleeding hearts were drawing up petitions when they weren't writing outraged letters to the Editor, the Department rejected such a simple curative measure as having the old folks carted off to jail for criminal trespass. Besides, statistics warned that even if all squatters in residence were removed (the last headcount showed the figure to range between 750 and 1,000 per day depending on the weather) there was an army of replacements waiting in the wings. Vacant seats never had a chance to cool off. The moment one of the regulars disappeared (going to his just rest, we assumed) a new one hobbled in to take his place. The waiting list was inexhaustible. More sophisticated measures had to be taken. The psychological warfare section of the Department was handed the job.

By chance, we had had some of our people doing research on geriatrics. Their findings seemed to offer an answer to why the oldsters were swarming to the bus terminals. One: the main complaint of mature adults was not poverty as one would have suspected. Poor food, dingy housing, lack of pocket money and medical care were way down on their list of gripes. Instead, loneliness and boredom were at the top. Two: even more startling (researchers had to use all the tricks of the trade to get subjects to admit it) the number two grievance was lack of sexual fulfillment.

Put one and two together, or, better, put two and one together and you have cause and effect. In other words, sexually unsatisfied people, be they adolescents or nonagenarians, are bored and lonely. Add to this the problems of advanced age and lack of funds, and you begin to understand why the busy terminals with their aura of excitement and vitality were so popular—the public-address system rattling off names of romantic places and distant vistas, the physical attractiveness of the long-haired youngsters of both sexes who drift in and out, carefree, footloose, taking to the life of the open road like migratory birds, and those well-dressed commuters rushing for the 5:04 to their split-level bowers of bliss or coming in on the 11:35 for lunch and shopping, for cocktails and assignations, square shoulders, flat bellies, straight legs, skirts blowing in the wind, hot eyes, cool mouths—a moving picture of all the good things in life denied to the watchers on their wooden benches, but to be enjoyed vicariously, to be smelled and inhaled. Enough visual excitement to blow the mind, to tire out a man fifty years younger. Five or six hours of watching and they could get through the long lonely night. Small wonder the aged fought for a seat, for a spot at the keyhole (so to say).

A mild form of nuisance, one would think. The old people presented no threat. Didn't accost passengers, didn't even try to talk to them. But they did take up all the space. And what was worse were not pretty to look at. Still, the bus company and commuters would have put up with them, as they had for a good number of years (as they had learned to accept an excess of pigeons in parks), if that muckraking reporter had not interfered, had not incited the wrath of professional do-gooders.

Once the ball was tossed into our laps we had to come up with something. For a while we were stymied. What good did it do us to know that the root of the problem was sexual?

Somebody suggested a campaign to pair the old-timers up and marry them off, an idea which was dropped when she was reminded that two out of four of the squatters were already or still bound in wedlock. Giving them free or reduced admission to the triple-X-rated movie houses might have helped, but a sister city agency was charged with harassing, if not closing down, such smut merchants. Ellis Island was up for grabs, someone else proposed. A free coffee house where they could be dosed with saltpeter and other tranquilizers. Covered grandstands facing the West Side Highway, the speeding cars providing continuous entertainment while their exhaust fumes lend Father Time a helping hand. One-way tickets to Florida.

We were scraping the bottom of the barrel when, at last, the senior psychiatrist in the brain-busting session spoke up.

"Masturbation," he said.

We asked him to repeat what we thought we had heard.

"Jacking-off," he repeated.

"What about it?" we demanded. "What do you mean?"

"It's coming back into fashion," he proclaimed. "Don't you know?"

We did and we didn't, not wanting to admit ignorance, but shying away from committing ourselves prematurely.

"It's healthy," he elaborated.

"For whom?"

"For everyone." He looked around the table. "Don't you find it so?"

"Well, yes." One of our braver members took the plunge.

The rest of us nodded in noncommittal agreement.

"Do you mean . . . ? Are you intimating. . . . ?"

"That's what I've just said."

"But how?"

"There are many ways," he sighed. "None by itself better than another, depending on individual preferences . . . I suppose, if we put our heads together, we could come up with a list of recommendations. Practical hints. Might be useful for those who don't remember due to anility, battle fatigue, the puritan ethic, and other assorted blockages along these lines."

"Would it work?"

"Don't see why not."

"But for a city agency to come out publicly for onanism!"

"You're jumping to conclusions," the lawyer in the group interjected. "We wouldn't be enforcing the program, only advancing certain possibilities. No collusion intended. An educational service is the way to think of it."

"Yes," the psychiatrist agreed. "I can give you a bibliography on the subject."

"Perhaps a test run first. Only volunteers."

"And if the pilot project is successful . . ."

"Then we could swing into full operation."

"A crash program."

"Two programs. One for men and a separate one for women."

"Great idea."

"When do we start?"

## II.

I started by drawing up a list of the various ways.

(1) The time-honored five-against-one method. My right hand does the work, moving up and down like a piston ring, slow or fast depending on my frame of mind, glissando or staccato. Prosaic but effective.

(2) Both Hands. Same technique, except my left hand is cupped

underneath, jiggling my twin ivories as if I were shooting craps.

(3) For a change I occasionally like to do it from the opposite side. My left hand. (Right if I were a southpaw.) The touch is different. Clumsier, a bit slower, but interesting.

(4) No hands. This takes me back to when I first started as a preadolescent who was ordered to keep hands outside the covers. I lie flat on my stomach and hump the mattress. A pillow under the vital area is good for additional leverage.

(5) Using a feminine garment. A pair of lace panties or a nylon bra, preferably used, can be particularly stimulating. The texture of the material itself makes a difference, but I suspect it's the emotional association between the intimate finery and the love-object (or even the general, nonspecific flesh for which it was intended) that makes this variation so special. My hand still does the mechanical labor, but the silky shield or glove creates the illusion of having a silent partner.

(6) In a related vein, a cored apple (I like mine chilled) may be used to simulate, to a certain extent, the moist orifice in one's mind's eye. Other possibilities for those who are not squeamish are a slice of raw liver, a filet of flounder, etcetera.

(7) A lubricated condom has certain advantages. Not only as a preventative against venereal disease, but no mess to clean up afterwards, no telltale stains. Again, the texture makes the difference. And, of course, the preliminaries: rolling the bag on slowly, gently, smoothing out the wrinkles till it fits snugly from tip to stem. I like to think of it as foreplay.

(8) A change of locale can be exciting. Doing it in the bathtub instead of in bed. I'd recommend adding a capful of fragrant oil (Sardo, for example) to the warm water.

(9) Or a change in position. Sitting in a chair, standing in front of a full-length mirror, leaning out the window.

(10) Another idea. Instead of opening my fly or undressing, I massage* it sheathed by the cloth of my pants (similar to what we used to do as boys, hands deep in pockets, playing pocket

---

*It goes without saying that electric or battery-operated vibrators could be substituted if desired. However, careless use might prove dangerous (e.g., in number 8 above); while continuous use might lead to over-dependency.

billiards). Such confinement, rather than irritating, can be keenly satisfying.

Obviously this list is not meant to be exhaustive. Other variations exist. Kinkier ways. No matter. Every man will find what suits him best. Just improvise. What does matter, though, is to feel free, and not to be held back by guilt. There's nothing dirty about it, nothing to feel ashamed of.

It didn't take me long to warm to the task. Especially when I remembered the suppressive attitudes in force when I was a youngster! (That wasn't too long ago either—I'm in my early thirties.) Suppressive in a subtle and thereby effective way. Not the old scare 'em to death tactics of my father's day ("*Cave, Cave, Deus Videt!*"—God's heavy-lidded, never-closing eye seeing all, damning the sinner to madness, to blindness, to premature balding) but scientific warnings from the hygiene teacher. Cold facts.

"It's not a matter of morals," he assured us. "Rather a question of mental health. Self-abuse lowers the chances for fulfilling marital relations. It perverts, debilitates, spoils! Habitual masturbators make inadequate lovers. They lack potency. Have poor staying power. Never achieve full erection. Are selfish, immature. Ejaculate prematurely. Fail to reach climax. Are unable to enjoy the real thing, having once mistaken the part for the whole . . ." Pausing for polite laughter—a regular fellow he. "Once a creature of that habit, it's next to impossible to break away. Like smoking, like alcoholism, like drug addiction. . . . Play now, pay later!"

His analysis was confirmed by the textbooks we read and by a series of free lectures at the New School (a hotbed of liberal thought in those days). "How do we know that the case is lost, that it is too late to effect a reversal?" the speaker, *the* expert on the subject, asked and, after a suspenseful minute of silence, supplied the answer: "Noticeable pleasure received via urination!"

That hit home. To this day, I feel pangs every time I have a good piss, even though I long ago stopped believing such nonsense.

Most likely it's because I myself had been victimized by the repressive pseudo-scientific propaganda of the Anti-Onanism League that I ultimately embraced the Department's enlightened view on the subject with a dedication far beyond the call of duty or ambition. Here, in a way, was my chance to get back at my erstwhile jailers.

Although my initial reaction to project FULL LIFE may have

been a mixture of cynical amusement, condescending pity and detached superiority (due mainly to what I thought was my privileged position, being a most eligible bachelor at the height of my sexual powers, leading a full life, having the pick of my fellow (female) social workers, not to mention the wives of colleagues who were eager to put themselves at my disposal), about six weeks into the project I began to shed my protective aloofness. Professional sympathy gave way to empathy. Before long I was actually practicing what I preached. Enthusiastically!

Admitted that "joining" is an old ploy of our trade, the quickest way to gain a subject's confidence, as well as the most effective way to illustrate the recommended process or to experiment with new techniques—but my association went much further. I took it more seriously than that, and more personally.

"Damn it, if self-pleasuring doesn't make sense!" my most persuasive peptalk began—the old men rising to the sincerity of my conviction, to the heartfelt zeal, rather than to logic. "Who doesn't want to be able to achieve satisfaction whenever and wherever the fancy strikes? Who wants to be dependent on the good will, so called, of another person? Who wants to be at the mercy of somebody's moods? To have to plead and please, to cajole and bribe. To keep oneself in check and say 'After you, my dear.' To be hamstrung by one's partner's limitations, to be governed by her hang-ups, her needs or whatever!

"Why pretend? Giving pleasure is not nearly as satisfying as getting it yourself. And that's true whether you're thirty-three or eighty-three.

"Who needs all the fuss and bother when instant gratification is at hand? Free, easy, neat and clean, as efficacious—if not better than the old enslaving dependent method . . .

"Which reminds me," switching to a more informal tone once I had the audience in the palm of my hand, "of the old story about the crazy scientist who killed and cremated all the cats he could get a hold of. Yes, cats. You know: kittens. Meow, meow! He sifted their ashes into empty coffee cans, or maybe it was baby-food jars, and tried to sell them to the hard-up dudes on 42nd Street.

" 'Psst! Want a piece of the best stuff in town?' he would buttonhole a likely customer.

" 'Sure. Where is she? How much?'

" 'Right here in the jar. Five dollars a spoonful. Just add some hot water. My invention—instant pussy.'. . .

"Now I'm no mad scientist, just an underpaid social worker. And I'm not out to sell you any instant pussy, patent medicine, cure-all or philosopher's stone. I'm not selling anything. We're giving it away. It's so easy, so available, as plentiful as the air we breathe. Let me illustrate . . ."

### III.

The success of our re-education program was greater than bargained for. Our illustrated pamphlet on your ten all-time favorite ways (blue cover for men, pink for women) climbed to the top of the government publications' best seller list a week after its release. Its sequel (minimally priced to cover printing costs; free to senior citizens) a slightly more ambitious work listing sample erotic fantasies to jerk off by, taken from both classic and contemporary literary masterpieces*, with full-color photographs (posed by TV and film stars, services donated in the public interest) did even better; the excuse for its issuance being preventative medicine against boredom from a steady diet of solo frigging and the consequent relapse to the longing for sexual congress—an imaginary danger judging by my experience both at home and in the field.

If anything, Project Full Life had won more faithful converts than we could handle.

---

*Herewith, a handful of abridged excerpts: "Resting on knees and elbows, *coitus a tergo, more ferendo,* she presents her symmetrically rounded buttocks for his pleasure." *Index Librorum Prohibitorum* "The upshot was that I let him have his way with me." *Confessions of a Lady of Leisure* "The sea shell cups of her white brassiere displayed ripe, quivering, twin black beauties, glistening with passion like oysters on the half shell." *Tidbits* "The blonde greedily stuffed my hard jockum into her bee-stung mouth while her brunette sister begged me not to neglect her. 'Bang my buns, lover!' she moaned. 'Save some for me.' " *Our Secret Life* " 'Open wide,' said the dentist to the prostrate, strapped-down captive in the chair, ignoring the unspoken plea in her tear-filled eyes." *Bedrock* "While his long wet tongue licks her dart-tipped titties, she expertly strokes his thingamabob. They finish in a dead heat." *Lewd Did I Live & Evil I Did Dwell* " 'Hold still!' the nurse cautioned, and straddling my loins with one leap (twisting expertly so as not to dislodge her breast from my mouth) she guided me smoothly past moist nether lips up into the soft core."

Even though my department staff quadrupled, we couldn't meet the demand. Retirement colonies, nursing homes, resident hotels, veterans organizations, and innumerable individuals—husbands as well as widowers—besieged us with applicants for the program. A village of golden agers converted in a body. Our speakers were sought by every social club, country club, bridge club, philanthropic organization and block association, by the Rotarians and the Salvation Army.

Old timers' day at Yankee Stadium turned topsy-turvy when some tens of thousands of senile citizens of the male persuasion mistook the sporting event for a rallying call to their cause. They descended on foot and crutches, on giant tricycles and chartered trains, breaking all attendance records. They ran the Full Life ensign up the centerfield flagpole and cheered a retired, double-jointed circus acrobat (a small, wiry man with plenty of vinegar) who could and did perform auto-fellatio on the pitcher's mound. They stormed the diamond, tore up the turf, and for a grand finale committed public nuisance according to directions blasted over the address system, coming jointly, one hundred thousand sparklers blasting off when the countdown reached zero. The action was a hit in the judgment of the official scorer, a new high-water mark, and was entered as such in the *Guinness Book of World Records,* where it still stands, as far as I know, along with the achievements of

---

*Twiddledum Twaddledum* "I'm a real swinging chick. Other than you-know-what I'll try anything. Lately, though, all my varied daydreams—I've had some lulus—leave me flat. Except one. I imagine myself visiting one of those sex shops and asking the salesman for a mouth. 'I want to buy a mouth,' I tell him. He doesn't know what I mean. I don't either, but the thought of it is enough to make my clit stand on end." *Her Secret Garden* "Her pubic triangle is meticulously groomed; hair slick; slit straight, shiny like a zipper." *The Golden Ass* "Her dress is wet, cool and wet. It looks liquid, as if she has been dipped into a vat of highgloss lacquer. She walks across the room, her vinyl-sheathed torso fluid, its surface rising and dipping, swelling as if about to crest." *The Skin of Pornography* "At full erection, the mean average expansion of the male member measures 7.5 centimeters from the in-repose length. Ejaculatory contractions between six and nine on the average, occur at intervals of zero-point-eighth of a second." *Facts on File.*

goldfish swallowers, unicycle riders, smoke-ring blowers, pogo-stick jumpers, yo-yo spinners, prune devourers and face slappers.

But back to serious business. Our zealous proselytizing had gotten us into one hell of a mess.

Contrary to expectations, contrary to intention, our campaign persuaded the young along with the old. Although we tried to hold the line at advanced middle-age, quinquagenarians and up, the mandatory cut-off point was ignored. And there was nothing that we could do to stop the stampede.

Small comfort that we had managed to empty the Port Authority waiting room (the long-forgotten immediate cause of our crusade); even less help that our agency's program had first been cleared by HEW (high functionaries have short recall). The blame fell foursquare on our heads.

It was our fault, they found, that the birth rate plummeted 90% below zero growth, that the marriage license bureau had to close its doors, that absenteeism among male workers reached an all-time high, that unbridled truantism galloped from the sixth grade up through graduate school, that the work ethic was jettisoned, that the inner cities began to look like ghost towns, that the gross national product went kaput, that only women ran for public office, that, in short, America was—and, alas, is—in retirement.

My fault, they claim, that we have become a nation of eunuchs. For it's the male population that has opted to quit the race.

Among women it's only grandmothers who have taken to exclusive self-gratification; the able-bodied continue to lust for and practice (if they can manage to come up with a stud) sexual intercourse. "A good sign," the government says. "Our sole hope for the preservation of the free enterprise system, for the perpetuation of the species. Thank God! . . . If clitoral masturbation ever wins the day, we can all pack it in."

I nod in agreement, but am not sure why we should thank God. Neither am I convinced that I, as director of the male side of our project, am responsible for the path my so-called brothers chose. To call me the "Pied Piper of Friggland," as some do, is a malicious exaggeration. I used no magic, no force. I promised nothing that I couldn't deliver. It seems obvious to me that I have been chosen as the whipping boy because of our city planners' total frustration. Rather than examine the root cause—precisely why did an overwhelming majority of able-bodied men elect early retirement from coition? what went wrong? where? when? how?—rather than getting down to constructive business, to positive action, they have taken the easy way out.

Anyway, there is nothing I can do to reverse the trend. I tried. I really tried (despite my heart not being in it). I approved the purging of my faithful staff, retracted my pro-onanism pronouncements, confessed my (supposed) errors, asked to be demoted, to be relieved of command, made public contrition (imperfect, I fear), painstakingly drew up detailed lists enumerating the superior joys of fornication, the physical and psychological advantages of interpersonal copulation (repeating the white lies like a well-disciplined parrot), gave live demonstrations on national television, preached against the dangers of self-love, damned it for being subversive revisionism, anarchistic nihilism. . . . I even offered to get married if it would help.

The men wouldn't listen. Won't listen.

And I, for one, can't blame them. What between erotic books, half an imagination, and a lively hand, there just is no need to go out and toil for one's pleasure. No need to grovel for it. Once in the know, how can one forget? Only a bloody fool would return to the old ways.

The result of my failure to stem the tide was predictable. A draconian contingency plan, long on the books, has been put into effect. It's involuntary deportation, the state farm, the old-age home for all of us who won't give it up. Every man jack of us, greybeard and cadet, whatever the chronological age, will be sent there. The terminal waiting rooms are once again filled with intransigents. Buses leave every hour on the hour.

Judging by my projection, it will take some time to empty the place (if it can be done at all). But the wait is rather pleasant. The terminal is warm and dry, as good as a furnished room, better than the park, more reliable, with overhead fluorescent lights burning as brightly as a never-setting sun in a cloudless sky. Although watched by closed circuit cameras, we are not interfered with, even when, now and again, we practice the passion which brought us here.

# THE ENDLESS SHORT STORY: DONG WANG

## *Ronald Sukenick*

He was glad to be back from his trip. But as soon as he said it he realized that being back was just the beginning of another trip. So where did that leave him? From where he sat he could see the curvature of the earth, just as he could from the plane, from where he sat way up in the mountains, overlooking the plains. He could see the horizon curving, very slightly, maybe forty miles away from where he sat, through a cleft in the mountains. He was making connections, as usual. He was trying to make connections between one trip and another, among trips, trips past and trips to come. He was starting off on still another trip, the connections trip. He liked making connections. He liked making connections because it slowed him down. It slowed him down and it made him feel connected. He didn't know if it was better to feel connected, but it make him feel better. But connected to what? Connected to other connections, he supposed. Alarming white stuff. What is that connected with? This might be good to read, he would read it aloud some time to try it out, the cadences seemed right. He had trouble reading. He'd always had trouble reading, even not aloud and to himself. When he was young reading was not allowed, not in bed, not late at night, late into the night when he wanted to read. Maybe the trouble was that he wanted to read but he didn't want to read in straight lines, he wanted to read two or three lines alternately, simultaneously, in his own order not the order that was already there in the straight lines. It takes years to find a style and once you

find it you go on to something else or else you're lost. Finding your
style is like being back from a trip, it's just the beginning of another
trip. In any case, this was what he found, he found the way he
wanted to read, or be read, and finally he would do it.

                                        brain granulated by
time                       covered by alarming white stuff
        old Juanitito          tomorrow he would see Dong Wang
back from the long voyage                                        after
                    labor day weekend   the word for today
                    clouds snow fog                           snert
        forty miles of plains
                            focus unfocus
        the binos                                   the rhinos
turn in the dust                    second baseman turns throws
                        focus unfocus
                            making the sound snert
from this distance              Dong Wang snorts
                    hocus pocus                 in his cave
            cuevas cuevas      montanas      eyes go blind
irregular              never              no rules
        focus                 unfocus              new focus
                            old Juanitito, a tiny old
man, blind, alarming white stuff filmed his eyes. He lived in a two-
room cabin in the mountains, the back room was actually built into
a natural cave, there aren't many here, granite, as opposed to
limestone of Sierras. He lived up at 8,000 feet, that cave came in
handy in five feet of snow or when the Chinook started blowing at
100 mph. There was nothing special he wanted to ask the old man,
he just felt drawn up there, and that's the kind of feeling you learn
not to ignore when you live here, in the montanas, in the southwest,
in the emptiness, in the power center of the country. Crazy talk for a
kid from Brooklyn, n'est-ce pas? The visits were ritualized in their
way. The old man was always there, never surprised to find him at
the door. Shake hands, sit for a cup of coffee, talk about the
weather in broken English, broken Spanish. Frankly, he sometimes
wondered whether the old man was all there. In a way he
undoubtedly wasn't, absent-minded etc., brain granulated by time,
talk disconnected. But in another way he just as undoubtedly was.
Let's say there was an energy field he created, like sitting in an
orgone box but not really, but some kind of energy, frightening at
the edges, like you could skid skid skid off into something very

weird, but basically benign, he had done the old man a good turn once, that counts make no mistake, if it weren't for that he wouldn't come. The old man wasn't all there, but whatever part of him wasn't there was definitely somewhere else. Where? Nothing happened. They talked. He left. And he realized he felt very different. Maybe it was this, that the things that had seemed important before were suddenly muted, buried under sand, under snow which he now skied across, the contours of the land very different from before the storm, the crucial landmarks changed, the feel of the landscape. There's a place there, on the ski trail, where you can see the skyscrapers of Denver, just make them out, tiny, below, and if you use your binos you can see a minute airport with microscopic jumbo jets taking off and landing. The inertial motion of his life suddenly altered, an abrupt turn, some heavy animal skidding in the dust, a redirection of forces. Let's say it comes to this, that things that once seemed important no longer seemed quite so important, and things he used to ignore he could no longer ignore. All those crazy little feelings, do this now, don't do that now, tuned out by the static and different energy of the city, that was the insane, magic way his life now began to organize itself. He became a sleepwalker.
ten-geek
sun bleeds up from horizon
dawn buck leaping
He found a new voice. A new sleepwalker voice. At dawn he took a new name, Dawn-buck-leaping. A new ten-geek name.
Dawn-buck-leaping, ten-geek sleepwalker
went down the mountain. He went to see his fat friend Madame Lazonga. Madame Lazonga was a sleepwalker, also she gave rubs. She was known locally as a rubber, that's how she made a living, but Dawn-buck-leaping also knew she was a sleepwalker. He wanted to ask her some questions about sleepwalking.

These mountains are magic, she explained. They go up and down. Since they go up and down the people who live in them also go up and down. It's partly the thin air, you have to breathe deeper in, deeper out, it affects the blood, everything is intensified, higher is higher and lower is lower and in-between is more in-between. It's a question of the flux of energies. In the mountains we become sleepwalkers, more attuned to energies than to comprehensions, like the animals. In the mountains there are many energies. The energy of the cosmic rays streams through you, the energy of the granite irradiates you, the push and pull of the moon, the lucid confusions of the stars. Watch out. In the mountains men jump off high cliffs out of exhilaration and women through despair are driven to erotic frenzy. One day you will wake up, but the reality you waken to will seem different, what was formerly reality will seem like another dream, a dream among dreams, and nothing will ever be the same.

What is ten-geek? asks Dawn-buck-leaping.

Ten-geek means everything is raised to the tenth power. Or lowered. Tenth is an exaggeration but sleepwalking numbers are metaphors and become fluid. For example you will probably already have noticed that your erections are larger and more painful. Be careful. If not assuaged they can lead to murder and suicide. The increase in size is due in part to lowered air resistance at higher altitudes, in part to increased energy streamings. The ancient Tibetans noticed this phenomenon and called it long duck. It is said that an oriental princess kept a pleasure palace in the Himalayas where she would excite her male slaves to the point of long duck and then have their organs severed and cooked. A version of this dish was brought back to middle Europe by the Mongols as sausage and is thought to be the origin of our own hot dog. Also ten-geek is a time. It's the name you give to the era as you now sense it, like twentieth century. For example this year would be ten-geek seven six. It's the kind of change in the time sense that happens after some kind of upheave, when everything turns over, when the words explode on the page, and you get 14th Brumaire or whatever. This means a major refocussing. Maybe what was worth it before isn't worth it now. A child dies or maybe something just clicks in your head one day. Suddenly the sphere of action seems pointless. Sex is no longer of great interest. Power is seedy. Money is boring. Friendship isn't serious, or isn't serious enough. Love is an exile's nostalgia. What remains is a kind of, let's say, painting. But painting of what? What is it that we sleepwalkers, in our trance, try to do? Let's try not to be frivolous about the thing, let's try not to evade the intelligence of it. What is that pure thing? Once a long time ago Juanitito and I were lovers, you didn't know that. He was what they call a great lover, I hesitate to use the cliché, even out here in the Rocky Mountains, but he was a great lover, believe me it was thrilling.

He came to me every day at dawn.

One morning he came and I knew he'd been with another woman that night.

This happened sometimes and I didn't care. He was a buck and I didn't care as long as he kept bucking.

Afterward he went to work, he worked in a hospital. As an orderly.

The woman was a nurse he started going out with after work.

They would go listen to a group called the Ten Geek Jazz Band.

The band was named for its leader, Jan ten Geek.

A Dutchman who came to this country after WWII.

He was in the Resistance as an adolescent, was caught by the Nazis in 1943, sent to a concentration camp.

He lived.

Learned to play horn in the Black ghetto in Detroit.

He had lost his voice in the camp. Shock.

That was the cool jazz era, he was sort of like a mute Chet Baker. Not great but sometimes he could really go crazy.

I mean he was really saying something, mostly to himself but not bad for Denver: fuck you, screw my pussy, eat my shit and I'll suck your tit.

That kind of thing. Wang wang wang wang. I mean what's this allabout.

Well at that time Juanitito was known as a great stud, that's why they called him Dong Wang.

Well the nurse was named Marge, a blonde, and that night Jan was just going crazy up there, too much, she got totally turned on.

Sonofabitch. Gogogogo.

Anyways she goes back to say hello at the break.

And Dong catches them outside the club in the back alley and she was doing something terrible and awful and obscene to him I won't even mention what it was.

She was sucking his cock.

Oh my god. The blower blowed.

Jan had a hard case of long duck, it was very embarrassing.

To make a long story short the three of them became good friends. There are little third-rate scenes like this going on all over America. You might say it's the essential flavor of the country.

It's so *good*.

I mean people just sort of break *loose*.

And then it turns out there's nothing to break loose *to*.

And that's *it*.

So Dong Wang ends up driving a delivery truck in Rapid City. So what?

It's the tip of that long line we keep drawing, each one of us.

It's part of the big picture we're all painting together.

The big picture is that there is no big picture. That's why we keep painting it.

The result is often "withdrawal of physical support, leading to separation of anxiety."

The result is often limbo of used band-aids.

The result is unexpected.

It is not even a result.

# NOTES ON CONTRIBUTORS

WALTER ABISH's latest book is *Minds Meet* (1975). He has just completed *Future Perfect* a collection of fictions which will be published by New Directions in Fall 1977. At present he is writer-in-residence at Wheaton College in Massachusetts.

GLENDA ADAMS was born in Sydney, Australia, and lives in New York City. Her short stories have appeared in *Transatlantic Review, Ms., Mother Jones,* and other periodicals. A collection of her stories, *Lies and Stories,* was published by Inwood/Horizon Press in 1976.

MIMI ALBERT is the author of *The Second Story Man,* a novel, *The Small Singer,* a collection of stories and poetry, and numerous stories published in literary journals. She has just completed a new novel, *A Daughter's Book,* of which "Rock Bottom" is an excerpt.

RUSSELL BANKS, a Guggenheim Fellow for 1976, is the author of *Family Life,* a novel, and *Searching for Survivors,* a collection of stories. "By Way of an Introduction to the Novel, This or Any" is the first chapter of his new novel, *Hamilton Stark.*

JONATHAN BAUMBACH is the author of four novels, *A Man to Conjure With, What Comes Next, Reruns* and *Babble,* and a book of criticism, *The Landscape of Nightmare: Studies in the Contemporary American Novel.* He has published short fiction in *Esquire, American Review, Iowa Review, Fiction International* and *TriQuarterly.* Co-director of the Fiction Collective, he is film critic for *Partisan Review* and directs the graduate creative writing program at Brooklyn College.

BURT BRITTON, ex-Marine, born in Brooklyn, presides over the caves of the Strand Book Store where he compiled his recently published *Self-Portrait: Book People Picture Themselves.*

JERRY BUMPUS's story collection *Things in Place* was published by the Fiction Collective in 1975. He teaches at San Diego State University. "Lutz" is an excerpt from a novel in progress.

JEROME CHARYN's most recent books are *Blue Eyes, Marilyn the Wild* and *The Education of Patrick Silver.* The fiction included in this anthology is an excerpt from a novel in progress, *King Jude.*

ROBERT COOVER is the author of two novels, *The Origin of the Brunists* and *The Universal Baseball Association: J. Henry Waugh, Proprietor,* and a collection of stories, *Pricksongs and Descants.* "The Clemency Appeals" is an excerpt from his new novel, *The Public Burning of Julius and Ethel Rosenberg: An Historical Romance.*

RAYMOND FEDERMAN is a bilingual writer who experiments with voices within voices in his novels, *Double or Nothing, Amer Eldorado,* and *Take It or Leave It* (Fiction Collective, 1976), and in his poetry, *Among the Beasts/Parmi les Monstres* and *Me Too.* "The Voice in the Closet" is from a work in progress, his "Season in Hell" or his "Text for Nothing".

B. H. FRIEDMAN is the author of five published novels *(Circles, Yarborough, Whispers, Museum* and *Almost a Life);* several art monographs; two full-length biographies *(Jackson Pollock: Energy Made Visible* and *Gertrude Vanderbilt Whitney);* and frequently contributes to art and literary magazines.

THOMAS GLYNN was born in Montreal, Canada. His Fiction has appeared in *Paris Review, Playboy, North American Review, Seems,* and *Modern Music & Hi Fi.* His novel, *Temporary Sanity,* was published by the Fiction Collective in the Fall of 1976.

RICHARD GRAYSON, born in 1951, earned an M.F.A. in Creative Writing from Brooklyn College. His stories have appeared in *Transatlantic Review, Texas Quarterly, Panache* and over twenty other magazines. He teaches at Long Island University and is currently at work on his first novel.

MARIANNE HAUSER's novels include *Dark Dominion, The Choir Invisible, Prince Ishmael,* and *The Talking Room,* published by Fiction Collective in 1976. Her short stories have been widely anthologized and collected in *A Lesson in Music.* She teaches in the Department of English at Queens College.

STEVE KATZ' books of fiction include *The Exagggerations of Peter Prince, Creamy and Delicious* and *Saw. Cheyenne River Wild Track* is his long poem. His novel, *Moving Parts,* has just been published by the Fiction Collective.

BRUCE KLEINMAN was born in Brooklyn, where he has lived ever since. He is a graduate of the M.F.A. Program at Brooklyn College.

ELAINE KRAF is the author of the novels *I am Clarence,* Doubleday, 1969, and *The House of Madelaine,* Doubleday, 1971. Her shorter works have appeared in many anthologies including *New Directions 31* and *Bitches and Sad Ladies.* Her third novel, *Find Oliver,* will be published by the Fiction Collective.

LAURA J. KRAMER has never been published. She was born 27 years ago in Brooklyn. She is presently working in a bookstore and teaching at Brooklyn College where she is enrolled in the M.F.A. program. "Shoes" will probably be part of a novel.

CLARENCE MAJOR is the author of three novels, five books of poetry, two works of nonfiction, an anthology, and hundreds of short works that have appeared in anthologies and periodicals.

URSULE MOLINARO has just completed a new novel, *The Autobiography of Cassandra, Princess & Prophetess of Troy.* She is the author of the novels *Green Lights are Blue, Sounds of a Drunken Summer, The Borrower* (which just came out in Japanese translation), and a number of short stories, one of which, "Tourists in Life," was published in *Statements 1.*

LEON ROOKE lives in British Columbia. His story collection *Last One Home Sleeps in the Yellow Bed* was published by LSU, and two new collections are due this year: *The Love Parlour* (Oberon Press) and *The Broad Back of the Angel* (the Fiction Collective).

STEVEN SCHRADER was born in New York City and is the director of Teachers & Writers Collaborative. He has published fiction in small magazines and anthologies. Inwood Press has recently published a collection of his stories, *Crime of Passion.*

ROGER SKILLINGS is the author of a book of stories, *Alternative Lives,* Ithaca House, 1974, and is chairman of the writers at the Fine Arts Work Center in Provincetown. The pieces printed here belong to an unpublished collection of told stories named *The Meatrack.*

PETER SPIELBERG, whose fiction has been widely published in literary magazines, is co-director of the Fiction Collective and teaches modern literature and creative writing at Brooklyn College. His books include *Bedrock: A Work of Fiction Composed of Fifteen Scenes from my Life* and the novel *Twiddledum Twaddledum.*

RONALD SUKENICK directs the creative writing program at the University of Colorado. His works of fiction include the novels *98.6, Out, Up,* and the story collection *The Death of the Novel and Other Stories.*

# FICTION COLLECTIVE

books in print:

*Reruns* by Jonathan Baumbach
*Museum* by B. H. Friedman
*Twiddledum Twaddledum* by Peter Spielberg
*Searching for Survivors* by Russell Banks
*The Secret Table* by Mark Mirsky
*98.6* by Ronald Sukenick
*The Second Story Man* by Mimi Albert
*Things In Place* by Jerry Bumpus
*Reflex and Bone Structure* by Clarence Major
*Take It or Leave It* by Raymond Federman*
*The Talking Room* by Marianne Hauser
*The Comatose Kids* by Seymour Simckes
*Althea* by J. M. Alonso*
*Babble* by Jonathan Baumbach
*Temporary Sanity* by Thomas Glynn
*Null Set* by George Chambers
*Amateur People* by Andrée Connors
*Moving Parts* by Steve Katz
*Statements 1,* an anthology of new fiction (1975)
*Statements 2,* an anthology of new fiction (1977)

available at bookstores
or from
GEORGE BRAZILLER, INC.
*(see next page for subscription offer)*